"WHY WOULD ANYONE KILL A REAL ESTATE AGENT?"

Up to that moment, I'd been thinking along the lines of "Why would anyone kill Trudi?" I hated to say it, but coming up with an answer to that one didn't seem terribly difficult. It was just as I was thinking this that I recalled something I immediately wished I hadn't. Good Lord. In her memo, Trudi had written that she was going to this very house to meet a client who'd asked for *me*. Did this mean that what had been done to Trudi had really been meant for me?

I went cold all over.

"We've got to call the police," I said to the couple who'd been looking at the house.

My voice still wasn't shaking, but it was getting oddly shrill. "The phone in this house was disconnected when the owners moved out, so I'm going to have to go get my car phone," I told them.

I'd gotten one of those cellular bag phones about a month earlier. The salesman who'd talked me into it had ticked off a variety of circumstances in which I'd find the thing unbelievably handy. Like if my car broke down. Or if I got lost. Or if I needed to check in with my office.

Oddly enough, he hadn't mentioned if I needed to report a murder.

A Killing in Real Estate

A SCHUYLER RIDGWAY MYSTERY

Tierney McClellan

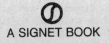

A SIGNET BOOK

SIGNET
Published by the Penguin Group
Penguin Books USA Inc., 375 Hudson Street,
New York, New York 10014, U.S.A.
Penguin Books Ltd, 27 Wrights Lane, London W8 5TZ, England
Penguin Books Australia Ltd, Ringwood, Victoria, Australia
Penguin Books Canada Ltd, 10 Alcorn Avenue,
Toronto, Ontario, Canada M4V 3B2
Penguin Books (N.Z.) Ltd, 182–190 Wairau Road,
Auckland 10, New Zealand

Penguin Books Ltd, Registered Offices:
Harmondsworth, Middlesex, England

First published by Signet, an imprint of Dutton Signet,
a division of Penguin Books USA Inc.

First Printing, May, 1996
10 9 8 7 6 5 4 3 2 1

 REGISTERED TRADEMARK—MARCA REGISTRADA

Printed in the United States of America

PUBLISHER'S NOTE
This is a work of fiction. Names, characters, places, and incidents
either are the product of the author's imagination or are used ficti-
tiously, and any resemblance to actual persons, living or dead,
events, or locales is entirely coincidental.

Acknowledgments

I would like to thank Randi Means, Realtor, of Century 21 Steve Hall and Associates, LaGrange, Kentucky, for taking the time out of her busy schedule to answer my questions so competently and with such good humor. Randi's help actually made my research fun. I'd also like to thank my editor, Danielle Perez, for her thoughtful guidance; my agent, Richard Parks, for his continuing patience; and my twin sister, Beverly Taylor Herald, for her perceptive critiques.

Chapter
1

I wouldn't have felt so bad about what happened if I'd liked Trudi Vittitoe. I know that sounds strange, but it's true. It was as if, long before awful things started happening, the way I felt about Trudi had already given my silent vote of approval.

I've never thought of myself as a particularly vindictive person, either. In fact, up until Trudi became the newest real estate agent working out of Arndoerfer Realty, I'd been under the impression that I could get along with just about anybody.

Trudi helped me see the error in that kind of thinking. But then again, Trudi could've made Mother Theresa want to punch her out.

Even now, amazingly enough, Trudi still has the power to make me angry. I'm angry now because I can't stop feeling guilty. I've told myself over and over that none of it was really my fault, and that it certainly wasn't as if I were personally plotting against anybody or anything. And yet, I still feel incredibly guilty.

It doesn't help to recall that I spent a good portion

of that last day looking forward to raking Trudi over the coals.

I'd been gearing myself up to do a little Trudi-raking ever since shortly after one that afternoon. That was the time I'd returned to Arndoerfer Realty after showing a house way out in Louisville's south end.

Once I pulled into the office parking lot, it hadn't taken Trudi ten seconds to make me furious, and Trudi wasn't even *there,* for God's sake.

Of course, her not being there was the problem. That, and its being ass-freezing cold, to put it—as we genteel Southern ladies always do—*delicately.*

Even though the temperature had been in the sixties just the day before, on this particular Tuesday it was thirty-five. With a wind chill of minus ten. This kind of sudden temperature change is not all that unusual for Louisville in March. Around this time of year, Kentucky weather often has all the ups and downs of a roller coaster. Only it's not as much fun.

You'd think, having lived here all my life, I'd have gotten used to the roller coaster weather. That by now I'd be tuning into the Weather Channel every single morning before I got dressed. But, no, I admit it, I'm not that smart. That Tuesday, for some odd reason, I'd actually been expecting another nice day just like the one before it. So I was wearing a lightweight wool suit. No coat, no boots, no gloves. Not even a sweater under my suit jacket.

The wind felt like tiny knives cutting into me as I ran across the parking lot from my car to the front door.

Which was, not at all incidentally, shut tight.

A bad sign if I ever saw one.

Jarvis Arndoerfer—co-owner, along with his wife, Arlene, of Arndoerfer Realty—has always insisted that the front door be left standing wide open during the day. Whether it's cold or hot, the only thing that's supposed to separate the front office from the elements is a storm door. Jarvis appears to be under the impression that if he doesn't make it incredibly easy for potential clients to walk in, they might just decide that having to reach out and turn a doorknob was too much of a strain.

I think I knew the instant I saw the front door shut that it was locked, too, but I gave it a try, anyway.

I believe the phrase "a complete waste of time" describes it best.

"Damn you, Trudi." As I said this, I realized I was looking straight at the small brass plaque located to the left of the door. It said, 9 TO 5, MONDAY THROUGH FRIDAY, 10 TO 2, SATURDAY. In plain English that even Trudi ought to be able to understand.

So where the hell was she?

Even if she hadn't been able to read the sign, I believe I'd made myself abundantly clear before I left. "Trudi, a client just phoned, and she wants to see one of my listings right away. So, even though this is my floor duty day, would you mind staying here until one of the others shows up?"

On days you have floor duty, you're supposed to man the office—answer the phone, greet walk-ins, that sort of thing. Asking another real estate agent to fill in for you was not, however, an odd thing. In fact, since Arndoerfer Realty is fairly small, with only four agents working here other than the Arndoerfers themselves, we cover for each other all the time. Trudi herself had asked me to do the exact same thing just last week, and I'd agreed. I'd even lied. I'd said, "Glad to." As I recall, she'd forgotten to thank me.

Judging from the look on her face when I'd asked

her, Trudi had not only forgotten to thank me, she'd forgotten the entire incident.

"What?" Trudi said, looking up from the latest issue of *Vogue* and brushing a wisp of blond hair off her forehead.

Trudi was one of the few women left on the planet who was still wearing her hair in a Farrah Fawcett tumble to her shoulders. I suspected that the reason Trudi still wore her hair this way was that, to be painfully honest, with her hair cut like that, Trudi looked a *lot* like Farrah Fawcett. Trudi certainly had all the necessary Farrah Fawcett attributes: thick blond hair, curvy figure, big blue eyes, and, of course, great teeth.

Before anybody starts thinking that the main reason I disliked Trudi was because she was gorgeous, let me hasten to add that I'm not that shallow. Well, okay, so maybe I *am* that shallow, but her being gorgeous was not the main reason I disliked her. It was only one of the reasons from a long, long list.

To tell you the truth, sometimes it seemed as if everything about Trudi irritated me. The way Trudi told everybody she was "thirtysomething," when I'd seen her driver's license, and she was two years older than my own forty-two. The way Trudi spelled her name. The way Trudi always lowered her voice to a breathy whisper whenever she answered the phone. And, let us not forget, the way Trudi always dotted her *i*'s with little hearts.

Lord. It even irritated me the way Trudi always wore scarves color-coordinated to her every outfit.

Trudi was fiddling with the end of a burgundy print scarf that exactly matched her burgundy suit as she said, "You mean, I'm going to be the only one here?" She looked around the office as if she were just noticing that she and I were alone.

Like I said before, there were two other agents—

Barbi Lundergan and Charlotte Ackersen—who worked here besides Trudi, me, and the Arndoerfers, but not one of these people had been into the office so far. That meant that Trudi and I had been here all by ourselves since nine. And now, two hours later, she was trying to make me believe it hadn't yet occurred to her that nobody else was here?

"Well, now, that's really going to be a problem," Trudi said, her tone petulant. "I wasn't planning on staying here *all* day, Shuler."

I just looked at her. I'd worked with the woman all of six months and every once in a while she still called me "Shuler." Just as if I hadn't told her quite a few times already that, although my name is spelled *Schuyler,* the *u* is silent. So you pronounce it "Skyler." Not "Shooler."

Oddly enough, Trudi always seemed to make this little mistake when I was asking her to do something. The last time she'd called me Shuler, for example, she'd been on her way to the Xerox. Already late for a closing and buried in paperwork, I'd asked her to make one quick copy of a single page for me. From the look she'd given me, you'd have thought I'd asked her to Xerox the phone book. "Oh, I couldn't possibly," she'd said, handing the page back to me, "but I tell you what, I'll let you go before me. Okay, Shuler?"

That time, even though I was late—and I still had one damn copy to make—I'd taken a moment to re-mind her exactly how my name should be pronounced.

This time, though, I decided to skip it. Mainly because *this* time I detected an unmistakable gleam in Trudi's big blue eyes.

As if she were actually looking forward to my having to go through it one more time.

I smoothly went on, as if I hadn't even noticed her

mispronunciation. "Do you have an appointment this afternoon to show a house, or—"

The gleam went out of Trudi's eyes. "Well, no, but I certainly don't want to get tied down here *all*—"

I interrupted her. "You only have to stay until one of the others gets here."

Trudi's eyes got wider, and her voice got higher. "But, *Shuler*—" This time she put a little extra emphasis on the name as her eyes darted to mine. I didn't even blink. Apparently, in a matter of seconds I'd developed a hearing problem. "—I'm not sure I can handle everything all by myself."

If I were male, the little-girl voice, the wide-eyed look of innocence, and the tone of abject helplessness might've worked. I was not, however, male. As a matter of fact, I've used the "I'm so dumb, you'll have to do it" gambit myself. I've used it most effectively when I've had a flat tire.

Not to mention, wasn't this the same woman who, whenever the phone rang, nearly broke a leg getting to it before anybody else did? Wasn't this also the same woman who immediately pounced on any walk-ins, with no regard whatsoever to who might possibly have floor duty on any particular day?

This was yet another thing I'd tried to explain to Trudi. How the policy at Arndoerfer Realty was that whoever has floor duty on a given day is supposed to greet *all* the walk-ins. *Every* one of them. The agent on floor duty then has the option of taking on the walk-ins personally as clients, or passing them on to another available realtor. This was, I'd tried to make clear, pretty much how floor duty was supposed to work. It was not supposed to be a footrace, with every agent in the place trying to beat the others to any prospective clients.

In fact, it was to avoid footraces that all of the realtors at Arndoerfer Realty alternate floor duty days. This way we could *all* have an equal opportunity to acquire new clients.

After I'd finished explaining the policy to her, Trudi had assumed the wide-eyed innocent look she was so good at. "I hope you're not suggesting that *I* would deliberately try to take somebody else's prospect." Trudi had actually looked close to tears when she'd added, "I'm just trying to be of service, you know, I'm just trying to make Arndoerfer Realty the best gosh-darn real estate agency Louisville has ever seen. *That's* all."

Jarvis, coincidentally enough, had been coming down the stairs at that exact moment. I couldn't help but notice that Trudi had raised her voice quite a bit toward the last. So that Jarvis could not miss a word.

Jarvis had beamed at Trudi as he went by.

I, on the other hand, had felt an almost overpowering urge to give Trudi the best gosh-darn punch in the face Trudi had ever seen.

This morning, asking Trudi to watch the office in my absence, I'd been once again fighting the urge. "You can handle the responsibility," I'd told her. "I've got real faith in you."

Trudi had not looked delighted by my vote of confidence. "Well, I'll *try*," she'd finally said.

Now, as I stood freezing to death in front of a locked door, I realized that Trudi's last little statement should've tipped me off. People never say "I'll try" when they're sure they're going to succeed. "I'll try" is what they say when they know they're going to fail.

"Trudi, you asshole," I said, taking my purse off my shoulder and unzipping the main pocket. I'd dropped my keys in there right after I'd locked my car. Believe me, I'd never have done such a thing if I'd had any idea that the office door was not going to be open.

Because dropping anything into my purse is like tossing it into a black hole.

My keys had apparently been sucked into a parallel universe, because they certainly didn't seem to be in my purse anymore.

As I began going through every inch of the damn thing, I also began calling Trudi every name I knew. While, of course, my extremities quietly turned blue.

In the interest of variety, I'd been reduced to calling Trudi a nerd-bird by the time I finally located my keys and got the front door open.

Once I was inside, my mood did not improve.

On my desk, printed in blue ink, was a note. It must've been torn off the pad in a big hurry, because a good quarter inch of the top of the paper was missing. Torn diagonally across, the note began, TO S.R.

After this warm salutation, Trudi must've decided that it was going to take too long to print the entire thing. Even though the rest of the note continued in blue ink, it was no longer printed. Written in bold, familiar scrawl, it said:

A client called, wanting you to show them the listing at 1422 Saratoga. Since you weren't here, I thought I'd help you out. Back soon. Trudi.

The *i* in the name Trudi, as usual, was dotted with a little heart.

I barely noticed that, though. What I was staring at was the second sentence. I knew very well that what Trudi meant was not *I thought I'd help you out*, but *I thought I'd help myself to your commission*.

This was not the first time Trudi had taken another agent's leads. Barbi Lundergan had complained to me more than once that she was sure Trudi had been stealing messages off her desk. And Charlotte Ackersen, who rarely had a bad word to say about anybody, had actually started referring to Trudi as "that thieving bitch."

Under the guise of being helpful, Trudi had walked off with several clients who'd initially come into the office looking *specifically* for either Charlotte, Barbi, or me. All three of us had complained to Jarvis about it, and yet his only response had been to say that he found Trudi "inspiring." But then again, I noticed that Trudi had always been very careful never to steal one of Jarvis's clients—or any clients, for that matter, belonging to Jarvis's wife, Arlene.

Trudi, in my opinion, was not dumb.

Leaving me this little note, however, had to be the height of arrogance. This time she was not only stealing one of my leads, she was flaunting it in my face.

The commission on the listing that Trudi mentioned in her note would not exactly be spare change, either. A brick colonial in one of the most desirable areas in Louisville, 1422 Saratoga Way was in the two-hundred-fifty-thousand-dollar range. The house was a multiple listing, of course—meaning that any realtor working at any agency on the multiple listing system could sell it, but the selling realtor would have to split the commission with the listing realtor fifty-fifty. Even still, at the current commission rate of seven percent, if I sold the Saratoga house, my half would be over eight thousand dollars.

I'd shown the house a couple of times, so I knew that its owners had been transferred to another state, and that the house had been standing vacant for quite some time. It had been listed originally with a small real estate agency located in the Highlands, much like Arndoerfer Realty. The owners had signed the standard listing agreement, giving this particular agency the right to sell their home for six months. Most homes sell within six months, but this one sure didn't.

In my opinion, its failure to sell might've had a little something to do with the way the owners had originally priced it about twenty thousand dollars over what it was worth.

When that first listing contract expired, the owners had switched to a medium-sized Century 21 agency in St. Matthews, an area not far from the Highlands. And, what do you know, they'd also lowered their price.

What this meant to me was that the owners were getting anxious—and more and more willing to consider any and all offers.

What this also meant to me was that Trudi stealing this one lead of mine could end up costing me thousands.

And she had the *gall* to leave me a note telling me she was doing it!

This turn of events was not a complete surprise. I already knew Trudi was not the least bit apologetic about her behavior. In fact, when I'd taken it upon myself to discuss it with her, Trudi had acted totally astonished that anybody would even *think* she was doing something wrong.

I'd even gone so far as to point out the exact section of the Arndoerfer Realty manual that specifically prohibits one realtor from going after another realtor's clients. Trudi, however, didn't seem to get it. She'd told me, with a straight face, "I have never, *ever* gone after anybody else's clients." I had to hand it to her, too. When she told me this, she'd actually managed to look hurt that anyone would accuse her of such a terrible thing.

According to Trudi, what few times she'd ended up with a client who used to work with another agent, it was the client himself who'd initiated the switch.

Uh-huh. Right. And if I believed that, Trudi no doubt had a bridge she wanted to sell me.

What made things worse for me was that up until Trudi got here, I had been Arndoerfer Realty's best-selling agent. Now Trudi and I were neck-and-neck for the title.

Trudi's success was all the more amazing since Trudi had only gotten her real estate license a scant two weeks before she came on board, and it usually takes months, at the very least, for a new agent to build up a client base.

Of course, you can acquire a client base a *lot* more quickly if you make a habit of stealing other agents' clients.

Now, standing there at my desk, staring at Trudi's note, I took one of those deep cleansing breaths that all the talk shows say are supposed to reduce stress.

It didn't help.

There was no indication on the note as to what time Trudi had left the office, so there was no telling how long the office had been unmanned. I myself had been out for over two hours, and for all I knew, Trudi easily could have left right after I did.

Other than Trudi's note, there were no other messages on my desk. Either none of my clients had phoned, or else there had been nobody here to take their calls.

I was suddenly so furious that my hand shook as I crumpled the note up and tossed it in the garbage can under my desk.

I guess I was so mad I only barely registered that Barbi Lundergan had just walked through the front door and was headed toward her desk.

As the crumpled note hit the wastebasket, Barbi glanced my way. I must've looked exactly like I felt, because Barbi's eyes widened. "Did Shitty-toe steal another one of your leads?"

"Shitty-toe" was Barbi's less-than-fond nickname for Trudi Vittitoe. Barbi was not exactly a rocket scientist—she'd once asked me how many quarters there were in a football game—but in this one instance, she'd shown real creativity. A couple of times Barbi had even been so bold as to call Trudi "Shitty-toe" to her face. Both times, strangely enough, Trudi had acted as if she hadn't heard a word.

Evidently, Trudi could develop hearing problems on a moment's notice, too.

For somebody I'd never thought was particularly smart, Barbi certainly seemed to have Trudi's number long before I did. In fact, Barbi seemed to dislike Trudi from the moment Trudi walked in the front door.

At first Barbi told me that she didn't much care for Trudi because Trudi also ended her name with an *i.* At the time I'd found this hard to believe, but Barbi kept insisting that she hated copycats.

Of course, one reason I found Barbi's sudden aversion to copycats difficult to swallow was that I was pretty sure I knew the real reason for Barbi's animosity. It was the same reason Barbi had often been rude to me. Particularly if an eligible male was anywhere in the vicinity.

Ever since the day Barbi turned thirty-nine, she had been on the Great Manhunt. That meant if you were an attractive female over the age of twelve within a five-mile radius of Barbi, she was going to view you as competition. And she was not going to be treating you kindly.

It didn't exactly take a private detective to deduce why on earth Barbi might not care for someone who looked like Farrah Fawcett.

Then again, after Trudi had been an Arndoerfer
Realty agent for about a week, Barbi had even more
reason to dislike Trudi.

Barbi had announced on her thirty-ninth birthday
that she was going to marry a wealthy man before she
turned forty, and until Trudi showed up, it looked as
if Barbi was right on target. Virtually overnight Barbi
had changed her office attire from tailored suits to
low-cut, clingy dresses, her office shoes from sensible
flats to five-inch stilettos, and her hair from brunet to
platinum blond. Barbi started speaking in a voice that
suggested severe asthma, she started putting on her
makeup as if Tammy Faye Bakker were her role
model, and she started wearing perfume so strong, I
half expected to see swarms of bees following her car.

Barbi's complete metamorphosis was pretty amazing to watch, but what was even more amazing was
that it actually seemed to work. The day Trudi signed
on with Arndoerfer Realty, Barbi had been dating two
wealthy men at the same time—Samuel Whitney of
Whitney Construction, Inc., and Mason Vandervere
of Vandervere Design Corporation. I myself always
referred to Samuel and Mason as S & M.

Back then, Barbi had been trying to make up her
mind which of the two was the better catch—meaning,
of course, which had the most money—when Trudi
put an end to both relationships.

By telling S about M. And M about S.

Trudi's story has always been that she had no idea
that Barbi had not *already* told both men herself, or
she would never have said anything. I, however, am
not so sure. Trudi's revelations to S & M came exactly
one day after Barbi called Trudi "Shitty-toe" to her
face.

Although at the time Trudi had acted as if she
hadn't heard, I believe I've already demonstrated how

easy it is to fake such a thing. Besides, I myself was in the office when Barbi called Trudi that, and I was sure that Trudi could not possibly have missed it.

I was also sure that I detected a triumphant look on Trudi's face when both men called Barbi—at the office—and broke it off with her.

Trudi, though, insisted it had all been a mistake. According to Trudi, she just couldn't *believe* that Barbi had not been completely honest with the two men all along, because *everybody* knows that good relationships are built on trust.

Trudi said this several times in Barbi's presence. Every time Trudi said it, she immediately took the opportunity to describe at length what a wonderful relationship she and her own husband, Derek, happened to have. According to Trudi, she and Derek had a marriage made in heaven because she and Derek had always been completely honest with each other. "Derek and I have a special closeness that most married couples just don't have," Trudi had told everybody in the office. More than once.

Barbi, on the other hand, had told everybody in the office more than once that *she'd* like to give Trudi a special closeness to a hot poker.

Trudi did seem to be speaking the truth about her husband, however. Derek had had flowers delivered to the Arndoerfer real estate office on Tuesday afternoon of every week since the day Trudi first came to work here.

You really couldn't miss their arrival, because every single time Trudi squealed, as if it were a big surprise, "Oh, that Derek! He is such a doll! He spoils me!" Then she would all but strut around the office for the rest of the day.

Barbi had been known to try to trip her.

Now I wish she'd succeeded. "You guessed it," I

said to Barbi, staring holes through the crumpled note in my garbage can. "Trudi has just stolen one of my leads, and when she gets back, I'm going to break her legs."

I meant that figuratively rather than literally, but that must've been a nuance lost on Barbi. She looked startled.

"What I mean is, I'm going to give Trudi a piece of my mind."

After I said this, Barbi actually looked a little disappointed. As if maybe she'd already started looking forward to Trudi's upcoming leg-breaking.

As the day wore on, I realized that I myself was looking forward to telling Trudi at last exactly what I thought of her. I even found myself going over it in my mind, again and again. Exactly what I intended to say to her the second she walked in the door. And exactly what I intended to tell Jarvis—in Trudi's presence. All about how Trudi, his "inspiration," had gone off, leaving the office unattended.

As it turned out, there was only one tiny problem with my little plan.

Trudi never did return.

Chapter
2

The phone calls began around two. To be exact, I suppose I should say the Trudi phone calls began around two. Because there were, of course, other calls that came in before then.

In fact, the phone had been ringing on a pretty regular basis ever since I'd gotten back to the office. As the only real estate agent on floor duty, it was my job to answer the thing. By two I'd taken at least one message for every agent in the office except Barbi, and the only reason I hadn't taken any messages for her was that she was still at her desk. All I had to do was buzz Barbi if the call was for her.

I'd even had a couple of phone calls myself. The Conovers—newlyweds in their late thirties whom I'd been helping house-hunt for the last several weeks—had phoned, asking to see the very house that Trudi had mentioned in her note. The vacant one on Saratoga. I'd made an appointment to show it to them the very next morning at ten. Assuming, of course, that Trudi had not already sold it by then.

I'd also made an appointment to show a listing of

mine. This particular listing, on Ashwood Drive, had been standing vacant for a while, too. Only it was vacant for a different reason. The current owner of the Ashwood house—a woman in her nineties—had moved to a nursing home, and now her children were in the process of selling her house.

According to the guy who'd called asking for the appointment—a Mr. Irving Rickle—he'd driven by the Ashwood house, gotten my telephone number off the sign in the front yard, and was very eager to see the interior.

Irving must not have been as eager as he said he was, though, because when I'd suggested seeing the house later today, he'd said, "Tomorrow evening would be better for me. How about meeting me there at seven? That way, I'll have just enough time to get there after I get off work."

Over the phone, Irving had sounded exactly like Don Knotts. When I hung up, I was picturing the guy wearing a deputy uniform, and maybe carrying around a single bullet in his shirt pocket.

The phone rang again as soon as I put the receiver down. I answered, expecting to hear Don Knotts on the other end again. No doubt asking how long it took to drive here from Mayberry.

It wasn't Irving, though.

"Hello?"

I recognized the deep, rumbling voice the moment he spoke. Lord knows, I'd spoken to him often enough during the last six months. Trudi's husband, Derek, had made it a habit to phone her at the office at least twice a day every day. I'd been impressed. Particularly since a lot of the time Trudi had practically barked into the receiver. "Look, Derek, I can't talk right now, okay? I'm busy." Either the man was not easily discouraged, or else he, too, had a hearing problem.

Now I made my voice as cheery as I could. "Derek," I said, "how are you?"

Maybe I was right about him having a hearing problem, Derek didn't answer my question. Instead, he went straight to: "Schuyler, is Trudi there? I've been waiting for her here at Lily's for almost an hour."

It didn't exactly surprise me that Trudi would choose Lily's for lunch. Around Louisville, restaurants are sort of like belly buttons. There are innies and outies. Lily's, an elegant five-star restaurant located on Bardstown Road, was most definitely an inny. Leave it to Trudi to want to lunch with the in crowd.

Derek was sounding tense. "I'm really sorry to have to bother you, but I thought, well, maybe Trudi had forgotten our lunch date."

I blinked at that one. The man had been stood up, and yet he was actually apologizing for having to phone to find out what had happened.

I couldn't help smiling. Because naturally what went through my mind immediately was: *Lord. Does Trudi have this guy well trained, or what?*

I wasn't at all concerned about Trudi. In fact, I checked my watch almost casually. "Well, Derek, Trudi was gone when I got back to the office, and that was about an hour ago," I said.

"An hour ago?" Derek said. "She's been gone an *hour,* and she hasn't shown up here yet?" Now Derek sounded even more worried.

"Actually, I'm not sure exactly how long she's been gone." As I said this, I leaned over and started rummaging through my garbage can for Trudi's little memo. "Before she left, Trudi wrote me a note. It didn't have the time written on it, so I don't know exactly when she left it. The note said, though, that she was going to show a listing on Saratoga." I was still looking through my garbage can for Trudi's memo. My garbage can was filled to the brim with paper wads—mostly because I'm the world's worst typist. Short of dumping the can out on the floor, it looked as if finding Trudi's little memo was going to be a lot more difficult than I thought. I gave up trying.

Instead, I reached over, got the latest multiple listings book I keep on the corner of my desk, and gave Derek the address of the listing on Saratoga. Derek repeated it slowly, as if he were committing it to memory. "1422 Saratoga Way? Well, I guess I'll drive out there. Maybe Trudi got hung up, writing a contract or something."

I actually winced. It crossed my mind to say, *Considering how many commissions she's been stealing lately, I wouldn't put it past her,* but I didn't. My voice, in fact, was as even as I could make it as I said, "Maybe so."

I told Derek good-bye, hung up the phone, and once again went over in my mind all the things I intended to tell Trudi the second she showed up.

I took another one of those deep cleansing breaths supposed to be stress-relieving—still no help—and I went back to the paperwork on my desk. Forty-five minutes later, I was completing a loan application for a client when Derek called again. "Schuyler, is Trudi there yet?"

"No, she isn't." It was a true measure of my profound concern that I continued to fill out the loan form as I spoke. "I take it Trudi wasn't at the house on Saratoga?"

"No, she wasn't," Derek said. His voice now actually sounded a little shaky. "Are you sure that's where she said she was headed? Because I drove by that address, and there's nobody there."

I don't know, but I guess his being so closely connected to Trudi made my feelings for her sort of seep over onto him. I felt a quick surge of impatience. "Derek," I said through my teeth, "all I know is, that's what her note said."

The implication here was that Trudi might not have been telling the entire story—Lord knows, the woman was not exactly George Washington when it came to telling the truth—but it went right over Derek's head. "Look," he said, "I hate to be a bother, but could you ask around the office? To see if anybody has heard from her?" He paused, and then added, "To be honest, I'm getting a little worried."

I drew another impatient breath, and thought, *Worried? About what, for God's sake? Trudi's obviously decided to take the afternoon off. It wasn't the first time she'd done such a thing, and it wouldn't be the last.*

Oh, yes, those were the exact words that flashed through my mind. *It wouldn't be the last.*

I held the receiver away from my ear, however, and did as I was told. Turning to look around the office, I said, "Anybody talk to Trudi lately?"

Charlotte Ackersen was in the office by then, along with Barbi. Both of them shook their heads.

"Derek," I said, "nobody's talked to her."

He didn't answer me right away, and for a moment I thought he'd hung up on me. "Derek?" I finally said.

"I'm here." If anything, he managed to sound even more worried than before.

There was another long pause. I was getting impatient again. I mean, what did Derek expect me to do? He wasn't talking, and I certainly had other things to do besides hang on the phone, waiting for him to think up something to say.

"Look," I said, "I'll have Trudi give you a call as soon as she comes in, okay?"

"Oh. Sure. That'll be fine," Derek said. "Have her call me right away. Please." He not only sounded distracted, he acted it. He didn't even say good-bye before he hung up.

Sitting there at my desk, with the dial tone sounding in my ear, I didn't have a doubt in my mind that Trudi was playing games with old Derek. She was probably mad at her husband for some imagined slight, and she'd decided to teach him a lesson by pulling a disappearing act for a few hours.

Playing games with people *was* a sport Trudi seemed to enjoy. She just loved to wind people up and set them spinning.

Hadn't she set my own son, Nathan, spinning a few months ago?

That's right. Shortly after Trudi started working at Arndoerfer Realty, Nathan had come by the office to have lunch with *me,* and Trudi had immediately glommed onto him.

Her desk was all the way across the room from mine, and yet the second Nathan walked in the door, Trudi had come rushing right over, tossing her head so that all those layered blond waves seemed to float around her head. "Why, hi, there," Trudi said, grabbing Nathan's arm. "What's a handsome guy like you doing in a place like this?" Her eyes were mocking.

Nathan, struck by the full force of Trudi's long-lashed gaze, said, "I, uh, I, uh, I, uh—"

Since it seemed as if Nathan's entire vocabulary had suddenly been reduced to just two syllables—and mumbled ones at that—I thought I'd better help out. "Trudi, meet my son, Nathan."

I wasn't sure if Trudi was acting or not, but her perfectly lipsticked mouth dropped open. Letting go of Nathan's arm and taking a step back so that she could gaze directly into his face, Trudi said, "You're Schuyler's *son*?" Oddly enough, on this particular occasion she actually remembered how to pronounce my name. Evidently, her memory went in and out like a radio on the fritz. "Why, goodness me," Trudi went on, "I—I just can't believe it!"

I could take that little comment two ways. The good way was that Trudi was implying that I was too young to have a son Nathan's age. Nathan was just twenty, but on this particular day, he was doing Corporate Nathan. Meaning that he was wearing a gray pin-striped designer suit. So that he looked older.

The bad way I could take Trudi's comment was that she was implying that I was too ugly to have a son this handsome.

I decided it would probably be better not to ask Trudi which way was correct.

When Nathan was finally able to say something besides "I" and "uh," he moved right on to "yeah" and "uh-huh." He was, of course, staring at Trudi the way he always stares at extremely good-looking women. As if he were about to drool.

I was now staring at *him.* I was pretty sure I'd seen doughnuts less glazed than this boy's eyes.

"That's right," Nathan went on. "I'm—uh—I'm—uh—" Nathan had been reduced to a two-syllable vocabulary again. He seemed to be searching for just the right phrase. What he finally settled on was, "I'm—uh—my mother's son."

Trudi laughed out loud, glancing over at me.

What could I say? Things like this make a mom proud.

Nathan must've immediately realized what he'd just said, because he went pink to his hairline. "I mean, I'm, uh, *her* son," he said, pointing at me. "*Hers,* yeah, that's right."

I was still staring at him. As a living example of the Ridgway gene pool, he seemed to be draining the shallow end *fast.*

Trudi laughed out loud again. "Oh, Schuyler, your son is *such* a doll!" she said.

I gave her a quick, tight smile.

Turning back to Nathan, Trudi went on. "You know, I've got a wonderful idea! You've *got* to meet my younger sister, Anne. You and Anne would make *such* a cute couple!"

Nathan, Lord love him, immediately asked what had to be the most important question on his mind. "Does your sister look anything like you?"

Trudi didn't laugh out loud this time. She giggled. Like a junior-high-schooler. "You mean, are there any more at home like me?"

That one apparently broke Nathan up. He stood there, all six feet two of him, laughing into Trudi's upturned eyes.

Trudi responded by batting her eyelashes. "Oh, you silly," she said, playfully tapping him on the arm, "you don't want someone like me. I'm too old for you."

Nathan was beginning to shake his head, like a total idiot, when Trudi hurried over to her desk. She returned immediately with a snapshot she'd dug out of her purse. "That's my sister, Anne. Isn't she precious?" Glancing over at me again, Trudi went on. "Schuyler, your handsome son and my precious sister would make the most striking couple!"

I stared at her. *Striking* was the word, all right. In fact, at that very moment, I was seriously thinking about *striking* Trudi. Hard. The last thing I wanted was any more of a connection to Trudi.

Nathan, however, evidently agreed with Trudi with regard to just how precious Anne was. Before I finally managed to drag him off to lunch, he'd let Trudi phone her sister and arrange a blind date for the two of them.

"You two are going to hit it off," Trudi had called

after Nathan as he and I were going out the door. "I guarantee it! I have a sixth sense about these things; I really do!"

To tell you the truth, I personally didn't give it a chance in hell. And yet—can you believe it?—Trudi seemed to be right on the money. Not only did Anne and Nathan indeed make a striking couple, the two of them had started going out regularly right after that first blind date. Now they'd been together for all of two months.

I wasn't sure, but I thought this might very well be a relationship longevity record for Nathan.

You'd think as Nathan's mother I'd be very supportive of his staying with just one woman for a change. And yet, that was not exactly my reaction when Trudi had walked up to me in the office just two days ago. Her big blue eyes had been dancing with excitement. "Look, I don't want to be telling tales out of school, but Anne is—well, no, I don't want to betray a confidence or anything like that, but—well, Anne is—no, no, I better not say anything—"

I'd been sitting at my desk, writing up a new listing, but Trudi had kept on like this until finally I'd had enough. "Okay, Trudi," I said, putting down my Bic and looking up at her, "what exactly are you trying to tell me?"

Trudi had giggled again. For a woman her age, she was amazingly good at giggling. "Well, I probably shouldn't be saying anything—not yet, anyway—but I've been told that wedding bells are going to be ringing *soon*!" The way she said that last word made it sound as if it had two syllables. Soo–oon. Clasping her hands together, Trudi had trilled. "Oh, won't it be wonderful? Just think of it, Schuyler, you and me—in-laws!"

I stared at her. The thought was enough to make me want to throw myself in front of oncoming traffic.

It wasn't merely the idea of Trudi becoming a relative of mine that made me think that this marriage wasn't the best idea I'd ever heard, either. To be honest, I wasn't at all sure either one of my sons was mature enough to be even *thinking* about getting married. Let alone actually going through with it.

Even though Nathan was all of twenty, only a year younger than his brother, Daniel, both my sons had amply demonstrated their vast level of maturity months ago by flunking out of the University of Louisville.

At—not at all incidentally—*my* expense.

Right after U of L requested that my sons do something else with their time besides enroll in classes, both Nathan and Daniel had assured me, at length, that they intended to go back to school. The next time they would even pay their own way.

They were going to return, in fact, just as soon as U of L would let them back in.

Yeah, *right,* as Nathan himself would say.

Two semesters had passed since their dismissal, and I knew very well that they could both petition the university to return if they wanted to. Neither of them, oddly enough, had even mentioned going back.

What a shock.

It also did not escape my notice that Trudi's *striking couple* had been dating for a mere eight weeks, for God's sake. It seemed to me that any talk of matrimony was more than a little premature.

And, in Nathan's case, I'd guess it to be, oh, about ten *years* premature.

If I were pressed, I'd also have to admit that there were a few things about Trudi's sister, Anne, that gave me pause.

To begin with, Anne was twenty-eight. That's right, *eight*—count them, one, two, three, four, five, six, seven, *eight* years older than Nathan.

Now, if Nathan were a model of maturity, I wouldn't think anything of this age difference. I myself happen to be an entire year older than the man in my life, so believe me, I'd be the first one to admit that maturity is not something you measure just in years.

On the other hand, no matter how you measured it, Nathan didn't measure up. In fact, if I were trying to come up with an antonym for maturity, I'd probably have to say, "Nathan."

Nathan, you see, is a kid who always says very loud, "Who turned out the lights?" when the theater lighting dims just before the movie starts. Nathan not only says this, but after he says it, he always laughs extremely loud. As if he'd just come up with something incredibly clever.

Even if Nathan did not misbehave in movie theaters, I'd still have my doubts about Anne. Anne has an M.B.A. and works as a marketing director for a small local bank. And yet, Anne seemed to be in instant, heavy-duty love with Nathan. Who has a high school diploma and works at a small local Burger King.

What was wrong with this picture?

I realize that maybe I couldn't quite see Anne's attraction to my son just because I can't quite picture Nathan as the object of *any* grown woman's desire. This inability could possibly have something to do with the way I could distinctly recall *diapering* Nathan at one time.

And yet, I had to admit, judging from the long list that Nathan's ex-girlfriends would make, quite of few young women have indeed apparently found him attractive.

For a while, anyway.

I, of course, was not the least bit surprised that Nathan found *Anne* attractive. Anne did happen to possess all the attributes that Nathan has always required in a girlfriend. One, Anne was female. Two, Anne was breathing. And three, Anne was pretty.

Anne wasn't as pretty, in truth, as Trudi, but she was still very attractive. About two inches shorter than Trudi, Anne didn't quite have Trudi's knockout figure. She did have the same huge blue eyes, and the same high cheekbones, but where Trudi's hair was blond, Anne's was so dark, it was almost black.

In fact, right after his and Anne's first date, Nathan had phoned me to say that "this time might be it, Mom, this might be the one. I've got a feeling."

I had not said anything at the time, but I was pretty sure that Nathan had had "a feeling" several hundred times since he'd gone through puberty.

What's more, as I mentioned earlier, the second Trudi mentioned the word "wedding," I had a few feelings myself. Some suicidal.

"It's so exciting, isn't it?" Trudi had hurried on. "We're going to be *family!*"

"Wow," had been all I could manage to say.

I was almost certain that Trudi had known exactly how I'd really felt about her little matrimonial news flash. Her mouth had still been smiling, but there had been a look in her eyes that seemed to relish my discomfort.

Oh, yes, I'd say Trudi derived a great deal of pleasure out of playing games with people.

In fact, I was so sure Trudi's leaving her husband to cool his heels at Lily's was yet another one of her little games that I didn't even get worried when I got the third Trudi phone call around four. "Is Trudi Vittitoe in, please?"

"No, she isn't. May I take a message—" I started to say, and then I recognized the caller's voice. "Anne?"

"Schuyler?" Trudi's sister sounded as worried as Derek. "Trudi was supposed to meet me to go shopping, and she didn't show up. Do you have any idea where she could be?"

I suppressed an exasperated breath. Was I Trudi's keeper, or what? "I don't have any idea where she is," I said. Too late, I realized I sounded a little testy.

Anne now sounded offended. "Well, I'm certainly sorry to bother you, Schuyler—"

Oh, God. Now I'd done it.

I'd been very careful ever since Nathan and Anne had started dating to be just as nice as I could be around both Anne and Trudi. I certainly hadn't wanted to put my son in the middle of a fight between his girlfriend's family and his mother.

Now I hurried to say, "Oh, my goodness, Anne, it's no bother. No bother at all! I'm sure there's nothing to be concerned about, but I'll be glad to have Trudi call you the second she walks in."

I went on to tell Anne what Trudi's memo had said, and I gave her the address on Saratoga, just like I'd done with Derek.

By the time I was finished, the edge had disappeared from Anne's voice. "Thanks for your help, Schuyler," she said. "I'm going to drive by the Saratoga house and see if she's there—"

I started to tell her that Derek had already done that, but Anne had hung up. Apparently, under duress, Anne—like her brother-in-law—didn't think good-byes were necessary.

By six o'clock that evening, there was no one left in the office but me, and I'd lost count how many times Derek and Anne had phoned. As time went on, their voices had gotten more and more tense, and their questions more and more anxious. During Derek's last call, he'd asked me, "Do you think I should call the police? Do you think we should report her missing?"

I had no idea, but I had to admit, Derek's and Anne's fear *was* catching.

I was actually beginning to wonder. Lord. Could something terrible really have happened to Trudi?

The first emotion I felt after that little thought crossed my mind was a quick flash of happiness.

The second emotion I felt was, of course, major guilt. I mean, how could I possibly feel happy about a thing like that for even a moment?

Around six-thirty, as I was closing the office for the day, Derek phoned one more time to tell me that he and Anne had indeed decided to contact the police. "The police won't officially list Trudi as a missing person until she's been gone forty-eight hours, but they have started to look unofficially for Trudi's car," Derek told me.

Trudi drove a bright yellow Karmann Ghia. "It shouldn't be hard to spot," I said.

I was just trying to sound reassuring, but as it turned out, I was absolutely right. I spotted it myself the very next morning.

Chapter
3

I wish I could say that worrying about Trudi kept
me up all night long, and that the next morning
Trudi was the first thing I thought of when I opened
my eyes.

The truth is, I slept like a baby, and the next morning the first thought that popped into my head was,
*Do I have a pair of panty hose that doesn't have any
runs?* If I didn't, I was going to have to hit a store
before I met the Conovers at ten.

That thought alone was enough to propel me immediately out of bed. While I was feverishly searching
through the laundry bag that I store my panty hose
in—trying on this pair and that pair, and finally finding
some No Nonsense ones that only had a rip in the
panty part—I did wonder briefly if Trudi had showed
up yet.

That was about it, though.

I took my shower, got dressed, wolfed down my
usual nourishing breakfast—a large glass of Coke,
heavy on the ice, and a few handfuls of Fritos—and I
didn't think of Trudi again.

In my defense, I'd like to make it clear that, at this point, I didn't think there could be even the slightest possibility that Trudi might not *ever* show up again.

To be painfully honest, one reason this particular possibility sounded so far-fetched was that it also sounded too good to be true.

The only thing, in fact, that worried me about Trudi on that Wednesday morning was the distinct possibility that she could've already sold the house on Saratoga, and that this morning's appointment with the Conovers might be a waste of time.

Standard procedure, of course, is that when you write a contract on a property, you enter the information right away on the computer back at the office. If the contract is accepted, you designate the property as "off market." Since our office computer is tied into a computer network linking all the other multiple listing offices, updating the office computer lets all the other agents in this area know a property's current status. If nothing else, it's just simple courtesy to keep other agents from putting in a lot of time on a lost cause.

Courtesy, however, seemed to be something that never troubled Trudi. It seemed to be standard procedure for Trudi, in fact, never to enter anything on the office computer—until somebody insisted that she do it. I'd never been able to decide if Trudi put off this little chore because she considered typing to be beneath her. Or if she put it off because she just wanted to play her cards close to the vest.

Whatever Trudi's reason, I knew checking the computer at the office would be pointless, so I didn't bother. In fact, I didn't even stop by the office on my way to the Saratoga house. I just got in my Tercel and headed straight there.

I'd made the appointment for ten, but I fully ex-

pected Carl and Becky Conover to be late. As I mentioned earlier, I'd been helping the Conovers house-
hunt for the last eight weeks or so. They'd been late
quite a bit more than they'd been on time.

I'd even brought along the latest Taylor McCafferty
mystery to read, just in case. Taylor McCafferty's novels are humorous, and if I had to spend a significant
amount of time cooling my heels, waiting for my clients to show up, I knew I'd need a good laugh.

I used to think that the Conovers were late so much
because they were unbelievably inconsiderate. Now,
after spending some time with them, I realize that it
wasn't because they were unbelievably *in*considerate.
It was actually because they were unbelievably considerate. Of each other.

Neither Carl nor Becky would even *think* of rushing
the other. Even if it meant that they were going to be
late for an appointment.

The very first time I took them out house-hunting,
Becky had mentioned that she and Carl had been married only three months, and that this was the second
marriage for them both. This definitely perked my interest because of my own situation these days.

Matthias Cross—you remember, the man in my life
who was a year younger than me—he and I had been
dating over nine months now, and lately he'd begun
saying those three special words that mean a relationship is getting serious. That's right, he'd been mentioning *moving in together.*

It had taken me a while, believe me, to say those
three other special words, but I had finally told him
how I felt about him. These days I didn't have any
doubt that I loved Matthias. I didn't even doubt that
Matthias loved me.

But, let's face it, was loving somebody any reason
to throw caution to the wind and start living together?

I can't say that the Conovers were exactly walking advertisements for the entire concept, either. Apparently, these two had made up their minds that the way to avoid divorce was to avoid arguments. And the way to avoid arguments was never to put any demands on the other one, and—oh, yes—never, never, *never* express a definite opinion about anything.

During those times I'd met with them so far, I'd had trouble getting either Becky or Carl to say that it was a nice day, let alone if they liked a particular house or not.

Of course, the two of them did have quite a lot at stake. Becky had also told me that she and Carl each have three children from their previous marriages. Six assorted kids in all. All under the age of thirteen.

Now I know why that Brady Bunch couple on television never seemed to argue—and why they both walked around with those bland smiles on their faces all the time. Mr. and Mrs. Brady had been terrified they might split up and one or the other might end up with complete custody.

I wish I could say that I found the way Becky and Carl constantly consulted each other on every single thing to be incredibly sweet—and, no doubt, an inspiring example of how marriage is supposed to work. To tell you the truth, though, after hearing Becky say to Carl for what seemed like the millionth time, "Honey, what do you think?" and after hearing him reply still *again,* "I don't know, sweetheart. What do *you* think?" I found it hard not to scream.

What I wanted to scream most was: *"For god's sake, think for yourselves! What are you, Siamese spouses?"*

Not to mention, trying to sell a house to these two was like trying to sell a house to a committee. A committee made up of just two members who steadfastly refused to make a decision. Apparently neither Becky nor Carl wanted to be responsible for making the final choice as to where their combined family was going to live for the next few years. You could also read that last statement as, Neither one of them wanted to take the blame.

Can you believe the vacant house on Saratoga would be the fifty-second house I'd shown these two? That's right, they'd had *fifty-one* chances before now to actually make up their minds. I do believe, if the choice to declare independence had been left up to the Conovers back in 1776, we'd all still be speaking with a British accent.

But the divorce rate could be lower.

My only ray of hope was that Becky had also mentioned, about the same time as she was telling me everything else, that the entire family was now living in a crowded townhouse apartment. Surely having six children bouncing off the walls was a situation that couldn't be endured for long.

Things must've been getting desperate, because I'd no more than pulled into the driveway than the Conovers—surprise, surprise—pulled in behind me.

They were out of their car before I was out of mine.

Becky was a petite brunette who obviously didn't have much time to spend on herself. She almost never wore any makeup, and she always looked as if she'd just run a comb through her curly dark brown hair and thrown on whatever she could grab first. Today she'd grabbed green corduroy slacks, a bright red turtleneck, and a white wool blazer. She looked like a Christmas decoration.

Carl was another story, however. Wearing sharply creased gray slacks, a navy blue blazer, a navy-pinstriped ivory shirt, a red tie in the same print as the handkerchief sticking jauntily out of his pocket, and shoes shined to a mirror finish, Carl looked as if he'd just stepped off a yacht.

I stared at him. Apparently, Carl had significantly more time to devote to his wardrobe than Becky did to hers. It could actually make you think that Becky was responsible for not only her own wardrobe but that of the six offspring. Not to mention, judging from the way she was now brushing lint off Carl's shoulder, she could be responsible for Carl's, too.

As I walked toward them, I couldn't help thinking that it certainly didn't take long to figure out who was benefiting most from their current living arrangement.

Particularly since both Carl and Becky worked full-time.

I gave them both a big smile, shook hands all around, and then we all headed up the sidewalk to the front door. Unlocking it, I stepped to one side to let Becky and Carl go in ahead of me.

As they passed me, I found myself doing what I always seemed to do lately when these two walked into a house. I held my breath.

More than once, you see, the happy couple had taken two steps inside a house and one of them had frowned. That was all it took to have the other one say, "If you don't like it, honey, I don't either." A couple of times they'd actually said this with the present owners standing right there in the foyer, their hands out, ready to greet them.

This time, however, neither Carl nor Becky frowned. Becky did murmur, "Hmmm," as she moved down the center hallway, but that was about it.

Wildly encouraged, I waved them both into the living room on the right and started pointing out the working fireplace, the genuine oak hardwood floor, and the extra-high ceiling. I went on for a while about how charming these older homes are, and how they don't make them like this anymore, and so on, but to tell you the truth, I've said this kind of thing so often before, I don't even listen to myself anymore.

When I finished, Carl echoed his wife. "Hmmm." Yet another encouraging sign, if I ever saw one.

While the Conovers were looking over the built-in bookcases on either side of the living room fireplace, I hurried back out into the hall and on into the kitchen. "So, honey, what do you think?" I heard Becky say as I left the room.

I tried not to grit my teeth.

In the kitchen I passed right by the door that I knew from previous visits led to the basement and went straight to the door that led to the garage. I unlocked and opened this one.

I believe up to that moment I'd been intending to leave the door standing wide open, so that the moment the Conovers walked into the kitchen they would be struck by how spacious the two-and-a-half-car garage was. And that, dazzled by the garage, they might overlook the fact that the kitchen cabinets looked as if they'd come straight out of the fifties.

That is, that's what I think I was intending. As soon as I saw what was parked in the garage, however, anything I'd been thinking before then went right out of my head.

There, parked a little sideways, as if its driver had pulled into the garage in somewhat of a hurry, was a bright yellow Karmann Ghia.

I stared at the automobile, my mouth going dry.

I hoped I was wrong, but this thing certainly looked an awful lot like Trudi Vittitoe's car.

I moved through the door, down the steps, and into the garage without taking my eyes off the car. I'm not sure why I kept staring at the thing. It was almost as if I actually believed that if I blinked the car might disappear.

When I moved around to the back of the vehicle, my heart actually gave a little jump. Oh, God. Unless there were two bright yellow Karmann Ghias driving around Louisville with bumper stickers on the back fender that said, WE OPEN ALL THE RIGHT DOORS—with the name Arndoerfer Realty and the office phone number printed right under it—this *was* Trudi's car.

My mouth was now so dry I could hardly swallow. I forced myself, however, to move even closer to the automobile so that I could take a good look inside.

Leaning over, I peered into the front seat. And then into the back.

The car was empty.

Thank God, I immediately thought.

In fact, both the front and back seats looked as if maybe they'd just been vacuumed.

I knew, in the interest of being thorough, that I should probably check out the trunk while I was at it, but I couldn't quite bring myself to do it. If there *was* something in the trunk, I was pretty sure that I didn't want to take a look at it.

Instead I turned and headed back into the kitchen. I had every intention of getting myself a large glass of water, because my mouth suddenly felt as if I'd just eaten a handful of sand. If there were no glasses, large or otherwise, left in the cupboard—and I doubted that there would be, since this house had been vacant for a while—I was going to get a huge gulp of water anyway, drinking it straight from the tap. Once I could speak without sounding as if I were doing a scene from *Lawrence of Arabia,* I intended to phone Trudi's husband, Derek, and tell him that I'd located her car.

The trip back to the kitchen, however, once again took me past the door to the basement. As I went past it, I noticed something I hadn't noticed when I'd gone by the first time.

The door was standing a little ajar.

I stopped dead in my tracks and stared.

Oh, God. My mouth no longer felt as if I'd swallowed a handful of sand. It felt as if I'd swallowed the Sahara.

To hell with even *looking* for a glass. I headed straight to the kitchen sink and stuck my head under the tap. Fortunately, the water had not been turned off. Unfortunately, however, I had my head in the sink and was glugging down water like a fish when Becky Conover's voice sounded right behind me.

"Is there a problem?"

There is no chic way to pull your head out of a sink and wipe water off your chin. I gave it a shot, though. All the while Becky was giving me the fish-eye, appropriately enough.

"Problem?" I repeated. "Oh, my goodness, no. Not at all. I was feeling a bit thirsty, that's all. Just a tiny bit thirsty."

I gave Becky a smile that felt a bit too bright even to me.

I don't know if it was that idiot smile or what I'd just said, but Becky started looking at me as if I might be in dire need of psychiatric help.

I waved a hand in the air. "You know what? I think I'll head on down into the basement now. It would be better, though, if you just stayed up here in the kitchen until I come get you, okay?"

Carl had followed Becky in as I was finishing, and

now he asked the question I was sure had to be on both their Siamese minds. "Why?"

I gave the Conovers another too-bright smile. "I need to make sure that all the lights are on before you go downstairs." My too-bright smile felt as if it were dimming by the second. "Hey," I said, trying for a light tone, "we wouldn't want you bumping into anything down there, now would we?"

Carl returned my smile, but Becky didn't. Instead, she just stared at me. I don't know. Maybe I looked strange, or maybe she could hear the tension in my voice. Becky was still staring at me as I turned to go down into the basement.

I made sure I flicked on the light at the top of the stairs before I started down.

Becky turned to Carl and said something, but to tell you the truth, my heart had started pounding so loud, I couldn't quite make out what she said.

I made my way slowly down the stairs, intending to turn on every light I passed. The only problem was, there didn't seem to be another light until the bottom of the stairs. Stairs that, wouldn't you know it, creaked with my every footstep.

I, of course, flashed immediately on every scary movie I'd ever seen in my entire life. Particularly the one called *The House at the Bottom of the Stairs.* In all those horror movies, the victims-to-be always go looking for the monster. Usually carrying something that would make a really great weapon. Like, oh, say, a penlight.

Watching these movies, I've always said that if I were ever in a similar situation, I'd never, never, *never* do such a thing.

Evidently, I must've been wrong about that, though, because here I was, making my way into a dark basement, with no idea what might be waiting for me down there.

I didn't even have a penlight, for God's sake.

Of course, it could be that my imagination was running away with me. The basement door could've been left open by another real estate agent showing the house. And yet, that didn't exactly explain what Trudi's car was doing out in the garage, did it?

I moved cautiously down the steps, but if anything, my heart seemed to be pounding even louder. I probably would've been even more uneasy, but I'd been down in this basement before. From previous visits, I knew that the basement had been finished, and that it was now a sort of underground rec room. The basement walls had been covered in wood paneling and the concrete floor in dark green carpeting.

As you came down the stairs, there was a long bar with a row of stools directly in front of you. Back against the far wall, under an overhanging Tiffany lamp, was a large pool table.

I also recalled that there was another light switch at the bottom of the steps, around the edge of the wall, on my right. Halfway down, I was already stretching out my hand, getting ready to flip it on.

In spite of everything that had been done to make it seem like just another room of the house, the basement still had the cold, clammy feel of a cave. There were also some smells I picked up on as I moved down the stairs—mildew, ammonia, and the smell of something spoiled. Like hamburger left out on the counter too long.

I was at the bottom of the steps by now, and I immediately turned to my right, groping for the light switch.

As soon as I found it. I turned it on.

I immediately wished I hadn't, though.

In the middle of the wall-to-wall green carpet, lying on her back, her large blue eyes staring fixedly at the ceiling, was—oh, my God—*Trudi*.

Her face was discolored, and the long silk scarf she had been wearing yesterday—the burgundy one color-coordinated to match her outfit—was twisted tightly around her neck.

I took one look.

And I screamed.

Chapter 4

If you see something truly horrible, you can't quite take it all in. At least, that's the way it was with me. I stood there at the bottom of the steps in that clammy, cold basement, staring at poor Trudi, and it seemed to me as if my mind started skipping, like a needle on an old LP record.

It started skipping the instant I saw Trudi. In fact, for a split second there, my mind-needle must've skipped completely off the track, because I went totally blank.

And then, my mind-needle started playing in short spurts. On very high speed.

Ohmigod.

That's somebody dead.

Oh, My God. It's Trudi.

It's really TRUDI.

After that, it took me another split second to totally comprehend what I was seeing. And then my mind-needle jumped into action again.

Oh, God.

Something's on her forehead.

Something's been DONE to—

Once again my mind-needle skipped away.

Staring at Trudi, my hand to my mouth, I wasn't sure if I said the words aloud, or just thought them.

OH, MY GOD.

It looked as if whoever had killed Trudi had also done something else. Something horrible.

He'd carved a little heart in the middle of Trudi's forehead.

Staring at that awful heart, I swayed on my feet as waves of nausea washed over me.

Who on earth could do such a thing?

My knees were really getting wobbly all of a sudden, so I took a quick step back, stumbling a little. Gripping the banister once more, I steadied myself.

As I did, I couldn't help thinking, Lord, the way Trudi dotted her *i*'s with those little hearts must've irritated somebody even more than it had irritated me.

I tried to look away, I really did, but my eyes wouldn't obey. They just kept focusing on one terrible thing after another.

On the horrifyingly deep cut in poor Trudi's forehead. On her large blue eyes staring fixedly at the light bulb overhead. And on her mouth. Her lips were slightly open as if she'd started to scream—and been interrupted.

A small trickle of blood had seeped from the heart-shaped cut on her forehead. It wasn't much blood, considering how deep the wound looked. Did this mean that Trudi had already been dead when this was done to her?

I hoped so. I hated to think of Trudi suffering through that.

I now found myself looking once again at poor Trudi's face. She looked so little, somehow. She may

have been one really irritating human being when she
was alive, but she sure didn't deserve this.

Nobody deserved this.

I'd seen enough. In fact, I'd seen far more than I
wanted to. I started to turn around, to head right back
upstairs, when a piercing scream sounded on the stairs
in back of me.

Apparently, my own scream had brought the Conovers running.

Glancing up, I saw Carl halfway down the basement
stairs, and in back of him, Becky, covering her mouth.
It had been Becky who'd screamed, but Carl definitely
looked as if, had Becky not thought of it first, he'd
have been glad to oblige.

The two of them were frozen, leaning over the banister, staring past me at Trudi, their faces masks of
horror.

I took a deep breath. From the looks on the Conovers' faces, I'd say I'd just chalked up number fifty-
two as another no-sale.

"Becky, Carl," I said, and amazingly enough, my
voice didn't even shake. "I really wish you two had
waited in the living room, like I told you." From my
tone, you might've thought I was a teacher, gently
reprimanding disobedient pupils.

Becky immediately nodded. In fact, her curly head
started going up and down like one of those dogs
people used to keep in the back windows of their
cars. "Oh, my, yes," Becky said, her eyes like blue
saucers. "Oh, my, yes, we should've waited in the living
room. Oh, my, yes."

It was the first definite opinion I'd ever heard out
of her.

Carl also had a definite opinion, would wonders
never cease. "That woman is dead," he said. His eyes
looked dazed.

There really didn't seem to be anything I could add. He'd summed up the entire situation nicely.

I began to herd them both back to the living room. It didn't take much doing. Not at all surprisingly, they seemed eager to go.

"Who *was* that down there?" Carl asked on the way. "Did you know her?"

I nodded. "I knew her," I said. "She was a real estate agent who worked with me."

"A real estate agent?" Becky said. "Somebody killed a real estate agent? Now, why would anybody kill a real estate agent?"

We were well down the center hallway, almost to the living room by then. I stopped not a foot from the doorway, however, to consider what Becky had just asked. Why indeed would anybody kill a real estate agent?

Up to that moment, I'd been thinking along the lines of, Why would anybody kill Trudi? I hated to say it, but coming up with an answer to that one didn't seem terribly difficult. Coming up with an answer to Becky's question, however, was another story. At least, I personally hoped so.

It was just as I was thinking this last that I recalled something. I immediately wished I hadn't. Good Lord. In her memo, Trudi had written that she was going to this very house to meet a client who'd asked for *me*. Did this mean that what had been done to Trudi had really been meant for me?

I went cold all over.

"We've got to call the police," I said.

My voice still wasn't shaking, but it was getting oddly shrill. Carl and Becky didn't seem to notice, though. They just stared at me blankly.

"The phone in this house was disconnected when

the owners moved out, so I'm going to have to go get my car phone," I told them.

I'd gotten one of those cellular bag phones about a month earlier. The salesman at Sears who'd talked me into it had ticked off a variety of circumstances in which I'd find the thing unbelievably handy. Like if my car broke down. Or if I got lost. Or if I needed to check in with my office.

Oddly enough, he hadn't mentioned that it would be useful if I needed to report a murder.

I started to move down the hallway toward the front door, but Becky's voice stopped me. "Since you're going to be busy with the police and all, I guess we'll be on our way. . . ."

I just looked at her. Apparently, it had not occurred to Becky that once she'd gotten a look at Trudi, the police would want to talk with *her,* too. I could tell from the look on Carl's face, however, that it *had* occurred to him. In the interest of continued marital harmony, however, he was apparently quite content to just stand there and let *me* pass on the good news.

"Uh, Becky," I said, "I don't think you're supposed to leave until the police get here."

Becky's eyes got round. She turned to look at Carl. Who, brave man that he was, just happened to be staring at the floor. "Wha–a–at? But we don't even know that woman!" She turned to look back over at me. "You're the one who knows her! So *you're* the one who should—"

I held up my hand. "I think it's sort of like leaving the scene of a car accident. If you run across a dead person, you're supposed to stay and give your statement to the police."

Becky looked back over at Carl. Who, at that moment, had begun to nod his head in agreement with what I'd just said. His eyes, however, were still fixed on the floor.

Becky threw up her hands. "I can't believe we have to talk to the police!"

I just looked at her. I wanted to say, "Believe it," but I didn't. Instead, while the Conovers waited at the front door, apparently unwilling to let me out of their sight, I hurried out to my Tercel. There I retrieved my cellular phone from its hiding place under the driver's seat and carried it back inside. I plugged the adapter gizmo into a wall socket in the living room, pushed the power button, and the phone lit up.

In no time at all, I was dialing 911.

After the woman who answered the phone assured me that we would be having official company very soon, I phoned Derek.

I've been in the real estate business nine entire years, and during that time I've had to tell people some pretty difficult things. Things like, "I'm terribly sorry, but your mortgage application has been turned down." Or, "You know, I believe your lovely home would show even better if you mowed your lawn, if you emptied all your garbage cans, and, oh, yes, if you swept up all those discarded condom wrappers lying next to your bed."

None of these things, however, even came close to what I now had to tell Trudi's husband.

I was tempted to wait and let the police break the news, but then I thought better of it. It seemed pretty mean to just stand by and let the poor guy hear what had happened from total strangers.

I intended, however, to leave out a few pertinent details. Like, for example, I had no intention of mentioning the words "heart" or "forehead."

As soon as Derek said hello, I plunged right in. "Derek, we've found Trudi," I said all in one breath.

I heard him sort of choke a little, and then he said, his voice sounding oddly flat. "What do you mean, you've found her?"

I've read somewhere that, when there are airplane crashes and people have been killed, the airline personnel are instructed to tell the next of kin that the passenger in question is "no longer alive." It's supposed to be easier somehow to hear those three words than the one word "dead." I didn't know if this was really true, but airline people had to have more experience than I did in this particular area. Thank God, I might add. So I decided to go with the experts. "Derek, I'm really sorry, but Trudi is no longer alive."

Those airline people must've known what they were talking about. For a moment there wasn't a sound on the phone. Then I could hear Derek take a long, long breath. Finally, he said in a voice that only shook a little. "I'll be right there."

I gave him the address on Saratoga Way, and then I called Anne.

Anne must've been the notable exception to the airline rule. I'd no sooner finished saying the phrase "no longer alive" when Anne let out a shriek that even the Conovers could hear, and they were standing across the living room at the time. The instant Anne screamed, both Carl and Becky jumped as if an electric shock had gone through them. They looked at each other in mutual horror.

I tried to hold the phone a little tighter to my ear, so that maybe my ear would act as a sort of muffler and the Conovers wouldn't be able to hear any more. "Anne?" I said. "Anne? *Anne?*"

It took a couple of minutes before she'd calmed down enough to be able to listen to me. Even then, I had to repeat the Saratoga Way address several times before I was sure she'd gotten it right.

"I'll be there as fast as I can!" At least, that's what I think Anne said. Her voice was distorted so much by sobbing and carrying on, I could barely make out what she was saying before she hung up.

I'm not sure why, but Anne getting that upset actually made me feel calmer. It was as if on some subconscious level, I decided that if Anne was going to do the Upset-Out-of-Your-Mind part, then it was up to me to do the Calm-and-Collected part. Standing there, still gripping the receiver, I actually felt as if I were thinking a little clearer. It even occurred to me that I ought to make one more phone call—to the listing agent for this house, a Mrs. Edmund Childers.

I'd already met Mrs. Childers when I'd shown the house earlier, and I'd talked to her just yesterday morning, of course, to make the appointment for the Conovers. A stout, short woman in her late fifties who apparently never went anywhere without a wide-brimmed hat and gloves, she'd seemed cordial enough. In fact she'd seemed positively sweet yesterday when she'd told me, "Look, honey, I've got several copies of the house keys, and I'll just leave a set in the mailbox for you. That way you and your clients can spend all the time you want going through the house—and I won't be in your way." What we both knew she was really saying, of course, was that she didn't want to meet anybody at ten in the morning just to unlock a front door, but I'd still thought she was sweet.

Sweet, however, was not the word I would've used to describe her right after I told her about Trudi. *"Wha-a-at?"* she bellowed over the phone. "You mean I entrusted you with the keys to one of my listings and you let another realtor get *killed* there?"

I had to interrupt. She sounded as if I'd been renting out the basement as a sort of OK Corral. "Mrs.

Childers, Trudi Vittitoe was dead when we got here. So what happened had to have occurred before—"

Mrs. Childers cut me off, her tone getting frosty. "Oh, no, it's *your* responsibility. *Yours.* Do you understand that? Now, was there any damage?"

I guess I was a little unclear about what she was asking. "Well, a woman *died.*"

Mrs. Childers now sounded impatient. "I'm not talking about *that.* I mean, to the property. The owners, you know, have entrusted me with—"

This time I cut her off. *"Look,"* I said. My own tone was now not kind. It might've been a little on the loud side, too. Across the room, Becky's and Carl's heads swiveled in my direction. They both looked startled. I turned away from them and lowered my voice. "A person is *dead.* Do you understand that? And if you're so worried about the condition of this house, maybe you ought to get over here and check it out yourself. Since *you're* the listing agent."

There was an audible intake of breath on the other end. "I don't believe I need *you* to tell me what I should or shouldn't do," Mrs. Childers said. The phone lines between us were definitely frosting up. "As the listing agent, I believe *I*—"

I cut her off again. I really didn't do it on purpose, but what she'd just said reminded me of something—something I really wanted to know. Right away. "As the listing agent, you made the appointment with Trudi Vittitoe to show this house yesterday morning, didn't you?" Every appointment to show a property was supposed to go through the real estate agent who'd listed it.

"Well, yes, I *did* make the appointment." Mrs. Childers sounded wary now. "But how was I supposed to know that—"

I didn't care to hear the rest. And what the hey,

Mrs. Childers sounded mad already. What did I have to lose? I interrupted her one more time. "Mrs. Childers, did Trudi happen to mention who she was showing the house to?"

I think I knew the minute I asked the question what the answer was going to be. As I said before, Trudi liked to play her cards close to the vest. To Trudi, giving another agent the name of one of her clients would've been like handing another agent a possible sale.

"No," Mrs. Childers said, "she didn't." The phone lines weren't just frosting up now, they were freezing solid. "I simply told Mrs. Vittitoe that she could find the key in the mailbox, and that was that." Mrs. Childers's tone had turned defensive. "You know, I don't think *you* gave me the names of the people you were taking through the house today, either."

Her point seemed well taken.

"Listen, Mrs. Childers—"

I had every intention of trying to smooth things over, but Mrs. Childers didn't give me the chance. She followed my lead and interrupted *me*. "I'm sorry to cut you off, but I really can't stay on the phone any longer. I will, of course, be there as soon as I can." She heaved a huge sigh at this point. "I hadn't intended to go out today, so I'll have to do my hair and iron something to wear before I can leave. I would appreciate it, however, if you'd stay there until I arrive. Thank you."

Oh, brother. She was doing the excessively polite routine that my mother always does when she's absolutely furious with me. Hey, lady, I hate to tell you, but you are strictly amateur night. My mom could polite you under the table any day of the week.

I probably would've been considerably more concerned about Mrs. Childers and just how angry I'd made her, except that I didn't have time. Five minutes later, Anne showed up. I couldn't believe it. Anne had gotten there even before the police. Unfortunately, when Anne showed up, she brought somebody with her.

Nathan.

Standing in the doorway, I watched my son hurrying up the sidewalk, holding hands with Anne. His jaw was set in a grim line, and he was wearing what he almost always seems to wear no matter what the weather or the occasion—shorts. Nathan does have nice-looking, muscular legs, but you'd think he'd confine himself to showing them off on days when the temperature climbs above seventy. Today was definitely not one of those days. In fact, it hadn't warmed up much since I'd first gotten to the office earlier this morning. Nathan's knees now looked almost as blue as the long-sleeved oxford-cloth shirt he was wearing under his leather jacket.

Watching Nathan's blue knees heading my way, I felt like running toward him, pointing my finger in his face, and telling him to get right back in his car, head straight home, and go to his room. This minute. No buts about it.

And while he was there, put on some jeans, for God's sake.

I wanted to tell him all this, and yet he didn't even live with me anymore.

In fact, there had never been a time in the boy's entire life when I'd wanted to ground him more than I had at that particular moment.

I really didn't want Nathan to see what I had seen. I didn't want Anne to see it either. "Look," I said, stepping in front of her as she came through the front door, "the police aren't here yet, and—"

Anne interrupted me. "And what?" she said. Her

voice had recovered some since I'd talked to her on the phone. "I want to see my sister. Where is she?"

I swallowed before I answered. "She's in the basement, Anne, but there's no need for you to go down there. Believe me, there's nothing that can be done."

Nathan looked more than ready to agree with me. He'd followed Anne in, and he was now standing in the hall right next to her. He turned to look almost pleadingly in her direction. Anne, however, didn't even glance his way. She was staring at me, shaking her head. "You don't understand," she said. "I have to see her. I have to see Trudi with my own eyes."

I stared right back at her. "Anne," I said, "it's bad."

Anne didn't even blink. "How do you get to the basement?" she asked.

"Through the kitchen," I said, "but, Anne, I mean it, you don't—"

"Yes, I do," Anne interrupted. She shoved right by me, headed down the center hall, and made a beeline for the kitchen.

Nathan tried to grab her as she took off, but with a quick movement, Anne dodged his outstretched hand and put some distance between them.

The Conovers were standing in the archway leading into the living room, taking in the entire scene. Their heads swiveled as Anne ran by them.

There didn't seem to be anything else for me and Nathan to do but follow her.

The door to the basement was still standing open. Anne didn't even hesitate. She disappeared down the steps before I could say another word.

Not at all inclined to take another look at Trudi, I did not follow Anne down. I just stood there in the open doorway, with Nathan right beside me, listening to my own heartbeat. My stomach burned.

You could tell the exact moment Anne laid eyes on

poor Trudi, because that's when Anne let loose with the most awful sound I'd ever heard. It was somewhere between a sob and a scream.

Nathan gave me a wild look and then rushed down the stairs after Anne.

I would've tried to stop him, too—much like I'd tried with Anne—but Nathan moved so fast, I didn't have a chance.

I really didn't want to follow the two of them down into the basement, but it looked as if I had no choice. I took a deep breath and started slowly down the stairs, swallowing hard and trying to steel myself against what I was about to see again.

As it turned out, though, I didn't have to steel myself after all. I'd gone down only two steps when Nathan came rushing back up, moving about as fast as his muscular legs could carry him. Anne followed right in back of him.

When Nathan came through the door, his eyes met mine. I could see how pale he'd gone.

"Gross," he said.

Nathan has never had any trouble expressing a definite opinion.

"Nathan," I said, and I know I sounded just like a mom, "didn't I tell you not to go down there?"

It had to be one of the dumbest things I've ever said.

The look Nathan gave me confirmed it. "Yeah, Mom," he said, "you told me." He gave me another look that said, And your point?

In back of him, Anne was now sobbing openly. "Oh, God," she wailed. *"Oh, God! Oh, God! O-O-O-OH, GO-O-O-OD!"*

I don't know. Something was obviously very wrong with me. Down the hall Becky and Carl were both staring at Anne, their faces filled with sympathy. I, on the other hand, was just staring at her. Period.

Anne had grabbed hold of one of Nathan's arms, turned him around to face her, and was now sobbing against his chest. There was no doubt about it. The woman certainly seemed terribly upset. And yet, there was something about her hysterics that didn't quite ring true. I don't know, maybe it was the four "Oh, God's." I mean, you might come up with, oh, say, two, maybe, or even three. But *four*? It seemed a bit excessive to me.

Even as all this was going through my mind, though, I was already scolding myself. I mean, can you believe I was *critiquing* the way another person grieved? For heaven's sake, who did I think I was? Emily Posthumous?

Anne's sobs had grown even louder as she continued to hang onto Nathan as if he were her lifeline. Those did seem to be real tears streaking Anne's cheeks. Genuine moisture, wet as anything.

And yet, I continued to wonder. Was this real, or was it Memorex? Was this actual grief, or a little something being played for the benefit of those watching?

There were, after all, quite a few watching. Indeed, the watchers who seemed most unable to tear their eyes away were the Conovers. They were now wearing identical looks of distaste, and yet, both of them had moved to stand very near the living room doorway where they had a clear view down the hall and into the kitchen. It was also where, no doubt, they wouldn't miss a single distasteful moment.

Of course, there was every chance that I was feeling suspicious of Anne just because of the way I personally felt about Trudi. Maybe, knowing Trudi the way

I did, it was difficult for me to believe that her demise could cause such despair.

Call me callous.

You can also call me a jerk.

I guess it'll be no surprise that this entire thought process caused yet another huge wave of guilt to wash over me.

A few moments later, Anne's sobs had subsided a little. It was a good thing, or I'd never have heard the car door slam out front. A glance through the curtainless double windows of the living room told me that a tall, dark-haired man in an impeccably tailored gray suit had just gotten out of a late-model black BMW and was walking up the sidewalk toward the front door.

Derek, Trudi's husband, had made it here ahead of the police, too.

Even with his face set in grim lines, Derek was still movie-star handsome. As a matter of fact, the first time he'd ever come into the office, I'd thought he looked exactly like somebody Trudi would've married. She certainly wouldn't have settled for anything less. Derek had dark, wavy hair that looked professionally styled, very broad shoulders, and a tan George Hamilton would've envied. To look like this during these gray days of March, the man had either just returned from a tropical vacation or he'd spent a significant part of his life recently lying on a tanning bed.

Anne's head lifted off Nathan's chest the second Derek walked into the room. "Oh, Derek!" she sobbed. "Derek! *Derek!*"

That's right, *three* "Derek's." This was almost as bad as four "Oh, God's."

After that little outburst, Nathan and I pretty much replayed the same scene we'd just played with Anne. Only we played it with Derek.

Unfortunately, we ended up with the exact same results. Derek, like Anne, finally pushed past all of us to go down to the basement to see Trudi for himself. And, yes, once again we could all hear his anguished cry at the bottom of the stairs.

Derek, however, unlike Anne, was not making a sound when he came back up the stairs into the kitchen. Walking jerkily, he actually looked shell-shocked. It took him a moment, but Derek finally managed to say, his voice a croak, "Who could do such a thing?"

That, of course, was the sixty-four-thousand-dollar question.

Who indeed?

Anne apparently did not want to ponder it long because, in the silence that followed Derek's question, she jumped in with, "I'll never forgive myself for not checking inside the house. Never!"

Derek was staring at the floor, but he nodded. "I just wish I'd gone inside," he said woodenly. "Or at least checked the garage."

It appeared to me these two were berating themselves needlessly. I mean, it was certainly easy to understand why Derek and Anne might've thought that Trudi had left. The garage had no windows, so with the doors locked, there was no way that anybody could've known that Trudi's car was in there.

Not to mention, what do they think they could've done? By the time Derek and Anne were driving past Saratoga, Trudi had been missing for hours. It seemed fairly likely that by then Trudi was probably already in her present condition.

"I should have known she was here, I should have known . . ." Anne's voice trailed off into more sobs.

Nathan was clearly out of his depth. When Anne began sobbing again, he actually winced.

Nathan didn't seem to be personally grieving at all. Mainly, he just looked vastly uncomfortable with the excess of emotion around him. Nathan also looked as if he'd really like to leave. Like, immediately.

He kept glancing over at me. As if maybe he was hoping I'd tell him he really was grounded.

When Anne briefly left to go to what she called "the little girl's room," Nathan quickly moved to my side, leaned down, and whispered in my ear, "Mom, what am I supposed to do?"

I stared at him. Either Nathan acts as if I know absolutely nothing, or else he acts as if I'm the world authority on everything. In this instance, I'd evidently been promoted to world authority on How the Boyfriend Should Behave in a Grief Situation. I wasn't sure I knew exactly what he was asking, but I started to whisper back, "Hon, I think your fiancée just needs you to—"

Before I could finish, Nathan interrupted. "Fiancée?" he whispered. "What do you mean, fiancée? Whatever gave you that—"

I actually stepped back so that I could look him straight in the eye. Was he kidding me? I was about to ask him that very question, but we were interrupted by Anne's return. "Oh, Nathan," Anne said, now holding a crumpled Kleenex in one hand. "My poor, poor, poor, poor sister."

That's right. Four "poor's." I found myself staring at her all over again.

Nathan cleared his throat, looking uncomfortable, but apparently Anne needed no more encouragement than that. She moved into his arms, burying her face once again against his chest.

Nathan patted her back. "There, there," he said. Over Anne's dark head, he gave me a helpless look.

What a rock the boy was.

Once Anne had grabbed Nathan, I was left standing off by myself for a moment. Everybody else seemed pretty occupied. Derek was still standing in the hallway, just outside of the living room, still staring at the floor, still looking positively dazed. And the Conovers were still standing just inside the living room, just on the other side of the archway, looking mutually quite anxious to get the hell out of Dodge at the first opportunity.

So I had a moment to think. What went through my mind almost immediately was, oddly enough, just one question. In retrospect, it was probably the least compelling thing I could've been considering at that moment. And yet, there it was. Pulling at me. Had Trudi been making all that up about Anne and Nathan being engaged? Had her telling me that been yet another one of her games? Looking over at Anne, who continued to dampen the front of Nathan's shirt, I decided that this was probably not the best time in the world to ask Anne about it.

I was sure of it when, in the next split second, the doorbell started ringing. I went into the living room so that I could see through the double windows again. There on the porch were two men, one in a light gray suit and the other in a navy blue suit so dark it looked black.

Unfortunately, I recognized both these guys the second I laid eyes on them. For a second there, I was tempted to scream even louder than Anne had a few minutes earlier.

Chapter 5

Of all the policemen on Louisville's force, why must the ones who always respond to my phone calls be Detectives Murray Reed and Tony Constello?

In this last year I have talked to these two policemen more than I ever expected to talk to any policeman in my entire life. It has not—I repeat—*not* been my fault. I have not had any car accidents, or parked illegally, or held up any liquor stores, or anything like that.

It's just that people who have been murdered keep turning up in my life.

Something, believe me, that I have not encouraged.

In the past, when Detectives Reed and Constello have dropped by, I have been extremely cooperative, and, yes, without fear of contradiction, I believe I can truthfully say that I've even been instrumental in bringing a couple of actual murderers to justice. Something that is not my job, I'd like to point out, but the job of the two men now standing on the porch of 1422 Saratoga Way.

So why, may I ask, when I first opened the front

door, did both detectives look at me as if I were Ma Barker, for crying out loud?

The one on the left, Murray Reed—the one in the light gray suit, with the hair so blond it almost looked white—said, "Oh, God, not you again."

And the one on the right, Tony Constello—the swarthy one in the navy blue suit who looked like an extra in a *Godfather* film—said, "What happened *this* time?"

I cleared my throat. When I spoke, I was a little surprised at just how calm my voice sounded. "A woman by the name of Trudi Vittitoe," I said, "has been strangled."

Putting it into words made the whole thing seem more real somehow. More real, and more horrifying. My God, it had really happened. Somebody had actually *killed* Trudi. In this very house. I shivered.

Reed and Constello exchanged a look. I didn't like the looks of that look.

After that the two detectives seemed to be in a race to determine which one could pull out a Bic and a small spiral notebook from inside his suit jacket the fastest.

It was close, but Reed won. He immediately began scribbling away. "Then you knew the victim, ma'am?"

Oh, brother. Reed was now doing Joe Friday—the detective Jack Webb used to play on that old classic fifties TV show, *Dragnet.* I should've known he'd get to it sooner or later. Reed always seems to do Joe Friday—speaking in staccato bursts and saying "ma'am" a lot—when he's asking me questions.

"Ma'am?" Reed prodded me.

I suppressed a sigh and nodded. "She was a real estate agent who worked with me."

That answer, for some reason, caused Reed and Constello to exchange another look. The way they kept doing that was making me nervous. I hurried on, saying, "If you'll follow me, I'll show you—"

Constello interrupted me. "Mrs. Ridgway," he said, "do you have any idea what the odds are that you'd get yourself involved in *another* murder?"

I just stared back at him, fighting the urge to reply, *Sir, do you have any idea that you and your partner look like salt and pepper shakers?*

This was a fact. Reed, with his squat, weight lifter's body bulging out of an almost white suit and his white-blond hair cut into a flattop, was obviously playing the part of the salt. And Constello, with his black, heavy-lidded eyes, his black hair and mustache, and his nearly black suit, was definitely playing the pepper.

I instinctively knew, however, that these two probably wouldn't be all that thrilled to hear how much they resembled condiments. So all I said was, "I am not *involved* in another murder. I just happened to have come across one in the basement of this house."

Apparently, this was a nuance lost on both detectives. Constello shook his dark head in disbelief. "*Another* murder," he said. "It's downright amazing." The man may have looked like an extra from *The Godfather,* but he talked like an extra from *Deliverance.*

I opened the front door a little wider. "If you'll follow me, I'll take you down . . ."

Neither detective moved. You might've thought their shoes had been nailed to the porch. I was actually beginning to wonder if they just didn't want to take directions from me.

Constello went on as if I hadn't even spoken. "This has got to be some kind of record." Turning to look at Reed, he said, "I mean, it's unbelievable, don't you think? *Another* murder."

I put my hand on my hip and just looked at the two of them. For homicide cops, they didn't seem any too eager to take a look at one. "Look, do you guys want to follow me to the basement or what?"

Constello's response was to heave a huge sigh. "Okay, lead the way. I reckon we'd better have us a look-see," he said.

I stepped back and held the door open even wider so that both cops could come through. This was a gesture that, in my opinion, proved beyond a shadow of a doubt that Southern hospitality is indeed alive and well in Louisville, Kentucky.

Because right after the two of them started moving, what I really wanted to do was slam the door in both their faces.

It was right after they started moving, you see, that Reed asked—just as he was going past me—"Ma'am, this one wasn't suing you, by any chance?"

I caught my breath. Reed's question was a not-terribly-veiled reference to the last time I'd had occasion to chat with him and Constello. It had been a little over six months ago. I'd been showing a house, and I'd found a man with a gunshot wound lying in the middle of the living room. What can I say? It's not exactly a fond memory. Not to mention—to look at the entire situation in an extremely selfish way—finding a gunshot victim on the premises pretty much eliminates all possibilities of making a sale.

What made things even worse at the time, as far as I was concerned, was that the man who'd been shot had just brought a lawsuit against me, as Reed had just been kind enough to mention. The lawsuit was, take my word for it, totally groundless, but this didn't seem to make much difference to Reed and Constello. In fact, that lawsuit had made the two detectives look at me *then* every bit as suspiciously as they seemed to be looking at me now.

Seeing that familiar look on both their faces once

again was irritating, to say the least. These two knew very well that I not only hadn't had anything to do with that guy getting shot, but I'd even helped them find out who did. I opened my mouth to tell them so, but out of the corner of my eye, I could see Carl and Becky Conover exchanging another anxious look. Relinquishing their post over by the archway leading into the living room, they were starting to inch down the hall in our direction. Obviously so that they could get a better earful of whatever it was that the detectives and I were discussing.

Oh, dear. If Reed and Constello said anything more, the Conovers might actually form what could very well be their first extremely definite *mutual* opinion. That I was the realtor equivalent of Typhoid Mary.

If this got out, I'd be lucky if I could sell cemetery plots.

I immediately discarded the angry reply on the tip of my tongue. "Why, no," I told Reed almost cheerfully. "I don't believe *anybody* is suing me at the present time." But, hey, thanks so much for asking.

To head off any more such comments from Reed and Constello, I hurried to add, gesturing down the hallway, right on past the Conovers, "Now, if you two will follow me, I'll take you down to the basement—"

I guess maybe I overdid it this time. In my zeal not to sound as irritated as I really felt, I ended up sounding sort of tickled. As if I were actually looking *forward* to showing these two the scene of the crime. I don't know, I guess I spend so much of my life showing things that without thinking I'd slipped into realtor mode. As if maybe on some subconscious level I equated showing poor Trudi to these two officers with showing a house to two prospective buyers.

Oh, yes, I must've sounded far too upbeat. Reed and Constello were exchanging yet another one of their looks. "Did *this* one leave you any money?" Reed asked.

I caught my breath again. This was yet another thinly—if at all—veiled reference to the very first time I'd had the misfortune to make Reed and Constello's acquaintance. I'd just been left over a hundred thousand dollars by a man I'd never met—a man by the name of Ephraim Cross.

That's right, *Cross,* as in Matthias Cross, the man I mentioned earlier who is currently trying to talk me into moving in with him.

Matthias is Ephraim Cross's son. Believe it or not, Matthias and I met at the reading of his father's will. It was there that I'd tried to tell everybody present that—even though Ephraim Cross had seen fit to leave me a substantial sum of money—Ephraim Cross and I had never been so much as introduced. Oddly enough, Matthias—along with Reed and Constello and pretty much everybody else on the planet—did not exactly take my word for it.

Nowadays Matthias insists he never truly suspected me of anything. Back then, though, it had been abundantly clear that Matthias not only suspected me of carrying on an affair with his dad, he'd also suspected that I might've been the one who'd shot the poor man.

If you'd told me back then that Matthias and I would end up romantically involved, I'd have laughed right in your face.

Now I felt like spitting in Reed's. "I'd be surprised," I said evenly, "if, in this instance, I was left a bread crumb."

Reed and Constello had been moving down the center hall, but now as they approached the archway opening into the living room, they apparently noticed for the first time that there were quite a few people standing around in there. For one thing, they couldn't miss Becky and Carl Conover, who were now standing out in the hallway, looking our way expectantly. Also, Anne and Nathan were standing just inside the archway, a little behind the Conovers. They, too, were looking our way.

Derek Vittitoe, in fact, was the only one not looking at me and the salt and pepper shakers. He'd gone into the living room and was now sitting on the sofa in there, staring at the floor, still looking dazed.

When Reed and Constello stopped in the middle of the archway leading into the living room, Derek did manage to lift his eyes from the floor and actually look Reed and Constello in the face. Derek made no move, however, to get up, or even to introduce himself.

Introductions did seem to be in order. At least Reed thought so. "Ma'am?" he said to me. "Who are all these people? And, ma'am? What are they doing here?"

For a moment I just looked at him. What did he think? That as soon as I'd found Trudi, I'd invited all these people over? That maybe I thought that homicide was a social occasion? Fortunately, before I could put any of these illustrious thoughts into words, Anne jumped in. Stepping forward, she said, "I'm Anne Forrester, Trudi's sister." Her voice quavered a little on Trudi's name, but other than that, she sounded amazingly calm. Turning to indicate Derek with a wave of her hand toward the sofa, she went on. "And that is Derek Vittitoe, um, Trudi's husband."

Reed began scribbling away the minute Anne started talking. "Then, ma'am, you two were here when—"

Anne was already shaking her head. "Oh, no," she said. Schuyler phoned us. To, um, let us know what had happened."

I wasn't sure why, but the second Anne said that, the eyes of both Reed and Constello darted again in my direction. "Yes, ma'am," though, was all Reed said.

The Conovers must've decided that it was now their turn, because both of them stepped forward at the same time. Carl gave Reed their names and then said, "We're not involved in this at all."

"That's right," Becky said. "We don't know anybody here. We were just looking at this house. That's all. That's the only reason we're here. On account of its being for sale. That's it. We're not really involved in any of this."

Well, now, that did seem to cover the subject completely.

Becky must've not though she'd done it justice, however, because she went right on. With a nervous glance in my direction, she added, "But I don't think we're really interested in *this* house anymore. I mean, I don't think we are. What do you think, hon?" she said, looking over at her husband.

I, of course, was now busy concentrating on not grinding my teeth. While Carl looked at Becky and shrugged his shoulders noncommittally, Nathan evidently decided it had come down to him. Stepping forward, my son stuck out his hand. "Hi, there," he said, his voice a tad too cheery under the circumstances. "I'm Nathan Ridgway—"

That was all he got out, however, before the heads of both salt and pepper shakers did this odd little jerking motion. *"Ridgway?"* Constello asked, his dark eyes darting in my direction and then back over to Nathan. "We've met before, haven't we?"

As a matter of fact, the salt and pepper shakers had met Nathan when they'd dropped by my house a few months ago to search the premises for incriminating evidence. How *sweet* of Constello to remember.

Nathan was now shaking hands quite vigorously, but I could tell having the police remember that they'd seen him before had unnerved him a little. Nathan was getting paler by the minute. Before Nathan confessed that he was indeed his mother's son, I thought I'd help out. "Nathan's my youngest son," I said. There really didn't seem to be any good reason to mention that the shakers had met him while they were going through my cupboards, looking for weapons. I hurried on. "Nathan is—" At this point I realized I wasn't really sure what the relationship was between him and Anne, so I decided to just say —"*dating* Anne, Trudi's sister."

"Your son is dating the sister of the victim?"

I wasn't sure what the significance of this could be, but I nodded.

I wasn't sure Reed even saw me nod. His attention seemed caught at that precise moment by Nathan's knees.

You could almost read his mind. *Shorts?* On a day *this* cold?

I probably should've felt apologetic—after all, Nathan did happen to be my very own flesh and blood— but it occurred to me that there was probably an advantage in Nathan's choice of winter wardrobe. If the shakers should try to accuse Nathan of anything, he could always go with the insanity defense.

Reed stared at Nathan's knees for only a moment, anyway. Then, blinking, he turned back to me. "So let me get this straight. *You* worked with the victim, *you* notified the next of kin, and *your* son is dating the victim's sister. Right?"

I wasn't totally sure where he was going with this,

but so far he seemed to be pretty much on the money. I nodded uneasily.

Reed whistled and shook his white head. "And you still say you're not *involved?*"

I just looked at him. He had a point.

I rather hoped that the entire subject would be dropped right there, but wouldn't you know it, Constello had to put in his two cents. "The way *I* see it," he drawled, "you're more involved in this one than you were in those other two. I mean, you didn't even know that first guy who was murdered, did you? And that second one—that was just somebody you'd sold a house to, wasn't it?"

Reed and Constello did not exchange any glances at all after Constello finished saying all this, but Becky and Carl did. After they exchanged their glances, Becky looked over at me, the whites showing all around her eyes. Oh, my, yes, I'd say I could not only chalk up number fifty-two as a no-sale, but there was every likelihood that I was never going to get the chance to show the Conovers number fifty-three. In fact, it was my guess I'd never see Becky or Carl again, once they screeched out of the driveway.

Thanks so much, Reed and Constello.

Talk about police harassment.

"Let me show you two how to get to the basement," I said through my teeth.

Wonder of wonders, this time Reed and Constello actually followed me. Before they headed down the stairs, Reed barked over his shoulder to the others, "Nobody leaves until we've taken your statement, got it?"

Then they were gone. Standing there at the top of the stairs after the shakers had moved past me, I think I was almost waiting to hear another scream. Instead, there was nothing but silence. In less than five minutes

Reed and Constello were back, coming through the basement door at a fast clip.

"Okay, before we got here, we called the coroner's office, and they should be here soon." Reed, in my humble opinion, was doing his best Joe Friday yet. "Until then, nobody goes downstairs, is that clear?"

Naturally, the second Reed said that, Nathan got this look on his face that he used to get when he was a kid and I'd caught him doing something he shouldn't. It's a look that had been transparent back then, and it apparently didn't fool anybody these days, either. Reed immediately zeroed in on him. "You haven't already been downstairs, have you?" Reed asked.

Nathan actually gulped before he answered. "Well, uh, yessir, I have," he said. "But everybody else went down there, too," he quickly added. "I—I wasn't the only one." This, I believe, was the exact same argument the boy had used when, in the fourth grade, he'd been caught shoplifting Tootsie Roll Pops at the convenience store next door to his elementary school.

Back then, little Nathan had seemed to believe that if you did something wrong as part of a group, you weren't anywhere near as guilty as if you'd done it all on your own. After the Tootsie Roll Pop caper, I'd explained to him at some length that guilt didn't exactly work that way. Now it seemed I'd been wasting my breath. Apparently, big Nathan continued to believe that guilt was something that could be spread very, very thin.

Reed's eyes widened. "*Everybody's* been down there? You mean, everybody in this room?"

Nathan gulped again before he nodded.

Can you believe Reed's reaction to this was to turn to *me* with his blue eyes flashing? "You let *everybody* troop down there?"

Good Lord. He sounded like Mrs. Childers. I was losing patience fast. "I didn't *let* everybody do anything. They all just went down there, that's all."

Reed rolled his eyes and turned to Constello. "Can you believe this?" he said.

I folded my arms across my chest. He was acting as if I'd conducted *tours,* for God's sake. "Look," I said, "I couldn't stop them. I tried, believe me, but—"

Reed was not interested in my explanations. "All right," he barked, cutting me off. He was sounding less and less like Joe Friday and more and more like Dirty Harry. "Everybody take a seat in the living room until we call your name."

Waiting in the living room turned out to be a lot like waiting to be called into the dentist's office.

Only I believe I personally look forward quite a bit more to a visit with the dentist.

I was interviewed last. I know I probably sound paranoid, but I was pretty sure this wasn't an accident. Reed and Constello were, no doubt, punishing me for letting their crime scene get compromised. So Derek, Nathan, and Anne had all gone in and out of the kitchen, *and* Becky and Carl Conover had also gone in and out of there—and straight out the front door without a backward glance—before Constello finally ambled out and drawled, "All right, Miz Ridgway, we're ready for you now."

Sitting across from them, at the knotty pine kitchen table, I tried to answer their questions in a calm and collected way. It wasn't easy, though, because by that time the coroner had been there a while, and every so often you could hear the guy moving around downstairs. It seemed as if every time I heard a noise, I could see poor Trudi's face all over again.

Still and all, I think I did pretty well up until I got to the part where I had to tell Reed and Constello about the note Trudi left me. I actually considered not mentioning it at all. The cleaning people always come in Monday nights, and the garbage is picked up early Tuesday morning. So that memo was long gone. Then, too, I guess I'd almost convinced myself by then that the note Trudi had left me really didn't have anything to do with what had happened to her.

On the other hand, I'd already told Derek and Anne about Trudi's note. I couldn't exactly *forget* to mention it to the police.

Wouldn't you know it, the second I told them, both men suddenly looked alert. Leaning forward, Constello said, "In this note, the victim said she was going to meet somebody who'd asked for *you*?"

I nodded. "That's right," I said. "Of course, I don't have the note anymore."

Constello exchanged another glance with Reed. *"Of course,"* Reed said.

My stomach knotted up. Did these men actually think for even an instant that I was just making this up? I sat up a little straighter in my chair. "Look, I didn't have any idea that something was going to happen to Trudi, so I didn't know to keep the note. Okay? I just wadded it up and threw it away."

I hurried on, telling them about the cleaning people and the garbage pickup. When I was finished, I thought—the way both of them were just sitting there, gawking at me—that they really did doubt my every word. Then Constello tilted his chair back until only the back two legs were touching the floor. He took a deep breath, then drawled, "You got any enemies?"

I could feel my neck get hot. Whenever I get extremely nervous or outright rattled, my neck breaks out in these big red blotches. Now, sitting there in the kitchen, staring at Constello, I had no doubt that I'd just come down with a bad case of Paisley Neck.

I lifted my hand to nonchalantly cover my throat as Constello brought his chair back down flat on the floor. "Any one person you've been having problems with lately?"

The one person I'd been having problems with lately was at that moment lying in the basement with a scarf tied too tightly around her neck. "I don't think so. At least, I can't think of any."

"None?" Constello asked. His tone seemed to imply that he found this hard to believe.

I gave him a level look. Apparently, Constello was of the opinion that I would not win Miss Congeniality this year. "I can't think of anybody. I have no enemies."

Unless, of course, you counted Mrs. Childers. After our little phone conversation, she would probably not be adding me to her Christmas list anytime soon. That conversation, however, had occurred long after I'd gotten Trudi's note. Unless Mrs. Childers was clairvoyant and somehow knew I was going to be annoying the hell out of her in the near future, I believe she really didn't count.

Reed was running his hand over his white hair. If his hair had been longer, I would've said he was running his hand *through* his hair, but with that marine haircut, running his hand *over* his hair was the best he could hope for. "Mrs. Ridgway, in the last few days have you noticed anybody strange hanging around?"

I shook my head.

"Have you had any strange phone calls?"

I shook my head again.

"Anybody you've argued with?"

I stared at him. The only argument I'd been having lately was with Matthias. And I wouldn't exactly call it an argument. It was more a discussion—about, as I mentioned before, whether or not I was going to move in with him. While I'll admit that Matthias did seem to be very much in favor of my moving in, I was pretty sure he wouldn't go so far as to murder somebody in order to scare me into agreeing.

I cleared my throat. "I haven't been arguing with anybody," I said. That is, of course, once you eliminated Trudi.

And, it seemed to me, she had clearly been eliminated.

Reed and Constello were now exchanging still another one of their glances.

Have I mentioned I wished they'd stop doing that?

Constello took a long, beleaguered breath. "Okay, then could you give us the names of anybody who might not have liked Trudi?"

I moved in my chair uneasily. For a moment there, I was tempted to just hand them the Louisville phone book. At the last second, though, I thought better of it. "Well, I really didn't know Trudi very well outside of work."

Constello was looking impatient. "Was she well liked at work, then?"

I stared at him again. Wasn't there supposed to be a rule about speaking ill of the dead? I cleared my throat. On the other hand, I do believe that there was also a rule about lying to the police. "To be honest," I said, "I don't think she was particularly well liked."

Lord. That was a lot like saying *Hitler* was not particularly well liked.

Constello looked interested. "Who disliked her?"

The answer to that was, of course, anybody who'd ever met her, but I really did hate to say that. Particularly with Trudi lying downstairs at that very moment.

"I'm not sure."

Constello leaned forward. "Did *you* like her?"

Well, now, there it was. Out on the table.

I hedged. "She was all right."

"All right?"

Reed and Constello exchanged yet another one of their looks. Would they *ever* stop doing that?

I squirmed a little in my chair. "Okay, so I guess maybe she wasn't exactly one of my favorite people."

Reed's head bent over his notebook. He actually seemed to be writing that down. "Not one of your favorite people," he said.

I felt guilty the second I heard him say the words. I mean, the woman was *dead,* for God's sake. "But she was an okay person," I added quickly. I wasn't sure either Reed or Constello believed me.

What I was sure of was that both of them were starting to scare me a little. They particularly scared me right after I'd thought our little interview was over. Both detectives had finally stopped writing, and I was reaching for my purse, getting ready to get the hell out of there.

"Ma'am?" Reed said. "If you do notice anybody following you—or anybody acting strange—or if you get any weird phone calls—let us know, okay? *Right away.*"

I froze right in the middle of picking up my purse from the floor. And I mean, *froze,* literally. A chill actually rippled up my spine as I lifted my head to stare at Reed.

I probably looked a lot like the skipper on the *Poseidon* looked just before the wave hit, because Constello immediately said, "We don't mean to alarm you or nothing. We just want you to be careful, is all. Particularly if you run into any strangers."

I finished picking up my purse, stood up, and just looked at him. Was he kidding? *If* I run into any strangers? That was pretty much my entire job description. I ran into strangers, and after I ran into them, I showed them a few houses. Hell, I'd made an appointment just yesterday with a total stranger to show the listing on Ashwood Drive this very evening. The stranger had told me his name was Irving Rickle, but how the hell did I know who he really was? It could be Irving the Ripper, or Charlie Manson, or— or *anybody*.

I really wished all this had not flashed through my mind. I cleared my throat. "I'll certainly be careful," I said. My throat had gotten awfully dry, so my voice cracked a little. Undaunted, however, I turned, and chin most assuredly up, I headed out the kitchen door and on down the hall.

When I passed the archway leading into the living room, I saw that Derek, Anne, and Nathan were all standing in there. They'd been joined by a short, stout woman wearing a wide-brimmed hat and white gloves who immediately turned and looked in my direction.

"Why, *there* you are," Mrs. Edmund Childers said. When I hesitated, she quickly added, "I am *so* sorry, Mrs. Ridgway, that we meet again under such tragic circumstances." Her tone was extremely polite.

I suppressed a sigh and headed into the living room.

"I am *so* glad to have the opportunity, though, to thank you for *all* you've done." Mrs. Childers's voice could've been poured on pancakes, but her eyes— shaded by the brim of her hat—looked straight at me with icy distaste.

What do you know. Mrs. Childers might actually give Mom a run for her money.

Chapter
6

"I was trying to somehow express my heartfelt sympathy to these wonderful people." Mrs. Edmund Childers actually clutched at her heart with her white-gloved hands as she said the words.

I had to admire the woman. I'd heard that once you can fake sincerity, you've pretty much got it made.

"How *terribly* kind of you," I said. I was thinking, of course, *Then I probably shouldn't mention what you said to me earlier over the phone. You know, when you seemed considerably more concerned about the damage to the* house *than the damage to* Trudi?

I don't know if Mrs. Childers read what I was thinking in my face, but she might've. She turned rather abruptly back to the others. "I know when I lost my own darling Edmund, well, I thought I'd never recover," she said. "But I take comfort from knowing that he is still by my side. Why, whenever I'm trying to decide what to do, I always ask Edmund, and right away he tells me."

I was beginning to wish she'd ask Edmund if maybe she should shut up. Her words of comfort were obviously not doing the trick. Fresh tears were now brimming in Anne's eyes, and even Nathan had started blinking a little. Mrs. Childers's words didn't seem all that comforting to Derek, either. The man was once again staring at the floor, biting his lower lip. Of course—to be brutally honest—maybe Derek felt as if he'd heard from Trudi quite enough when she was alive.

"Our loved ones never really leave us, you know," Mrs. Childers was now saying. "They've just gone to a better place, that's all, to wait for us to join them."

At least, this was the gist of what the woman said. To tell you the truth, I wasn't exactly hanging on her every word. I was watching Derek. The man did look strange. His dark hair looked as if he'd run his hands through it about a million times, his handsome face was white and drawn, and he was sort of twisting his hands together. Every once in a while, he'd glance over at Anne, and from the look on his face, you could actually get the idea that he didn't even recognize her. His own sister-in-law.

Lord. Trudi's death must've hit the man even harder than I'd thought. Staring at him, I wondered if maybe he didn't need a sedative or something.

I guess I was feeling a little dazed myself, because I jumped when I heard the salt and pepper shakers walk into the room behind me. I turned just in time to hear Reed say, as he directed a pointed look at Mrs. Childers, "Who is this?" You could tell by the way he paused for a long moment right after he said "Who" that Reed really wanted to say "the hell" right after it, but somehow he'd managed to refrain.

Mrs. Childers immediately stepped forward, extending a white-gloved hand. The hand, wouldn't you know it, held a business card. How the woman got a business card into her hand that fast, I'll never know.

She was, in fact, almost as good at it as Jarvis, and I'd often suspected *him* of having one of those magician contraptions under his suit coat that shot a card into his hand whenever he wanted one.

Reed took Mrs. Childers's card and started reading the thing.

I knew what it said. She'd pressed one into my own hand the first day I'd met her—when I was showing this house for the first time. It said *Mrs. Edmund Childers* in an elegant script. I should've known then that she wasn't quite what she at first appeared to be—a sweet little middle-aged lady. Particularly when I'd introduced myself as Schuyler Ridgway and she'd immediately told me that she was—yes, you guessed it—Mrs. Edmund Childers. There is something a little strange about a woman who wants to be known solely by her husband's name.

At the time, of course, I hadn't thought a thing about it. I'd just assumed she was one of those women who are so tickled to have gotten themselves married, they want to continue to remind everybody that they'd really done it. Either that or she just didn't want to be on a first-name basis with me.

Hey, I could take the hint. It didn't exactly break my heart that a woman in her late fifties didn't consider me buddy material. Besides, I wasn't so sure I could ever feel on the same wavelength with somebody who always wore a hat and gloves.

Mrs. Edmund Childers was now introducing herself to Reed and Constello. "I'm with Norwood Realty." Her tone implied that surely the two detectives had heard of it.

I glanced over at Reed and Constello. They were looking at her blankly.

"I'm the listing agent of this lovely abode," Mrs. Childers went on smoothly, "and I know I convey the feelings of the owners when I say how truly sorry we were to be apprised of this regrettable tragedy."

I had to hand it to Mrs. Childers. Reed and Constello were both staring at her, their mouths slightly open. They stood like that for only a moment, though. Then, looking less than delighted to be doing so, they took out their little spiral notebooks and their Bics all over again and started writing. "The names of the owners, ma'am?" Reed asked. Joe Friday sounded weary.

I just looked at him. Hey, join the club. I don't think I'd ever felt so bone-tired. Fatigue, however, would not have stopped me from shamelessly eavesdropping on every single thing that the shakers and Mrs. Childers had to say to each other. Unfortunately, though, I got distracted when Nathan moved quickly across the room to stand at my elbow.

"Mom?" he said. Lowering his voice, he all but whispered in my ear, "I'm, uh, going to be tied up around here for a while."

I blinked at that one. The last time I checked, Nathan didn't live with me anymore. So why was he telling me this? He didn't exactly need my permission to stay.

Nathan was hurrying on. "Anne *needs* me." He put a little extra punch on the word "needs," so I knew it was significant. I turned to look at him. The boy was actually looking proud, as if maybe he'd worked very hard for this, finally achieving the lofty status of A-Person-Whom-Anne-Needed.

I wasn't sure what to say. Well-done? Bravo? Congratulations? Nothing that came to mind seemed appropriate. Of course, like I said, I *was* tired.

"Yeah," Nathan was saying, "Anne says she just can't get through all this without me by her side."

He was trying to look solemn—as if this new responsibility were weighing heavily on his shoulders—but Nathan's eyes were practically dancing. It was easy to see just how tickled pink he was over the entire situation.

Staring at my son, I realized that this was probably the first time in Nathan's life that he'd ever actually been needed. That is, of course, if you didn't count those multiple occasions when his brother had needed Nathan to slip him a ten spot to see him through till payday. Come to think of it, you might not want to count those occasions, after all. On most of them, Nathan had not been able to meet that particular need.

I gave up trying to think of something appropriate. Patting Nathan on the arm, I said, "That's nice, dear."

Nathan ducked his head, smiling a little and nodding. For a second there, the way he was moving his head, he reminded me of Keanu Reeves when Keanu was playing Ted in *Bill and Ted's Excellent Adventure*. My reaction, of course, was probably the same reaction Keanu's own mom had experienced when she saw Keanu in that movie: *Dear Lord, give me strength.*

Anne had been talking in low tones to Derek, mumbling something in comforting tones, but she had apparently finished. By the time Nathan had stopped doing his Keanu impression, Anne had joined us. Clutching my arm, she said, tears still glistening in her eyes, "Oh, Schuyler, oh, Schuyler . . ."

Have I mentioned how abysmal I am in these kinds of situations? I never know what to say when a person passes away naturally, let alone when somebody has seen fit to help them along. I felt even more at a loss when Anne continued with, "I know how you must be feeling. You and Trudi had a special relationship."

I just stood there, looking at her. *Special.* Well, yes, that was one word for our relationship. Other words, perhaps more appropriate, were *antagonistic* and *hos-*

tile, but I supposed you could call it— "Special," I repeated weakly, nodding my own head now. I probably looked more like Keanu than Nathan had.

Nathan must've misinterpreted the quaver in my voice. He immediately put his arms around my shoulders. Tight. "It's okay, Mom. Really." He gave me a squeeze then that felt as if it might've cracked a few vertebrae. "After all, Mom, we're all family here."

I raised my head and just looked at him. Every time Nathan has had a new girlfriend that he has thought might be the one, he has always started talking about the girl and her relatives as if they were a part of our family. With all the girlfriends Nathan has had over the years, the population of our family was now—in my estimation—roughly equivalent to that of Rhode Island.

Nathan gave me another squeeze, no doubt cracking several of the vertebrae that had been spared earlier. "Come on, Mom. I'm telling you, it's okay. You can let it all out if you want to."

I could've hit him. It was like being asked to cry. Immediately. In front of an audience.

I gave Nathan a little pat on the front of his chest. "That's all right, hon," I said. "I'm fine."

Nathan looked over at Anne. "That's my mom for you. She's a real trouper."

This trouper was backing out of Nathan's arms. As I did so, though, I realized that Anne was still standing there, looking at me expectantly. Apparently, if I wasn't going to cry, I was supposed to say something. I cleared my throat. "We're certainly going to miss your sister," I lied.

That lie, however, must've been one of my better ones. It caused Anne to start weeping all over again. Nathan, thank God, immediately turned away from me and took *Anne* into his arms.

That left me just standing there, looking around at everybody. The salt and pepper shakers were occupied with Mrs. Childers, Nathan was occupied with Anne, and Derek—well, Derek was once again occupied with staring holes into the floor.

Looking at everybody there, I made up my mind. There really wasn't any reason for me to hang around. I lifted my hand at Nathan, he gave me the briefest of nods over Anne's head, and I made tracks for the front door.

I didn't quite make it.

"Mrs. Ridgway?" It was—who else?—Reed.

For a split second, I was actually tempted to hit the afterburners and run full tilt straight out to my car. Fortunately, before I did such a thing, it occurred to me that it was probably never a good idea to run from the police. I shut my eyes for a second; then, taking a deep breath, I turned around to face Reed.

He immediately moved so that he was standing right next to me. Ducking his white-blond head so that he was practically whispering in my ear, he said, "Ma'am, don't forget what we talked about earlier." Joe Friday actually sounded concerned this time. "If you notice anybody strange—or if you get any strange phone calls—let us know, ma'am."

I was already nodding, but evidently that wasn't good enough.

Reed pointed his Bic at me. "I mean it, ma'am, let us know *right away*."

I nodded again and started to turn around. This time I actually made it through the door.

I didn't realize until I got to my Tercel just how unnerving that last little conversation with Reed had been. I actually had trouble getting my key into the door lock of my Tercel, my hands were shaking so bad. Hell, I hadn't even known they were shaking until I tried to open the door.

I started the car, backed out of the driveway, and pulled away. I was doing all the things I was supposed to, but my mind was racing. Lord. Reed actually seemed to think that I could be in danger. What's more, Reed did seem to be a law enforcement professional who really should know about such things. So if Reed thought somebody could be after me, then—good Lord—*somebody really could be.*

When I stopped at the intersection of Saratoga and Douglass Boulevard, I found myself glancing anxiously at the car doors, making sure every one of them was locked. Sitting there, staring at those stupid locks, I realized, my God, I was *afraid.* Really. My heart was pounding like a trip-hammer, and I was having a little trouble pulling my mind together to concentrate on driving. In fact, I was still sitting there listening to my heart pound, when some guy pulled up behind me in a blue Chevrolet and honked.

When the horn sounded, I jumped so high I almost cracked my head on the roof of my car. Before I got myself together enough to step on the accelerator, the guy honked one more time. This time I believed I amply demonstrated the kind of patient, forgiving nature for which I am, no doubt, well known. I rolled down my window just about an inch and yelled through the opening. "Oh, for crying out loud, *shut up!*" Right after I got *that* off my chest, I rolled my window back up.

Yelling at a total stranger didn't help me feel any better. It also didn't help to recall that in a few short hours I was supposed to meet another total stranger all by myself. Lord. I was actually afraid to meet a guy with a name like Irving.

And yet, hadn't the Boston Strangler been named Albert?

I made the right turn off Douglass Boulevard onto Bardstown Road, and now I found myself glancing in my rearview mirror and in my side mirrors again and again. At this time of the day Bardstown Road was three lanes heading away from downtown Louisville and one lane heading toward downtown. That meant that, since I was in the middle lane, every once in a while a car would pull up on one side of me or the other.

This is not exactly an unusual occurrence. It happens all the time, every day of the week. And yet today, every time it happened, my heart felt as if it were jumping out of my chest.

The first time, in fact, that a car pulled up beside me on the driver's side, my heart sounded so loud I thought for a split second that it was the engine of my Tercel—and that something had gone wrong with the thing. That maybe it had thrown a rod. I probably should point out here that I have no idea exactly what throwing a rod entails, but because I'd had two dates with an auto mechanic back in college, I did know it involved your engine making a loud knocking noise. It took me a second to realize that there was nothing wrong with my car. There was something wrong with *me*.

By the time I was pulling into the parking lot of Arndoerfer Realty, I hate to admit it, but I was a wreck. My mouth was so dry I could hardly swallow. My hands were so damp they slipped a little on the steering wheel as I pulled into an empty parking space near the front door. *And* my heart was going so fast it was difficult to get my breath. I braked, turned off the ignition, and then just sat there in the parking lot for a little while, waiting for my heart to slow down.

One thing was abundantly clear. In the real estate business, developing a fear of *strangers*—a word for which you could easily substitute the phrase *potential clients*—is not a great career move.

Unfortunately, when I finally got myself calmed down enough so that I could actually walk into the office without my knees knocking together, Charlotte, Barbi, Jarvis, and Jarvis's wife, Arlene, were all there. I guess it only took one look at my face for everybody to know that something was wrong. I'd heard the hum of conversation as I approached the entrance, but the second I opened the storm door and stepped into the office, a hush fell.

I walked directly to my desk without looking in anybody's direction, but I could feel their eyes. I tried to act normal, dropping my purse into the bottom right file drawer, just as I usually did, but I must not have pulled it off. When I straightened up, Jarvis was already moving toward me, his eyes riveted to my face.

I watched his approach, and frankly, I wanted to hide. I would've liked to have gone into the kitchen and fixed me a little something before I had to talk to anybody. It was long past lunch, but the thing I wanted to fix wasn't food. I wasn't the least bit hungry. I suppose abject terror is an excellent appetite suppressant. No, what I wanted was a large, bubbling glass of the Real Thing, extra heavy on the ice. I think of Coke as sort of my own personal carbonated pacifier, and believe me, after the morning I'd just had, I needed a pacifier *bad.*

"Schuyler," Jarvis said, when he was standing right in front of me, "are you okay?" Before I had a chance to answer, he added, "You don't look good."

I turned to give him a level look. Jarvis has a bulbous nose, lips like those wax ones they give out at

Halloween, and a pot belly, and he was telling me I didn't look good?

"I mean it, Schuyler," Jarvis hurried on, "you look *terrible*!"

Standing five feet five in his stocking feet—and that's only when he was wearing very thick socks—poor Jarvis has been suffering from Short Man's Disease for as long as I've known him. Lest anybody get the idea that I'm prejudiced against short men, let me hasten to add that not all short men suffer from this affliction. However, those that do generally have it bad. The symptoms are unmistakable. The SMD sufferer labors under the delusion that he alone has the definitive word on everything. He also believes that if there are more than two people in any given room, he has to be the center of attention.

A couple of beats after he'd spoken, I do believe Jarvis's voice was still echoing off the walls. That's how loud it was. Arndoerfer Realty shares a parking lot with Radigan's Meat Market next door. No doubt, the people over there waiting in line to have their tenderloins sliced had heard Jarvis's kind comment on my appearance.

I opened my mouth to thank him properly, but once again he didn't give me the chance. "Schuyler, come on now, you can tell me. Is something the matter?"

Poor Jarvis is not only short in stature, he's also a little short in the hair department. To give him credit, however, he doesn't do like a lot of balding men do—grow his hair real long on one side and then stretch it across the top. What Jarvis does, however, is constantly swipe at his forehead as if there is a lot of hair up there, falling into his eyes. He seems to think that if he goes through the motions of having a lot of hair, he'll convince those around him that it's really there. Sort of like a variation on "The Emperor's New

Clothes." He was swiping at his Emperor's New Hair as he waited for my answer.

I guessed my carbonated pacifier could wait, and that I might as well get it over with. I took a deep breath. "Something's the matter, all right," I began. "Trudi—"

Can you believe it, Jarvis interrupted me *again*. Of course, this isn't exactly unusual. Jarvis interrupts a lot. Apparently, if you're sure you have the definitive word on everything, you want to make damn sure you get every single one of those words in. "Now, if you're going to start complaining about Trudi again, I'm not going to hear it," he said. To illustrate what he was saying, he actually stuck his fingers in his ears.

I just looked at him. Remind me not to shake his hand anytime soon.

Removing his fingers from his ears—having made his point, apparently—Jarvis went on. "You may not agree with me, but I think that Trudi is an—"

I knew that if he said the word *inspiration,* I would scream, so I interrupted *him* this time. "Jarvis," I said, "believe me, I have no intention of ever complaining about Trudi again."

Oh, my, yes, he could take *that* one to the bank.

Jarvis, for his part, looked surprised. And pleased. "Well, now, that's more like it—"

I interrupted him again. "Trudi's dead."

I didn't mean to just blurt it out like that. I mean, the phrase *no longer alive* could definitely have been used in this instance, too. Even if it hadn't worked all that well with Anne, I probably should've once again given it a shot. Anything would've been an improvement over the reaction my words immediately got from everybody in the room.

First, there was this prolonged group intake of breath. Which sounded a lot like somebody had just shut off oxygen to the building. And then everybody started talking at once.

"What?"

"What did Schuyler say?"

"Oh, my God."

"Did you hear what she just said?"

"She said Trudi's *dead*!"

I'm not quite sure exactly who said any of this. All the voices in the room pretty much ran together. In fact, it was like being in a roomful of televisions, all set on different stations, all playing at once.

I do know, however, that the reactions of Barbi, Charlotte, and even Arlene, Jarvis's wife, to that last statement were virtually identical. Every one of the women immediately covered her mouth.

Either Barbi, Charlotte, and Arlene were all identically horrified, or they were all trying to cover tiny smiles as they rushed over to my desk.

Chapter 7

Jarvis, for his part, staggered backward a little. "Wha-a-a-t?" Jarvis has beady brown eyes that bulge when he gets upset. At that moment his eyes looked like swollen raisins. "Are you telling me that one of my agents is—"

Apparently, I was supposed to fill in the blanks. "—no longer with us?" I finished for him. I nodded.

Jarvis looked stricken. "Oh, dear Lord," he said. As the full implication of what I'd just said hit him, he looked even more stricken. "Then what you're telling me is that one of my very best selling agents is—is—?"

I didn't even blink. It was not a surprise that Jarvis would immediately see Trudi's death in terms of how it directly affected his business. Not too long ago, believe it or not, I myself had been shot at. It had happened right in front of this very building. The thing, I believe, that had disturbed Jarvis most about the entire incident was the possibility that it might discourage would-be clients from dropping in.

"—is—is—" Jarvis was still trying to finish his question, but he couldn't seem to bring himself to say the word I myself had blurted.

At this point, I decided maybe it wasn't too late to take the airlines' advice. "—no longer alive," I finished once again.

Evidently, I was wrong. It *was* too late. I suppose if you've already said the word *dead,* the damage has been done. You can't soften the blow.

"Oh, my God! Trudi's *dead*?" Jarvis shrieked. "OH, MY GOD! TRUDI'S DEAD!" Lately, Jarvis has gotten into the habit of repeating himself when he's excited. I believe it might have something to do with how many replays he watched on ESPN during football season. Apparently, it affected the poor man's mind. Now he seems to be convinced that every dramatic moment in his life has to have at least one replay. "This is terrible," Jarvis said. "THIS IS TERRIBLE!"

Charlotte, Arlene, and Barbi were all standing around my desk, on either side and in back of Jarvis by then; but in the face of his near-hysterics, the three women did absolutely nothing. They just stood there and stared at him. Arlene was the first to speak, but what she said was clearly not directed at her husband. "How did it happen?"

I looked over at Arlene. She was one of those women everybody always describes as "good-looking for her age." Meaning that if she were still in her twenties, she'd have been in awful shape, but since she had to be in her thirties—or, perhaps, even in her forties—she looked terrific.

Of course, if you knew exactly how old she was, you could pinpoint exactly how terrific Arlene looked; but Arlene evidently didn't want you to be that precise. She didn't carry her driver's license in her wallet like the rest of the world, but kept it under lock and key in the glove compartment of her car. Moreover, the fastest way to get Arlene to leave a room was to start discussing when you graduated from high school, or if you knew anybody who'd gone to the first Woodstock, or anything that might somehow pin down her age.

Arlene wore her dark brown hair in a shoulder-length pageboy, and not a single gray hair marred its glossy sheen. Her makeup always looked as if it had just been applied—and, indeed, it probably had been. Arlene, I'd noticed, did seem to spend a significant part of her day—in the ladies' room and at her desk—checking and rechecking, doing and redoing, all the stuff she puts on her face. There was speculation around the office that she even wore her makeup to bed. All I can say is, I'd hate to be the one responsible for cleaning Arlene's pillowcases. It would probably be like trying to launder the Shroud of Turin.

Now, as Arlene spoke, I thought I heard a note of something in her voice. A little trill of unmistakable *satisfaction.* I must've started staring at her a little too pointedly, because Arlene immediately shrugged, patting at her pageboy. "Not that I'm asking for all the gory details, or anything—"

She did a little cough at this point, but it sounded forced. I think everybody in the room knew that the gory details—as Arlene so quaintly put it—were indeed exactly what she was asking for. When Charlotte Ackersen also gave Arlene a pointed look, Arlene shrugged. "I just wanted to know," Arlene explained, her tone defensive, "in case it turned out to be work-related. I mean, since the woman worked out of our firm, I think Jarvis and I really ought to be informed—"

I sort of wished Arlene had not brought this particular topic up. Jarvis interrupted her with a wail. "Oh, my dear God in heaven! It *wasn't* a work-related injury, was it?" He turned on me, the blood draining from his face. Apparently, to Jarvis, the prospect of his firm facing a lawsuit was even more appalling than losing one of his most successful agents. What could I say? The guy was all heart.

"Jarvis," I said flatly, "Trudi was strangled. Would you call that work-related?"

I guess I should've given that a little more thought before I spoke. My comments brought on another group intake of breath. Not to mention, all three women raised their hands to their throats.

Arlene was again the first to speak. "Poor, poor, *poor* Trudi."

I stared at Arlene all over again. Three "poors." *Three*. I could be wrong, but once again—just like with Anne earlier—this struck me as a bit excessive.

"It's such a terrible, terrible, *terrible* tragedy," Arlene went on, shaking her dark head a little, but not so much that a single strand of hair moved out of place.

I continued to stare at her. I could've been wrong, but I'd bet that Trudi's death was not all that terrible, terrible, *terrible* a tragedy to Arlene. At best, she couldn't care less. At worst, Arlene was ·delighted.

God. I was beginning to feel really sorry for poor Trudi. I mean, didn't anybody she'd worked with *care* that she was dead?

I glanced over at Barbi. Apparently, when Barbi had raised her hand to her throat, she'd noticed she had a hangnail. Now, her platinum hair falling across one eyes, she was busily chewing on a fuschia-lacquered fingertip. Not exactly a portrait of inconsolable grief.

Next I looked over at Charlotte. Charlotte Ackersen has always reminded me of Alice in Wonderland. Today, in fact, she was wearing the exact kind of outfit a grown-up Alice would wear to work—a pastel blue jumper, white lace-trimmed blouse, white hose, white heels, her long, straight blond hair pulled back with a pastel blue headband.

I guess I was expecting a lot out of Charlotte. I'd worked with her for over a year, and during that time I'd found her to be that rare thing—a genuinely nice human being.

Charlotte, at that moment, was checking her watch.

Finally, I looked back over at Arlene. Of all the women in the room, she was the only one who looked the least bit emotional. The emotion that seemed to be dominant in her face, however, was not grief. It was anger. As a matter of fact, when I glanced her way, her gaze was burning through Jarvis—almost as if she were trying to gauge just how upset her husband was over Trudi's demise.

I stood there for a moment, watching Arlene watch Jarvis. Could it be that Jarvis had found Trudi "an inspiration" one too many times to suit Arlene's liking? Had Arlene suspected that there could be something more than just an employer-employee relationship going on?

The thought was chilling. Of course, my contemplating *anybody* having an intimate relationship with *Jarvis,* of all people, was the mental equivalent of having ice water thrown in my face. I had to admit, though, that there *was* the distinct possibility that Jarvis's own wife might not feel this way.

Arlene had not yet taken her eyes off Jarvis. Jarvis, on the other hand, had not yet stopped whimpering. In fact, it seemed safe to say that our esteemed leader was the only person in the room who looked truly upset at what had happened to Trudi. He was swiping at his eyes, his hands shaking a little, as he turned to me. Taking a deep breath, as if making a monumental effort to regain control, he said in a rush, "All right, Schuyler, tell me the truth: Do you think they'll mention the name of this firm in the newspaper?"

I blinked at that one. "What do you mean?"

Jarvis looked impatient. "*I mean,* do you think that the paper will say where Trudi worked?"

I just stared at him. Was the man hoping for free advertising? Did he actually think that being mentioned in the account of a murder might do wonders for business?

And then Jarvis hurried on. "Because we can't have that. We just can't." He swiped at his Emperor hair again. "I mean, it will be awful. Just *awful.*"

I took a deep breath. Apparently, I'd been wrong about the advertising bit.

"Do you think, if we called the paper right this minute," Jarvis went on, "that we could talk them out of mentioning where Trudi worked? Because I really don't think that it's necessary that they tell *that.* Where the woman worked doesn't really have anything to do with ..."

Oh, yeah. I got it now. Jarvis didn't think a mention in the paper would drum up business. He was afraid it might scare business away.

This, then, appeared to be the main reason Jarvis was upset about Trudi's death. Lord. He was as bad as everybody else. Hell, he might be worse.

I was beginning to fume. Good Lord. If you didn't know better, you might actually get the idea that everybody who'd worked with Trudi truly believed she'd gotten what she deserved. And, hey, nobody deserved that. *Nobody.*

I didn't really mean to say anything, but before I could stop it, my mouth had started spouting off. "Look, you all, I know Trudi had her problems, but what somebody did to her was horrible." I looked straight at Arlene. "Somebody *strangled* her with her own scarf." Arlene's eyes got big. I knew I should stop, but I was suddenly so angry at all of them that I found myself hurrying right on, actually *wanting* to shock them. "*And,* as if that wasn't cruel enough, after he finished doing that, he *carved* a heart in her forehead."

If I'd wanted to shock everybody, I'd say I certainly succeeded.

Jarvis was making this sort of choking noise. "Carved?" he whispered. "What do you mean, *carved*?"

I didn't even hesitate. "I mean carved—like with a knife. The asshole who killed poor Trudi cut a heart in her forehead."

Maybe I'd gone too far. Charlotte was now looking a little green. "A—a heart?" she said. Charlotte normally has a high-pitched Minnie Mouse voice, but now it was even higher than usual.

Arlene was grimacing. "Yuck," she said.

"Wha-a-at?' This came from Barbi. What do you know; she was no longer chewing on her fingernail. Her face had gone almost as white as her hair. "Schuyler, are you sure?"

I wasn't quite certain what Barbi meant. *"Sure?"* I repeated.

With all the liner and mascara she was wearing, Barbi's eyes had been large already, but now they seemed to fill her face. "I mean," she said, and this time I think her breathy voice wasn't faked, "you know, are you sure she was—uh—cut like that?"

Evidently, Barbi needed convincing that things like this do indeed happen in the real world. "Barbi," I said, "I know a heart when I see one. And this particular heart you really couldn't miss."

Barbi's response was to do something I wouldn't have thought possible. She went even paler.

"Good Lord," Arlene said, looking first at me and then at the others. "Do you think that this means that whoever killed Trudi had to have known her *personally*? I mean, since whoever did that to her had to have known how Trudi always dots her *i*'s? I mean, isn't that so?"

Charlotte's own blond hear jerked in Arlene's direction. "Oh, my God, that's right. Trudi always dotted her *i*'s with those little—those little—" Her Minnie Mouse voice faltered.

"—hearts," Arlene finished for Charlotte. This time Arlene didn't glance around at anybody. Instead, she seemed suddenly fascinated by the electric pencil sharpener I keep on the edge of my desk. I knew, of course, why Arlene wasn't looking at anybody. Because if you started looking for somebody who knew Trudi well enough to know how she dotted her *i*'s, everybody in the room qualified. Arlene wasn't looking at anybody, because she didn't want her glance to be interpreted as accusing.

"But that doesn't make sense," Barbi said. She looked a little startled as every head in the room turned in her direction, but then she swallowed once and hurried on. "I mean, didn't Trudi go off to answer a lead of *yours,* Schuyler? Isn't that what you told me?"

I just looked at her. As I mentioned before, Barbi has never exactly been a brain trust. She has a vanity plate on her car that says TRU LUV, and sometimes I've been sure that she thought those words were spelled correctly. And yet, now her logic seemed right on target.

I turned back to the others. "Barbi's right," I said.

"Trudi did leave me a note saying she was going to meet somebody who'd phoned for me."

Can you believe, Arlene actually looked relieved? "Oh, thank *God*," she said. Patting at her pageboy, she added, "That's a load off my mind."

It was at this point that Arlene seemed to realize that everybody in the room was now staring at her. She shrugged. "I mean, otherwise you could get the idea that there was a serial killer out there, murdering real estate agents at random." She tried to give this little nonsensical snicker at the end, as if what she'd just said was ludicrous.

I directed a flat, level gaze at Arlene. It may have been a load off Arlene's mind, but it certainly wasn't a load off mine.

"No, no, NO." Jarvis was now lifting an index finger, no doubt preparing to deliver the definitive word on this particular subject. "The killer could *still* have been targeting people at random. Because we don't know for sure that Trudi really went to that appointment at all."

I turned to look at him. Trudi was found in the house she'd mentioned in her note, and yet Jarvis didn't think she'd gone to that appointment? Perhaps Jarvis had helped Barbi spell the inscription on her license plate.

"In fact," Jarvis was going on, swiping one more time at his imaginary hair, "the way I see it, Trudi had to have been taken from this office at gunpoint. She *had* to have been. After, of course, she was coerced into writing you that note."

I was getting tired of standing, so I sat down on the edge of my desk. "How do you figure?" I asked Jarvis, folding my arms across my chest.

Jarvis gave me a condescending look. "Simple," he said.

Oh, brother. If he said, "Elementary, my dear Watson," I was going to throw up.

Jarvis lifted his index finger in the air again. "Trudi had to have been taken by force, because a top-notch agent like Trudi would *never* have left this office unmanned."

Uh-huh. Put Jarvis down as one superb judge of character.

I had no intention of telling him any different, however. I was already feeling guilty enough as it was. I didn't need to add "Bad-mouthing her after she was dead" to my ever-growing list of Trudi offenses.

It looked as if I didn't have to say anything, anyway. From the way Barbi, Charlotte, and Arlene were all exchanging knowing looks, I'd say they all knew exactly how reliable Trudi had been.

The only problem with this, of course, was that once you accepted that Trudi had indeed gone off to meet whoever it was who had called for me, then you also had to accept something else. There was the distinct possibility that what had happened to Trudi had really been meant for yours truly.

My mouth suddenly felt as if I'd just eaten an entire box of crackers. "I think I'll get me a Coke," I sort of mumbled to the others. Then, easing off the edge of my desk, I more or less bolted for the kitchen. There I poured a long, tall, bubbly one, heavy on the ice. Nobody followed me, and I sincerely hoped that everybody had more or less gone about their business by the time I got back.

No such luck. They were all still clustered around my desk when I walked back out. I was considering walking right past all of them, glass in hand, straight out the front door, when Charlotte said, "Now, Schuyler, just because Trudi went off to meet somebody who was supposed to meet you isn't necessarily bad."

I took a sip of Coke, staring at her. Minnie Mouse had to be kidding. If it wasn't bad, what was it?

Charlotte had picked up on my uncertain look, because she immediately jumped in with, "What I mean is, Schuyler, there are a thousand things that could've happened."

I almost smiled. This was so like Charlotte to try to make me feel better. I had no doubt that if she ever ran across my picture on a Wanted poster in the post office, she would be quick to point out how simply gorgeous I'd looked in it. My goodness, *what* a photogenic criminal I was. "Okay, Charlotte," I said, my tone indulgent, "what could've happened?"

I did notice that Barbi, Jarvis, and Arlene were all now looking at Charlotte with skeptical expressions on their faces, that no doubt mirrored my own.

Charlotte's big blue eyes kind of wandered for a moment. Then she lifted her chin and said, "Well, uh, whoever Trudi was supposed to meet might not have shown up. I mean, it happens all the time, doesn't it, us agents getting stood up?" She turned to look at the others for verification.

They all just stared back at her.

I was staring at her, too. Somebody *had* clearly met Trudi. Or was Charlotte now actually trying to make me believe that Trudi had done an Isadora Duncan down in the basement, strangling herself with her own scarf by accident?

Charlotte may have been headed down that path, but she must've realized that nobody was going to follow her. Particularly since, as I recalled, Isadora's scarf accident had actually involved a car—a thing pretty difficult to get down into a basement. Charlotte paused for a long moment, eyes once again wandering, and then her chin went up again. *"And,"* Charlotte said, her Minnie Mouse voice sounding victorious, "somebody else could've followed Trudi—somebody who didn't even know you, Schuyler—and when he saw that Trudi was alone, since she'd been stood up, well, then ..." Minnie Mouse didn't seem to want to go any further.

"Uh-huh," I said. I hated to rain on Charlotte's parade. I mean, I did appreciate what she was trying to do.

Charlotte once again picked up on my skeptical tone, because she quickly added, "Okay, well, how about this? Maybe Trudi wasn't meeting anybody at all. Maybe she just put that in her note, just to get out of the office." Charlotte said this last with a quick, sideways glance at Jarvis. Really. She actually acted as if this were something that had never occurred to him.

That's right. Charlotte apparently truly believed that Jarvis had never once entertained the notion that any of us, his very own agents, would ever say that we were going to appointments when, in fact, we were not. When, in truth, we were headed straight to Oxmoor Center, a mall located mere minutes away, to take advantage of the final clearance at Lazarus Department Store. Oh, God, no. I'm sure Jarvis had never suspected any of us of doing such a thing. I mean, hell, how could he? Good God, man, didn't he have any trust?

I cleared my throat. "Charlotte," I said gently, "I talked to Mrs. Childers, the listing agent for the house Trudi was found in. Trudi made the appointment. She *was* meeting somebody," I said again.

Charlotte blinked. Then, undaunted, Minnie Mouse tried again. *"Or,* it could be that—"

I held up my hand. "That's all right, Charlotte," I

said, "I know what you're trying to do, and I really do appreciate it."

In another minute Charlotte would be trying to convince me that Trudi could have been spirited away by aliens, and that they'd beamed her down, coincidentally enough, to the exact location Trudi had happened to mention in her note to me. Come to think of it, this sounded about as likely as the scenarios Charlotte had come up with so far. What's more, I knew Charlotte herself didn't really believe what she was saying, because her eyes were now following me worriedly.

"It's okay, Charlotte," I said, trying to smile at her convincingly. "I'm not worried. Not a bit. Really."

I believe everybody, right down to Jarvis himself, knew I was lying. Fortunately, however, they all went along with the ruse.

"Oh, yeah," Arlene said, "there's really no reason to get all in a dither over this. I mean, whoever did that to Trudi is probably long gone by now."

Barbi, Charlotte, and Jarvis all nodded in unison.

I, on the other hand, took another sip of Coke.

Eventually, everybody did sort of wander back to their desks. Leaving me, of course, to take a seat behind my own desk and busily start going through the paperwork on my desk. Of course, I gave it up after about five minutes, and then I just sat there, staring at nothing, thinking wonderful thoughts. Like, for example, I pretty much made up my mind while I was sitting there that I didn't want to find out if the killer carved the heart on your forehead before he strangled you—or after.

Call me *not* inquisitive.

As the time got closer and closer to seven—the time I'd told Irving the Ripper I'd meet him—I realized that my heart was beating faster and faster. And my hands were getting damp again.

As were my underarms.

Good Lord. Unless I did something fast, I was going to be totally dehydrated before I even *met* old Irving. I'd have to take him through the house dragging an IV drip behind me.

About six-fifteen I finally admitted it to myself. I couldn't do it. I could *not* go all by myself to meet a total stranger at an empty house. The simple truth was, I was just plain too scared.

Even as I was realizing the truth, though, I could hardly believe it. For the first time in all of the nine years that I'd been working as a real estate agent, it really struck me that my job could be *dangerous*. Meeting total strangers in vacant houses was not exactly the safest thing in the world for a woman to do for a living.

This was certainly a fine time for this to occur to me.

I hated to do it, but there didn't seem to be any choice. I reached for the phone on my desk. As I dialed, I could almost hear my mother back when I was in high school. Every single time I'd been tempted to call up some boy, she'd said, "Now, Schuyler, Southern ladies do not ask men out. Southern ladies wait for their man to call."

Uh-huh. Well, Mom, it looks like it's finally come down to this: I'm no lady. Southern, or otherwise.

"Hello?" Hearing the familiar deep voice was unexpectedly comforting.

"Matthias?" I said. "Are you doing anything tonight?"

Chapter
8

Matthias pulled into the parking lot not ten minutes after I phoned him. Of course, he lives in a condo over on Douglass Boulevard—not on the side across Bardstown Road, but on the side closest to Cherokee Park. The land Arndoerfer Realty sits on backs up to Cherokee Park, so Matthias is not far away. Still, in order to get here this quickly, Matthias would've had to have left almost the minute he put the receiver down.

This is something else about Matthias that is very different from my ex-husband, Ed. When I tell Matthias I need him to do something for me, he actually acts as if it could be important. It wasn't even necessary to tell Matthias why I'd wanted him along with me tonight. He'd just said, "Be there as fast as I can," and what do you know, it looked as if he'd actually hurried.

Ed, on the other hand, would've needed some kind of documentation that there really was a pressing reason to "accommodate my latest whim." That's what Ed always called anything I ever asked him to do—

one of my *whims*. Like, for example, the night I went into labor with Daniel. On a whim—and, oh, yes, because my pains did happen to be coming ten minutes apart—I suggested that we ought to leave for the hospital right away. Ed had been watching *Mission Impossible* at the time, and according to Ed, if we left before the show was over, he'd never know exactly what the mission had been. As I recall, that was pretty much the way *Mission Impossible* worked. They didn't tell you until the end exactly what it was they were trying to achieve. If my water hadn't broken right in the middle of our discussion, *my* mission probably would've turned out to be driving myself to the hospital—or maybe having Daniel in the middle of the living room. When I started dripping all over the Oriental rug in front of the television, however, it was just the sort of documentation that Ed seemed to need to get him moving.

What a sweetheart.

Speaking of which, when Matthias pulled into the parking lot outside, I knew it immediately. I didn't even have to get up from my desk to go look out the front window. Matthias drives a beat-up 1964 MGB that he tells me he's restoring. I'd like to believe him, but he's been working on it the entire time I've known him. The only thing he seems to have restored is something I don't think it had in the first place—a loud roar announcing its arrival everywhere it goes. Come to think of it, the Roar Hog makes this announcement several blocks *before* it arrives.

Today, however, was the first time that I'd ever fully appreciated this particular Roar Hog feature. I appreciated it mainly because Jarvis, Arlene, Barbi, and Charlotte were all still in the office, each one of them anxiously glancing over at me about every other minute. Under that kind of scrutiny, I would've hated to have kept getting up every so often and going to the window, looking for Matthias. If I'd had to do that, I know damn well that everybody in the office would've no doubt concluded that I was so scared out of my wits I couldn't sit still. Poor pathetic little me had to keep getting up and checking outdoors just to make sure that there were no killers lurking in the shrubbery, waiting to pounce. Knowing that the Roar Hog would be loudly announcing its arrival to everybody within a ten-block area, at least I was spared that.

I was not, however, spared Barbi's glomming onto Matthias the minute he walked in the door. I couldn't believe how fast that woman could move. Clearly Olympic material, Barbi was out of her desk chair and across the room before Matthias even had the chance to take more than a couple of steps in my direction. His eyes were on mine, he'd just lifted his hand in a little wave, and then Barbi was suddenly by his side.

"Why, hi–i–i, there," Barbi said. I was across the room, but I could tell that Barbi's asthma was acting up again. No doubt, when Matthias came through the front door, an enormous cloud of pollen and dust had blown in with him. Uh-huh. Right. That *had* to be it. Barbi was now holding onto Matthias's sleeve. "Long time, no see–e–e, handsome."

I just looked at her. What an original approach. Barbi's clever opening remarks were all the more impressive when you considered that it had not even *been* a particularly long time since she'd last seen Matthias. Barbi had seen him in the office just last week when Matthias had come by to pick me up for lunch.

Of course, that could be why Matthias was now staring down at Barbi, a confused expression in his green eyes. After a moment, he nodded uncertainly. "Yes," he said.

That's all Matthias said. Really. Even if I hadn't

been able to hear him—which I could, very clearly—
I could read his lips. They'd formed only the single
word.

Barbi's face, however, lit up. Giving her platinum
curls an emphatic shake, she said, "Oh, my, yes, it *has*
been a terribly long time, hasn't it?" Her asthma was
getting worse. She obviously needed one of those little
inhalers. "Matthias, I just don't get to see *enough* of
you." She leaned closer to him. "If you know what
I mean."

You could pretty much surmise from the terror-
stricken look on Matthias's face that he did indeed
know what Barbi meant. His eyes darted over to me
in silent appeal.

I just stared back at him blankly, as if I didn't quite
get the message. I knew, of course, what Matthias was
trying to tell me. He wanted me to trot right over
there and rescue him. Somehow, though, I couldn't
quite bring myself to do it. It seemed too much like
something you'd do back when you were in high
school. Back then, when your steady started talking
to another girl, you immediately ran to his side and
staked your claim.

That kind of behavior might not be so bad when
you're seventeen. But when you're forty-two? Are we
kidding? By the time you're my age, you realize that,
if a man really cares about you, it doesn't matter how
many other women hit on him. Ultimately, he will still
want to be with you. You also realize that if a man
doesn't care about you, it doesn't matter how much
you try to keep other women away. Ultimately, he
will still want to be with someone else.

Matthias had given up looking at me pleadingly, and
was now saying to Barbi, "Well, it's certainly been
nice to see you—"

Matthias looked as if he had every intention of

starting to move toward me again, but Barbi was not giving up his sleeve. "I wonder," she interrupted, looking up at him through heavily mascaraed lashes, "if anybody has ever told you that you look like Fabio?"

The confusion in Matthias's eyes got worse.

Barbi leaned closer. "You know, *Fabio*—that gorgeous hunk who's on all the paperback romance covers?"

I almost choked. Matthias is six three, he has very broad shoulders, and he's in great physical shape for a man who's forty-one. He's got the greenest eyes I've ever seen, a smile that lights up his entire face, and the hands of an artist. Of course, he *is* an artist—he teaches printmaking at the Kentucky School of Art.

Bearing all this in mind, I still have to say, if Matthias looks like Fabio, I look like Sharon Stone.

If nothing else, Matthias has a *beard*—a thick, neatly clipped one that I love running my fingers through. I don't believe I've ever seen Fabio with a beard. What's more, if you can believe all those paperback covers, Fabio doesn't even have hair on his chest. Matthias, *I can testify*, has thick hair on his chest that—yes, at the risk of repeating myself—I love running my fingers through.

In fact, there was only one thing I could think of that Matthias and Fabio did have in common. Other than, of course, that they were both male. They both have thick, shaggy hair. Matthias's hair is darker and not as long as Fabio's, though. Matthias's hair barely touches his shoulders.

So exactly how did Barbi come up with this one?

Even Matthias was looking mystified. Of course, he could've been looking that way just because he didn't have the faintest idea who the hell Fabio was. "Fabio," he repeated. "Hmmm. Well, well ..." He gave Barbi a quick smile, and then once again started to move in my direction.

Barbi actually stepped in front of him. "You do know who Fabio is, don't you? He looks just like you. You two even dress alike."

I blinked at that one. Matthias was now wearing faded blue jeans, a navy blue sweater, scuffed boots, and a fleece-lined blue wool jacket. In all the pictures I'd ever seen of Fabio, he was wearing pants a little tighter than a tourniquet, and no shirt. Uh-huh. Matthias and Fabio could be twins.

Like me and Sharon.

"You two have the same huge shoulders," Barbi was now saying, "the same muscular arms, and the same—"

Can you believe, all the time Barbi was listing Fabio characteristics, she was running her hands over Matthias? Touching his shoulders, his arms, his chest. Lord knows what she would've gotten hold of next, but Matthias stepped away. "Barbi, Schuyler's waiting for me, so—"

Barbi's response was to grab his sleeve again. This time, though, it didn't work. Matthias's face was determined as he started once again in my direction.

Barbi suddenly had a choice. She could either let go of Matthias's sleeve, or she could hang on and be dragged bodily across the floor. Fortunately for everybody concerned, she let go.

Matthias no longer looked determined, he looked relieved.

Barbi, on the other hand, looked furious. Not, of course, at Matthias. Oh, no, I have never seen Barbi look furious at any person of the male persuasion. No, Barbi went back to her desk, sat down, looked across the room, and glared at—you guessed it—yours truly. I could almost feel Barbi's piercing gaze. This was not a new experience. Barbi has been glaring at me off and on ever since Matthias and I started dating. She seems to think that I set my cap for Matthias the very first day he walked into the office.

It seems to have completely slipped Barbi's mind that the reason Matthias showed up in the first place was to find out who was responsible for his father's death. Barbi also seems to have forgotten that the person Matthias considered number one on the suspect hit parade was me.

Call me oversensitive, but to my way of thinking, that entire scenario does not bode well for romance. While I confess that back then it had been quite a while since I'd even *met* a really attractive man, I still hadn't reached the point where I was so desperate that I would consider as a possibility the one guy in the world who wanted to put me on death row.

While I might not have set my cap for Matthias, Barbi certainly had set *hers*. She'd announced days before Matthias turned up that she intended to catch herself a wealthy husband, and it was clear right from the beginning that, in Barbi's opinion, Matthias fit the bill.

I've tried to explain to Barbi several times since then that Matthias is not the wealthy man a lot of people seem to think he is. His family's money is now completely in the hands of his mother, and Matthias prides himself on being self-supporting. He's told me, "I've never taken one thin dime from my parents, and I never intend to."

Barbi, however, seems to think that I'm just saying all this so she'll back off. She obviously believes that I've poached territory she herself had staked out.

I do feel bad about it. Before Matthias and I started going out, Barbi and I had been pretty good friends. I suppose it had been almost inevitable—after all, she and I did have an awful lot in common. We were both real estate agents, we were both divorced, we were even close to the same age—although Barbi, of course, would be quick to tell you that she's a mere thirty-nine to my all-but-elderly forty-two. Barbi has two children, Jennifer, nineteen, and Shawn, Jr., twenty—both, as you can see, very close in age to my own two sons.

Even if we hadn't had so much in common, Barbi had endeared herself to me right away—by referring to my ex-husband, Ed, as "Mr. Ed." I was never sure if she was doing it on purpose, or if she even got the joke herself. It really didn't matter. Those times Barbi had actually called Ed that to his face, I'd almost had a stroke, trying to keep from laughing.

Now I guess I wasn't laughing anymore. I'd thought that Barbi and I were good friends, and yet the minute Matthias began to concentrate all his attention in my direction, Barbi actually seemed to view me as an enemy.

Under the present circumstances, I'd sort of hoped that Barbi might forego the hostilities. Apparently, though, a little thing like the distinct possibility that a murderer could be targeting me as his next victim wasn't enough to get Barbi to let up. She looked holes through me right up until Matthias and I started to head out the front door.

When Matthias held the door open for me, Barbi abruptly stood and walked out of the room. She headed toward the kitchen in the back, her stiletto heels making little explosions on the floor as she went. I suppressed a sigh and went on out the front door.

Instead of the Roar Hog, Matthias and I took my Tercel to the appointment, for obvious reasons. Matthias, however, drove. I know. I know. As an independent woman of the nineties, I'm supposed to be grabbing for that steering wheel every chance I get. The truth is, with all the time I spend in my car, driving all over the place to closings and open houses and appointments, I'm delighted when I get to be a passenger.

I was hoping I'd be able to get Matthias to come with me to show the house on Ashwood without my having to tell him exactly why I wanted him along. I should've known I was kidding myself. Matthias had no sooner pulled out of the parking lot onto Taylorsville Road when he turned to me and began, "Okay, Sky—"

Matthias has only just lately started calling me Sky. Short for Schuyler, I guess. Every time he says it, though, I immediately flash on the only other person I've ever heard of whose name was Sky. That was Sky King. Sky King was the name of this cowboy on television back in the fifties. Multitalented, Sky King not only sang songs, rode horses, and caught bad guys, he also flew a plane. Hence, the name, I suppose. Matthias always calls me Sky so affectionately that I haven't ever had the heart to tell him that I've always considered Sky to be a boy's name.

"—so what's the deal?" Matthias finished.

I gave Matthias one of my best innocent looks. "Why, whatever do you mean?"

Matthias actually laughed. "Don't give me that Southern lady innocent bit. You know exactly what I mean. Why do you want me along? Is there something about the guy you're showing this house to that worried you?"

For a long moment I just sat there. Fighting temptation. Because, believe me, it would've been so easy to just tell Matthias a lie. I could just say that, yes, this guy had said something vulgar to me over the phone, and Matthias would've believed it. In a heartbeat.

Of course, he might also punch the living daylights out of Irving Rickle the minute we got to the house on Ashwood. Carting Irving off to the emergency room would probably not be the best way to start off a realtor-client relationship. Then, too, none of the self-help books I'd ever read over the years had ever endorsed lying as a good way to cement a relationship.

It also didn't help to recall exactly how I myself had felt all the times I'd caught my ex-husband, Ed, lying to me. Trudi's story would be in tomorrow's *Courier-Journal,* without a doubt. Once Matthias read that little news item, he'd know exactly why I'd wanted him along tonight.

So, after an admittedly too-long moment of real temptation, I ended up turning to Matthias and more or less spilling my guts. I told him all about what had happened to Trudi, what she'd said in her note, and what the salt and pepper shakers had asked me. I did notice, as I went on, that the knuckles of Matthias's hands on the steering wheel were turning whiter and whiter.

"Good Lord, Schuyler," however, was all Matthias said.

He was looking so worried, though, that I found myself also telling him all the theories that Charlotte in Wonderland had come up with. As if I actually thought Charlotte's theories could have some validity. I told Matthias how Trudi might've been stood up, how Trudi might've been followed, and how Trudi might not even have been meeting anybody at all— but just been trying to get out of the office.

Oddly enough, Charlotte's theories didn't seem to make Matthias feel any better than they had me.

"So, of course," I finished, "you can't be sure. Trudi's death might not have anything whatsoever to do with me."

Matthias, wouldn't you know it, immediately agreed with me. He agreed so fast, without even a split second of hesitation, that I knew he really didn't believe a word of what he was saying. "You're absolutely right. There's no use jumping to conclusions." Matthias reached over and patted my hand. "I'm sure it's nothing to worry about."

Have I ever mentioned how much I hate having my hand patted? I knew Matthias was trying to be sweet, but I couldn't help it. There is something about being patted that makes me feel like a dog, waiting patiently at its master's feet for scraps off the table. I pulled my hand away.

Matthias gave me a quick, sideways glance.

I gave him a quick smile. "Hey, I'm not really worried," I said. "Not really. It's just that this guy I'm supposed to show the house to, well, he did sound a little scary on the phone."

Now this was not strictly a lie. There were, no doubt, tons of instances in which Don Knotts could be scary. Like, for example, if he ever turned out to be your blind date.

"I mean," I went on, "this guy sounded kind of odd, you know, and, well, I just thought, if you weren't doing anything, then it would probably be a good idea if I didn't meet this guy all by . . ."

Unfortunately, it was about then that Matthias and I were pulling into the driveway at the house on Ashwood, and we could both plainly see the guy waiting for me up on the porch. My voice sort of trailed off.

Standing on the top step, with his hands in his pockets, was a man at least two inches shorter than my own five six and at least ten pounds lighter than my own 120. What's more, this guy looked *exactly* like somebody who'd be named Irving Rickle. In fact, looking at him, you could almost see this guy's mom on the day he was born, holding her newborn baby, and knowing instinctively that one day this baby would be standing on a porch somewhere wearing the exact same getup he had on today. The new mother, no doubt, visualized all of this, snapped her fingers, and said, "I've got it! *Irving!*"

Irving Rickle was wearing a red-striped dress shirt, blue plaid slacks, white socks, and black dress shoes with blue plaid laces. How did I know he was wearing white socks? Easy. Irving's plaid slacks were what my sons refer to as "high-waters." According to my sons, high-waters are slacks so short that if you ever have to wade through high water in them, you won't get the cuffs wet. I stared at Irving up there on the porch, and I realized that he was wearing the exact outfit both my sons have feared all their lives I would one day make them wear.

Matthias stared at Irving as he shut off the engine. "Oh, yeah," he said, "this guy's scary, all right."

I was staring at Irving, too. Either the man had just swallowed a Ping-Pong ball, or he had one of the largest Adam's apples I'd ever seen.

I cleared my throat. "You can't judge a book by its cover." I'm ashamed to admit it, but, yes, I did actually say that. Hey, when it came to originality, Barbi had nothing on me. "I mean," I hurried on, "didn't Ted Bundy look like just your average guy?"

Matthias's green eyes got a little bigger, but he didn't say a word. In fact, all he did was glance pointedly at Irving.

I followed Matthias's gaze.

Irving, at that moment, was scratching his right ear with a pencil.

Okay, so maybe Irving here was below average.

Chapter
9

After Irving Rickle finished using his pencil as an ear-scratcher, he tucked it into the plastic pocket protector lining his left shirt pocket.

I know. I watched him. As I watched him, I made a mental note never to ask the man to borrow anything to write with. *Ever.*

"Mr. Rickle?" I said, extending my hand. "I'm Schuyler Ridgway." The smile I put on my face felt as if I'd cut it out of cardboard and pasted it on.

Irving's smile wasn't all that much of an improvement over my own. His smile sort of wiggled at the corners. When the little man introduced himself, his voice sort of wiggled, too. "I–I–I'm glad t–to m–meet you," he said. Irving didn't sound glad. He sounded as if he were standing in the middle of something that might register six or seven on the Richter scale.

The way he shook hands was as bad as the way he talked. His hand was limp and slightly damp. What's more, when Irving and I stopped shaking hands, Irving's hand kept right on. Shaking, that is.

Oh, my, yes, I could see it now. Ted Bundy. Jeffrey

Dahmer. And Irving Rickle. Names that would live on in infamy. Uh-huh. *Right.*

I introduced Matthias, identifying him as my "associate," which was, of course, absolutely true. Matthias and I associated with each other all the time. Irving must've doubted our association, however. His watery hazel eyes seemed to linger uneasily on Matthias's face, even after I'd finished the introductions.

It occurred to me that if Irving's hand was damp and trembling when he was shaking *my* hand, there was no telling what Irving's hand would be doing when he was shaking Matthias's. Matthias towered over the guy, and he had to outweigh Irving by at least seventy pounds. The entire handshaking experience must've been pretty bad, because I noticed that Matthias's eyes widened the second Irving took hold of his hand. I also noticed that Matthias released Irving's hand as fast as he possibly could, and that the instant Irving glanced away, Matthias wiped his palm on his jeans.

"Well," I said brightly, "shall we go inside?"

Irving's head bobbled up and down, an action immediately echoed by his Adam's apple.

I gave Irving another cardboard smile, avoided Matthias's eyes, and led the way. Unlocking the door with one of the house keys I'd been given when I'd taken the listing, I waved Irving inside with a little flourish.

Irving going inside meant that he had to walk directly in front of Matthias, who was at that moment standing on my right. As Irving did so, he gave Matthias the sort of look you might give somebody wearing a ski mask and carrying a chain saw.

As a cold-blooded killer type, I'd say Irving could stand a few lessons.

And yet, even if the little man didn't appear to be the least bit threatening, I was still glad to have Matthias with me. Irving might not look like somebody to be afraid of, but how could you be sure? I mean, if all would-be killers looked like killers, nobody would ever get killed, would they?

I also remembered reading somewhere that Albert Desalvo, of Boston Strangler fame, had been an extremely shy sort. At the time, of course, I'd been amazed, having been under the impression up until then that shyness and a tendency to strangle were mutually exclusive personality traits. As soon as I read that, though, I'd realized it didn't necessarily follow that just because you were shy, you were incapable of murder.

It also didn't necessarily follow that men wearing plaid high-waters were incapable of murder, either. In fact, now that I thought about it, if I were a serial killer, I'd dress *exactly* like Irving here. I mean, who could possibly expect violence from a guy wearing high-waters and a pocket protector? If anything, Irving's choice of wardrobe would certainly give him the advantage of surprise. Hell, he probably wouldn't even have to *do* anything to his victims. He could just *tell* them that he planned to kill them, and they'd all die of shock.

The more I went over it in my mind, the more it seemed to me that Irving was the perfect murderer type. After all, wasn't the guy who did it in all the mystery movies always the guy you least suspected? I'd say Irving here qualified on all counts.

And, let us not forget, Irving had been the first person to call me for an appointment after Trudi disappeared. Had Irving called to make the appointment after he'd discovered that the wrong real estate agent had showed up to meet him? Could it be that the reason Irving was acting so nervous wasn't that he was shy, but that he was thrown off balance because I'd brought Matthias along?

Unfortunately, all this started going through my mind just about the time I was showing Irving the walk-in closet in the living room. Matthias was waiting outside at the moment, mainly because he had taken a quick look inside and obviously reached the same conclusion I had. It was going to be a tight squeeze in there for three people.

So, as it happened, Irving and I were alone. I didn't think our being alone bothered me, though. Everything certainly seemed like business as usual. I was pointing out the recently installed modular shelving and going on about the convenience of the roll-away bins, just like I'd done all the other times I'd shown this house.

Then Irving made a sudden move in my direction.

And my heart did an equally sudden lurch.

I immediately felt like an idiot. Because, of course, I realized right away that all Irving appeared to have in mind was getting past me as quickly as possible. So that he could get a better look at the roll-away bins I'd just been raving about. I even stepped back so that Irving could get to the bins without having to go around me, and yet my heart kept right on hammering away.

"N-n-nice," Irving said, pulling out the topmost bin and rolling it back in again.

I couldn't seem to help myself. When Irving spoke, I actually jumped. I managed to cover it up by moving quickly toward the door. There I had to clear my throat once before I could trust my voice to say, "Matthias? Could you come here, please?"

Even though I was trying my best to sound normal, Matthias must've heard something in my voice—some note of alarm—because he came through the doorway in a rush. Of course, once he got through the door, he came to an abrupt halt. This was fortunate, considering that if he'd come any further, I would've been shoved right up against Irving. And right then, if that had happened, I would most definitely have screamed my head off.

Matthias, for his part, just stood there, looking first at me, then over at Irving, and then back at me again. Irving was still playing roll away with the bins. He was admiring the lowest bin now, bending over, his plaid rump in the air, his back to both me and Matthias. "V-v-very n-nice," Irving mumbled.

Since there was obviously nothing happening that could make my voice sound the slightest bit alarmed, Matthias's green eyes began to look puzzled. "Schuyler?" he said.

I just stared back at Matthias for a split second. I certainly didn't want to tell him that the reason I'd *sounded* frightened was that I *was* frightened—of a little man who was now mumbling. "Goodness, yes, th–these bins are very, *very* n–nice."

I cleared my throat again. "Matthias, I just *had* to show you these nice bins." I gave him a wide smile.

Have I mentioned that I pride myself on thinking fast on my feet?

Maybe I should've thought a little slower. Matthias's eyes stayed on my face. "Bins?" he said. His eyes traveled over to Irving again, and then returned to me. "Bins?" he repeated.

I nodded. "Aren't these roll-away bins nice?"

Matthias was now looking at me as if he was beginning to fear that the only bin I should be taking a close look at was one described by the word "loony." "Yes," he said uncertainly, running his hand over his beard. "Those bins *are* nice, all right."

In my opinion, that certainly seemed to cover the

entire bin situation quite adequately. I moved as fast as I could past Matthias, and—not incidentally—right out of that damn closet. Once out in the living room, I took a deep breath. I also began to feel even more like an idiot, particularly when Irving came out of the walk-in closet right after that. With the sun streaming in the front windows, I got an even better look at the man, noticing little things I hadn't before. Like, for example, he was wearing a *polka-dot* bow tie, for God's sake. And he had ink stains on *both* shirt cuffs. And the elastic was evidently gone in his socks—they sort of bagged around his thin ankles.

Even so, I knew I wasn't going to be able to bring myself to go alone into any small enclosed space with Irving again. Which meant I might actually have to skip the pantry and the utility room. Or else I'd have to show them while standing outside in the hall.

I know. I know. I was obviously tired. And, no doubt, the events of the day had shaken me up even more than I realized. That had to be why all of a sudden I was actually feeling afraid of a man whose only crimes seemed to be of the fashion variety.

That also had to be why I acted the way I did in the next several minutes. Because, would you believe, before I could stop myself, I started asking Irving a few questions? Nothing really blatant like, "Oh, now that I think of it, wasn't that you who murdered Trudi yesterday?" No, I believe I was a little more subtle than that.

Not a lot. But a little.

It was shortly after Matthias had followed Irving out of the walk-in closet in the living room, and we'd all moved into the dining room across the way. I had just pointed out the built-in window seat, and while Irving was looking it over—lifting the cushions and checking out the storage underneath—I asked, "Oh, by the way, Mr. Rickle, did you ever meet Trudi Vittitoe?"

I'd meant that to sound casual, as if I were just making idle conversation. I must not have pulled that one off, however. Matthias was standing to my left, and the second I spoke, his shaggy head sort of jerked in my direction.

Irving also looked my way, his eyes watery as ever. "Tr–Trudi who?"

I was watching Irving intently, but I didn't detect even a flicker of recognition when I said Trudi's name.

I shrugged. "Trudi Vittitoe," I said. "Another real estate agent in my office? I thought you might've talked to her."

Irving was already shaking his head, his eyes returning to the storage area inside the window seat. "N-no, I-I don't think so—"

I nodded. "Oh. Well, I was just wondering," I said. "Somebody called the office yesterday, and Trudi took the call, so I just thought . . ." I let my voice trail off. It was just as well. Old Irv seemed considerably more interested in the interior of the window seat than in whatever I was talking about.

I stared at him. Either the man deserved an Academy Award, or Trudi's name meant nothing to him. Of course, I thought with a little shiver, maybe he'd never even known her name. It could very well be that finding out your victim's name might not be a high priority to your average killer.

I could feel Matthias's eyes on me, but I purposely didn't look in his direction. "Mr. Rickle," I said, "what kind of business are you in?"

This time I think I really did sound as if I were just making polite conversation, because Irving didn't even lift his head. He was replacing the cushions on the window seat when he said over his shoulder, "I own my own computer repair business."

"Oh, really?" I said. "How interesting. Well, I guess as the owner of the business, you can probably leave your office just about anytime you feel like it—"

Irving's head jerked in my direction, much like Matthias's had earlier. Irving's watery eyes looked horrified. Apparently, I'd just been guilty of blasphemy. "Oh, my Lord, no," Irving said. "There's only me and a secretary. Half the t-time I don't even take lunch."

I stared right back at him. So much for trying to establish that the man could come and go at will—that, indeed, he'd had all the time in the world to meet Trudi.

Of course, there was always the possibility that Irving was lying. Murderers probably didn't draw the line at telling a few fibs.

I cleared my throat. "Then," I said, "what you're saying is that you *never* get away from your office during the—"

Oddly enough, at that moment, Matthias interrupted me. "Schuyler, don't you think we ought to show Mr. Rickle the upstairs now? I think it's the best part of the house."

This last comment was something of a surprise, since Matthias—to my knowledge—had never been in this house before. I turned and just looked at him.

Matthias met my gaze head-on. "I *believe,*" Matthias said, "that Mr. Rickle is anxious to see the upstairs."

I looked back over at Irving. He was looking anxious, all right, but I wasn't sure it had anything to do with the upstairs.

I knew right then what Matthias was trying to do. Matthias was trying to tell me that now would be an excellent time for me to quit quizzing Irving and get on with what we were all here to do in the first place.

"Certainly," I said, perhaps a shade too brightly. I led the way toward the stairs.

I wish I could say that from that point forward, I just concentrated on showing Irving the house. And that, by the time I'd gotten upstairs, I'd realized that Matthias was absolutely right, and that my submitting poor Irving here to an inquisition was probably a little out of line.

Unfortunately, however, there is something about me that I might as well confess right now. That something is: I don't respond well to somebody telling me what to do. Even when, let's face it, that somebody could very well be absolutely right.

I particularly don't respond well if the somebody telling me what to do happens to be a man. I know. I know. I'm a sick puppy. I have no doubt that this little difficulty of mine is a leftover from being married to Ed for so many years.

Ed and I got married in the early seventies, you see, back before women's liberation really got going. Ours, in fact, was probably one of the last ceremonies in America that still had the word "obey" as part of the vows. I know it's hard to believe, particularly considering what I just confessed, but for *years* I actually took that "obey" vow seriously. Of course, if during any of those years I'd ever found out that Ed was not taking seriously the part of the ceremony that said "forsaking all others," I might've behaved a little differently.

I didn't find that out for some time, though, so for most of my married life I took a great many orders. I also got extremely tired of taking them. Eventually, of course, it dawned on me that what Ed really wanted

was not a family, but a platoon. Either that, or a small
Latin American country he could rule with an iron fist.

I bring all this up to explain why I didn't immediately follow Matthias's lead. I not only didn't follow
his lead, but by the time I'd gotten upstairs, I'd decided that, having asked Irving as much as I'd already
asked him, a couple more questions couldn't hurt. I'd
just pointed out the original porcelain hot and cold
handles in the bathtub in the master bathroom when
I cleared my throat again. "Incidentally, Mr. Rickle,"
I said, "what do you think of hearts?"

I guess I should've been a little less blunt, because
suddenly I had two men staring at me. Matthias's eyes
were bugging out a little.

Irving's voice cracked when he answered me.
"H-hearts?"

I stared at him intently, trying to make up my mind
whether the way his voice had cracked was significant
or not. "It's a simple question, Mr. Rickle," I said.
"What do you think of them?"

Okay, I admit it, this was not my finest hour. Or
even, *minute*.

Irving was now giving me the loony-bin look Matthias had given me earlier. "I like hearts okay," he
said weakly. His eyes traveled to Matthias.

Matthias just stared back at him, his face
expressionless.

Irving looked back over at me. "Of course," Irving
went on, "I l-like spades and diamonds and c-clubs
okay, too. I mean, I really can't say I *prefer* hearts."

I blinked at that one. Oh, boy. I could be leaping
to conclusions here, but it did seem as if Irving might
not be the least bit sensitive with regard to the subject
of hearts. In fact, you could actually get the idea that
Irving didn't have the slightest idea what the hell I
was talking about. Particularly after he cleared his own

throat once, and asked, "Why do you w–want to know?"

That one gave me pause. And then, without looking over at Matthias, I began doing what my sons have often referred to as shoveling it big-time. "Oh," I said, waving a hand in the air carelessly, "I ask that of everybody I meet these days. It's because I just read a book all about how you can tell a whole lot about somebody just by which suit of cards they prefer."

Irving didn't even blink. "Really," he said. His tone was oddly flat.

I nodded. "Really," I said. "This book said that hearts people are, uh, warm and friendly. And spades people are, uh, let me see now, down to earth; yes, that's right. And diamonds, well, they're, uh, motivated mainly by money. And clubs, uh, they're joiners, you know, the kind of people who need people. . . ."

I think it was lapsing into the title of a Barbra Streisand song that pretty much blew it. Can you believe that Irving actually started looking at me as if I were making all this up? I mean, really, the *nerve*.

"You read this in a book?" he said. His Adam's apple bobbed up and down a couple of times. "What's that book called?"

I didn't even pause. "You know, I don't recall the title right off hand." I tilted my head to one side and tried to look as if I were straining to remember. "It was a very interesting book, though. Really."

Irving just looked at me without a word. The expression on his face reminded me uneasily of a kid I used to know back in high school. I don't remember this kid's name—if indeed I ever knew it—but he used to ride the same school bus I did. Awkward and gangly, with a bad complexion, this poor kid was always the brunt of the jokes. He was always the one who got his coat hidden, or his homework thrown out the window, or his books tossed around the bus. Every single time something like this happened, this kid looked exactly like Irving right now. Infinitely sad. And bewildered. And hurt.

I swallowed, staring at the little man. Oh, dear. Did Irving think I was putting him on? Just for fun? Looking at him, I realized if I had indeed been doing such a thing, this was probably not the first time it had happened to him. In fact, judging from the look on his face, it was something he had to put up with a lot.

I suddenly wanted to tell Irving the truth. And yet, how could I? What would I say? *Look, Irving, I don't want you thinking I was acting this way because I thought you were a geek. No, I was acting this way because I thought you were a murderer.*

Oh, my, yes. *That* ought to ease his mind.

After that—no surprise—Irving suddenly seemed to pick up speed. In fact, Irving all but sprinted through the rest of the rooms. I didn't have to worry about going into the pantry or the utility room with him because he wasn't interested in seeing them. In fact, mere minutes later, when we were all standing downstairs at the front door once again, Irving mumbled very quickly, "I-I don't think this is w-what I'm looking for." Then, without looking back once, he turned, headed for his car, got in, and pulled away.

Even more significantly, he pulled away without asking to see any more properties.

I stood there on the porch, next to Matthias, watching Irving's car disappear in a blur of exhaust down the road. For a long moment, neither of us said a word. When Irving was out of sight, Matthias said, "Clubs are *joiners*?" His tone was amused.

I couldn't help smiling. "Hey, I was just trying to—"

Matthias raised his hand. "I know, sweetheart," he said. "I know what you were trying to do."

"I guess I just lost a client," I said.

Matthias didn't say a word, so I knew that he had to agree. I drew a long, weary breath. Now I not only felt like an idiot and a bully, I felt like an incompetent. I'd sent a perfectly good client scurrying for cover, and for what? What in the world had I hoped to accomplish? Even if Irving had been a murderer, did I really think that at some point he was just going to nod his head and say, *You know, I'm glad you brought this up. I'd been meaning to tell you—I strangled Trudi yesterday.*

I went back inside, got my purse, locked the front door, and headed back out to the car with Matthias. On the way, Matthias put his arm around my shoulders.

After a second or so, it seemed like the most natural thing in the world to put my head against Matthias's broad shoulder and lean against him a little as we continued toward my car. Matthias's arm tightened around me as we went.

What can I say? It was a nice moment.

Unfortunately, the moment ended right after Matthias opened the passenger door of my Tercel. As I started to get in, Matthias said, "Sky, I know all this is really bothering you."

I stopped and turned to look at him. I didn't have to ask what he meant by "all this."

Matthias's green eyes were dark with concern. "It's bothering me, too," he said. "Hell, I don't know what I'd do if anything happened to you." His voice actually sounded a little ragged.

I made a scoffing noise. I got in and busied myself putting on my seat belt. "Nothing's going to happen to me," I said, without looking at Matthias.

I wished I believed me. I also wished I'd been able to say that with a little more conviction, because clearly Matthias didn't believe me, either. He leaned against the frame of the car and stared in at me.

"Sky," he said, "we need to talk."

Oh, dear. In my experience, when a man says, We need to talk, it usually means, I need to talk, and you need to listen.

It was all I could do to suppress a groan.

Chapter
10

If Matthias had just started in when he was still standing right outside my car window, whatever he was about to say wouldn't have seemed like such a big deal. But, no, he waited to begin until after he'd gone all the way around the car, gotten in on the driver's side, locked the door, and put the key in the ignition. Finally, turning to face me, he ran his hand over his beard and took a deep breath.

By then, I was pretty much equating what was about to be said as something on a par with that little chat Grant and Lee had at Appomattox. My mouth had actually gone dry.

"Sky," Matthias began, "I love you."

I blinked. I couldn't say I hated the way the conversation was starting out.

"I love you very much."

Goodness. Maybe I was wrong. Maybe this conversation wasn't going to be so bad, after all.

"I love you, too," I said. As I mentioned earlier, it had taken me a while to finally be able to bring myself to tell Matthias this, but I believe I was making real strides in this area. These days the words fairly rolled off my tongue. No hesitation whatsoever.

Matthias gave a little nod of his shaggy head, as if to acknowledge that, yes, he'd heard me, and then he hurried on. "In fact, it's because I love you so much that I think that you and I should go ahead and do what we've been talking about doing for quite some time now. We ought to move in together. Right away."

Uh-oh. This conversation had just taken an ugly turn. This, as a matter of fact, was the very reason I hadn't been able to bring myself to tell Matthias how I felt about him for so long. Because the second you start saying the L word to somebody, you're taking the chance that he'll start saying other words right back to you. Words, like, oh, say, "move in together," and other phrases of that ilk.

I stared at Matthias. "You want us to move in together *right away*?" The second I said those particular words, I wished I could take them back. I sounded about as enthusiastic as I would've if Matthias had just suggested that he and I move into his *car*.

I believe Matthias immediately picked up on the subtle nuance of my tone, too, because there was now a sort of kicked-puppy expression in his eyes. My stomach wrenched. Matthias was opening his mouth to say something, but before he could get it out, I jumped in. Reaching over to touch his arm, I said, "Look, I didn't mean that the way it sounded. What I meant was that *right away* seems kind of—" I scrambled in my mind for the right words, while Matthias just sat there, that kicked-puppy look still in his eyes. "Well-l-l," I finally said, "it seems kind of—soon."

"Soon?" The green of Matthias's eyes seemed to deepen a little as he repeated the word. "Schuyler,

we've been dating almost a year." His tone wasn't argumentative. He was simply stating a fact.

"Nine months," I said. "We've been dating only nine months."

I was simply trying to keep the facts straight. That was all. Matthias, however, did not look all that appreciative of my efforts. He took another deep breath. "People have *babies* in nine months, Sky," he said, giving me a level look.

What in the world that had to do with anything was beyond me. "They certainly do," I said, giving him a level look right back.

Matthias closed his eyes for a moment. I couldn't be sure, but he might've been counting to ten. "Sky," Matthias said when he opened his eyes again, "I don't mean to be pressuring you or anything—"

I didn't say a word. However, it did cross my mind that if he didn't want to pressure me, he probably needed to stop talking.

"—but," he went on, "don't you think the time is right for moving in together?"

I blinked again at that one. *The time is right for moving in together?* Lord. Matthias was making this sound like a political campaign. What was next? Bumper stickers on my car?

However, the kicked-puppy look was gone, and I really didn't want to say anything that could make it reappear. So all I said was, "Well, it seems to me that we might be going a little too fast here. . . ."

Matthias ran his hand over his beard again. "A little too *fast*? Sky, I'm trying to move slow." He cleared his throat. "I mean, I realize that you've had some really bad relationships in the past, and so you've got this real fear of commitment."

I moved uneasily in the front passenger seat. Now

wait a minute here. He was making me sound like some kind of emotional basket case.

"Otherwise, I wouldn't just be talking about us moving in together," Matthias continued. "I'd be talking about us getting married."

It was all I could do to keep my mouth from dropping open. *Married?* Oh, my God. This conversation had just taken an even uglier turn.

I know. I know. Single women my age are pretty much assumed to be all but beating the shrubbery, hoping to flush out a husband. There was even that study a few years back that was supposed to depress us—the one that said that we women over forty were more likely to be shot by a terrorist than to get married again. Far from being depressed, I found that study delightfully upbeat. Of course, I was also pretty sure at the time that the reason that study's findings were interpreted the way they were was that nobody ever asked the women in that study if they *wanted* to get married again. I believe, if you factored in their desire to get married, the real significance of that study would turn out to be that women in their forties would *prefer* to be shot by a terrorist than get married again.

"Matthias," I said. "I—I—I—" Lord. I sounded like Irving Rickle. And yet, how could I explain that, even though I was sure that I loved Matthias, I was not sure I ever wanted to march down the aisle again. With Matthias or anybody else.

I mean, for one thing, there was the slug factor to consider. Right now, every time Matthias saw me, I was wearing makeup, my hair was freshly shampooed and styled, and usually I was wearing something that I knew looked pretty terrific on me. Even when I was dressed casually, I always wore my favorite Liz Claiborne jeans—the ones that fit as if they were made for me, instead of the ones that were so tight they unzipped themselves every time I sat down.

What I'm trying to get across here is that, let's face it, at this very moment there was a good chance that Matthias could actually be under the impression that I was good-looking. I really hated to disappoint the man.

Not to mention, I couldn't help recalling that the last time we'd gone to dinner, Matthias had actually looked at me across the table and said, "Schuyler, you are that rare thing. A natural beauty." At that particular moment, my natural beauty had been dimly lit by candlelight—a thing, I'm pretty sure, that could make a chimpanzee look like a natural beauty. I, of course, had immediately smiled at Matthias, genuinely touched, but I couldn't help thinking, Sweetheart, you are so right. A natural beauty *is* a rare thing. You might even say, *nonexistent*.

Oh, my, yes, the nice thing about just dating was that I didn't see Matthias every day. It was pretty easy to keep up with the makeup and the hair styling and the flattering wardrobe when you didn't have to maintain the illusion every damn minute of the day. On days I didn't see Matthias, I could still revert to type and be the slug I truly am. I could schlepp around my house in a shapeless sweat suit, wearing my extremely comfortable, but truly ugly, fuzzy blue slippers. I could wear Clearasil dabbed in big globs on the blemishes that keep showing up as if I were still a teenager. I could forget to put on makeup or even to comb my hair, and the beauty of it—no pun intended—was that Matthias was not there to take one good look at me and run screaming into the night.

I couldn't exactly tell Matthias this, however.

I also couldn't tell him that in addition to some general concerns regarding marriage itself, I had some concerns regarding him specifically. Well, not exactly him. Him I found wonderful and sexy and a terrific cook. But, as they say, no man is an island. You find that out big-time when you move in with somebody. Because that's when you become *family*. And once you're family to him, there's no getting around it, you're family to the *rest* of his family.

These days Matthias's family pretty much consists of three people—his daughter, Emily, who lives in Boston with his ex-wife; his sister, Stephanie; and his mother, the recently widowed Mrs. Harriet Schackle-ford Cross. So let me see now. My new family would consist of Emily, a teenage daughter I'd never met—so no telling what she was really like—and Stephanie, a teenage sister who, unfortunately, I *had* met and who had recently been very supportive when she thought I'd killed her dad. My new family would also include the widow Cross, a woman who to this day still harbors doubts as to my innocence in the murder of her husband, and who in the not-so-distant past called me some really adorable names, like slut and whore.

I hate to be a wet blanket here, but it didn't sound to me as if my new family was going to be a rerun of *The Waltons*.

And yet, how could I tell Matthias any of this? "I—I don't know," I said. "I'm just not sure I'm ready. . . ."

Matthias immediately turned away from me and started the car, so I couldn't be sure if the kicked-puppy look was back in his eyes again or not. "I said I wasn't going to pressure you, and I'm not," he said. He cleared his throat. "So why don't I make dinner at your place, okay? How do steak and mushrooms sound?"

To be honest, they sounded like maybe we were

changing the subject, and that sounded great. "Wonderful," I said.

Matthias nodded. "We'll have us a nice dinner, and we'll talk this over, and we'll decide what to do."

Oh, dear. It looked as if the breed of that kicked puppy might be bulldog. He wasn't going to let this one go.

"In fact, now that I think about it, I'm really hungry, aren't you?" Matthias went on. "I don't think we'll go back to the office right now for my car. I think we'll just head straight to your house."

Matthias had not glanced over at me once since he'd started the car, and he now sounded a bit too cheery, considering the circumstances. Coward that I was, however, I decided there was really no reason to re-open the discussion. So I didn't say a word.

Matthias didn't say a word for the next several minutes, either. I didn't have to ask, of course, what he was thinking about. His jaw was now set in that hard line I'd come to recognize as his Schuyler-is-driving-me-nuts-but-I-don't-want-to-fight expression.

Sitting beside him in my Tercel, I almost smiled. Because, to tell the truth, I get quite a bit of comfort out of this particular expression of Matthias's. It's kind of nice to be with somebody who doesn't want to fight for a change.

It's particularly nice if you had an ex-husband like Ed who absolutely loved to fight. Ed would go at you tooth and nail over such earthshaking things as, Did you really *need* that bra you just got on sale for three bucks? Oh, yes, that was *three,* count them, one, two, *three* buckeroondoes, and Ed would spend hours haranguing me about it.

Ed wanted to fight about three dollars here and five dollars there so often that I finally had to put my foot down. I told him that I'd gotten too old to spend any more of what was left of my life arguing over sums that small. I actually had to set a floor for arguing. Nothing under ten dollars. I tried to make it twenty, but—you guessed it—Ed argued.

Ed loved to argue so much that, once we'd set the floor for the money arguments, he tried to get me to fight over, What was the name of Mary Tyler Moore's boss? And, What Was Dick Van Dyke's name on *The Dick Van Dyke Show*? Looking back on our marital lack of bliss, I now realize that those last years of living with Ed had been a lot like being a perpetual contestant on *Jeopardy*. Unlike Alex Trebek, however, if you didn't know the answer—or, worse, if you *did* know the answer, and it didn't happen to jibe with what Ed said was correct—then Ed argued with you. In the interest of keeping the peace, I once actually agreed that the name of Marlo Thomas's boyfriend on *That Girl* was Ted Danson.

Now, glancing over at the firm line of Matthias's jaw, I felt a rush of affection. What a sweet, easygoing man he was. I reached over and gave Matthias's arm a quick squeeze.

This, unfortunately, was a mistake. Because Matthias, of course, immediately interpreted that as signaling that I might be open for a little more discussion on the moving-in issue.

"You know, Schuyler," Matthias said, "it's not as if we're kids."

I just looked at him. If he was going to tell me that I was now so decrepit that I needed somebody to live with me, he probably needed to rethink his entire approach.

"I mean," he went on, "at our age, we don't need a lot of time to know how we feel."

Oh. Thank goodness *this* was what he was driving at.

I nodded. "Right," I said.

"Not that nine months isn't a lot of time. Nine months is *plenty* of time."

"Uh-huh," I said. Nodding again.

"People who love each other just naturally want to be together."

"Uh-huh," I said again.

I knew, of course, what Matthias was doing. It's a proven sales technique that you get your prospect to keep agreeing to one point after another so that when you hit them with the thing you're trying to sell, they'll agree to that one, too.

"So," Matthias said, his eyes fixed on the road ahead, "don't you think that the next logical step in our relationship is moving in together?"

This time I didn't say anything. It may be the next logical step, but who said I was logical?

Matthias went right on as if he didn't notice I hadn't answered him. "Okay, Schuyler, I didn't want to bring this up, but you know damn well it isn't safe right now for you to be alone."

That got my attention. I shot a quick glance over at Matthias.

"I mean, for God's sake, Sky, there's a killer out there, and he could have you in mind as his next victim."

I folded my arms across my chest. Well, now, *this* was dirty pool, trying to use my fear for leverage.

On the other hand, I had to hand it to Matthias, fear *was* an excellent motivator.

Hell, hadn't fear been one of the reasons women had men move in with them in the first place? I mean, back in prehistoric times, hadn't it been the man's role to keep the wild animals away from the entrance to the cave?

On the other hand, the only time I'd ever lived with

a man was when I'd been married to Ed, and toward the end, if given the choice, I'd have picked a few wild animals over Ed any day of the week. Of course, my feeling this way might've had something to do with what kind of man Ed was. A philanderer. A bully. And a quiz-show host.

Matthias did seem to be none of the above.

I turned to look at Matthias again. At his strong hands, his broad shoulders, at the streaks of gray throughout his beard.

I am very much in love with this man, I thought. He is gentle, and kind, and he's done wonders for my kitchen. He's terrific in bed, he makes me laugh, and I adore the way he smells.

And yet, knowing all this to be true, I still wasn't sure I really wanted to live with him.

I'd finally gotten my life exactly the way I wanted it. I was reasonably successful in my career, I'd finally paid down my MasterCard to where I didn't wince every time I got the bill, and I liked coming and going on my own without having to consult anybody else. My house was filled with a hodgepodge of furniture, ranging from English country to antiques I'd found dirt cheap at thrift stores. My walls were hung with a hodgepodge of watercolors and original intaglio prints. And my floors were covered with a hodgepodge of rugs mostly the color of Coke—the thing I personally was most likely to spill on them. The point was, they were all *my* hodgepodges. All handpicked by me to suit my taste.

My entire life, in fact, suited my taste. It was just fine, exactly as it was. And, as some of my Kentucky kinfolk say, If it ain't broke, why fix it?

Matthias, however, obviously felt that my life did need fixing. The knuckles on his hands were turning white as he said, in a tone of extreme patience,

"Schuyler, you're not listening to me. A murderer is running around loose, and you might be the one he's after. If that isn't reason enough for us to move in together, I don't know what is."

What could I say? He had a point. What's more, having a warm man in your bed all night long is a truly wonderful thing.

That was just about the only thing I missed about marriage.

Speaking of which—

"You're right," I said. "I really should *not* be alone. Not with God knows who out there prowling around."

Matthias glanced over at me. I guess he knew I wouldn't give in this quickly, because he looked suspicious.

"I think, solely in the interest of safety, you ought to spend the night," I went on.

A little smile began pulling at the corners of Matthias's mouth. "Solely in the interest of safety?" he repeated.

I nodded.

"Then you think maybe I should spend the night on the sofa in your living room? So that if anybody breaks in, I'll be right there to catch them just as they come through the front door? Or, God forbid, through a window?" Matthias's smile was getting wider.

I smiled in return. "I think that could be carrying safety a little too far," I said.

We were both grinning at each other like two fools as Matthias pulled my Tercel into my driveway. He got out, went around to open my door for me, and then walked me up to my porch with his arm around my shoulders.

What can I say? His arm felt good.

As it turned out, it was a good thing Matthias's arm was around me as I walked up to my front door.

I had my key out, ready to unlock my door, when I saw it.

And, for a moment, my knees buckled.

Someone had carved a small heart deep into the wood just above the lock.

Chapter
11

Whoever had carved that heart in my door had wanted to make damn sure I didn't miss it. Well, I certainly didn't. I took one look, let out this pathetic little chirp of a scream, and then actually swayed as my knees gave out from under me.

Matthias must've felt me go, because he tightened his grip. "Schuyler?" he said.

Then, of course, he, too, saw it.

"What the hell—" Matthias turned to look from side to side, his eyes darting this way and that, as if he actually expected to see our wood-carver standing nearby, waiting for us to admire his handiwork. Fortunately, while Matthias was doing all this looking around, he didn't let go of me. My legs were still shaking a little, and I wasn't sure I could stand on my own just yet. "Is this somebody's idea of a joke?" Matthias asked.

I swallowed and looked back at that awful little heart. "I'm pretty sure whoever carved this didn't do it to make me laugh," I said.

I guess I was so stunned by it all I wasn't thinking

clearly. I was feeling steadier, though. I reached out and once again started to insert my key into the lock, but Matthias grabbed my hand. "No," was all he said.

I just looked at him.

Matthias closed his eyes for a moment, as if he really hated to elaborate. "Sky, I don't think we should touch anything." He ran a hand over his beard before he went on. "And I don't think we should go inside. At least not until the police have gotten here."

I gave him a startled look. "You don't think that whoever did this could still be *around,* do you?" I peered into the long, narrow windows on either side of my front door, but I could hardly see anything through the semisheer curtains.

I was about to move even closer to the window, but then I stopped. Wait a minute. What did I think I was doing? I didn't really *want* to see anybody moving around in there. I also didn't really *want* to see anybody standing on the other side of the semisheers, looking back through the window at *me.*

The instant that last little image crossed my mind, I took a quick step backward, trying to shake off a sudden shiver of fear. Oh, for God's sake. Now I wasn't just afraid to go inside other people's houses. I was afraid to go inside my *own.*

I was also afraid to let Matthias go inside. Instead, I insisted that we both go call the police, using the pay phone up at the convenience store about three blocks away. Matthias wanted to use one of my neighbor's phones, but thank God he let me talk him out of that one.

Matthias doesn't know my neighbors. Almost all of them are elderly, almost all of them are just as sweet as they can be—and almost all of them have a lot more time on their hands than I do. A couple of weeks ago I'd dashed over to take the lady across the street a letter of hers delivered to me by mistake, and I hadn't gotten back home until midnight. On the up side, however, by the time I'd left my neighbor's house, I'd been brought up to date on everything that had happened in this neighborhood since 1952.

Besides wanting to avoid another conversation marathon like that one, I had another reason for wanting to call the police from a location farther away than just next door. If the phantom carver *was* still in my house, I wanted him to have plenty of time to get the hell out of there before Matthias and I returned. I realize, of course, that there are those who would say that this certainly sounded cowardly of me. I have an answer for them, though. It's this: Okay, so I'm cowardly. I mean, let's face it—while I was indeed anxious to discover the identity of the phantom carver, I was even more anxious that Matthias and I survive that discovery.

Once I finished calling the police on the public phone just inside the entrance of the convenience store, Matthias drove us back to my house. He pulled into my driveway, turned off the ignition, and then we both just sat there, trying to act as if we had to phone the police every day of the week to come out and check my house for murderers. Can you believe, we actually started talking about television shows we'd seen and books we'd read and whether or not the last *Die Hard* movie was as good as the first. Anything, I guess, to keep from thinking about an ugly little heart gouged into the wood of my front door.

I think I already knew, even before they showed up, exactly which detectives it was going to be. Sure enough, about ten minutes after Matthias and I had pulled into my driveway, an unmarked tan Ford Mustang pulled in behind us. Murray Reed got out on the driver's side, and Tony Constello got out on the passenger side. The salt and pepper shakers were pulling identical spiral notebooks and Bic pens out of their inside coat pockets as they headed toward us.

"Ma'am?" Reed said, leaning over and opening the car door for me. "What seems to be the problem?"

He didn't say "this time," but he might as well have. The words seemed to hang in the air between us.

Matthias was out of his side of the car by then. He came around, stuck his big hand out, and introduced himself. Reed and Constello both shook Matthias's hand, and then Reed said, his pale blue eyes narrowing, "Haven't we met somewhere before?"

Wouldn't you think that Reed would get tired of asking that question?

Matthias, however, didn't seem the least bit reluctant to refresh Reed's memory. "You investigated the death of my father almost a year ago."

Reed's reaction to that one was predictable. He exchanged a look with Constello, glanced over at me, and then turned his attention back to Matthias.

I took a deep breath. Now I knew how Bill Murray must've felt in that movie, *Groundhog Day*. Was I going to play the same scene with these two over and over again?

Constello had his Bic poised to take notes. "And you live *here* now?" Constello asked, jerking his dark head toward my house.

Leave it to Constello to bring up a sore subject. I noticed that Matthias cleared his throat once before he answered. "No, no, I'm just a friend," Matthias said. His eyes never left Constello's face.

"A *friend*," Constello repeated. He exchanged another glance with Reed.

"The reason we called you," Matthias said, "is over here." He started toward my house then, leading the way up to the porch so that the salt and pepper shak-

ers had to stop exchanging looks and follow him. I
trailed after all three men, feeling not at all inclined
to take another look at the thing Matthias was now
pointing at. "Somebody did this to Schuyler's front
door," Matthias said.

Both detectives immediately moved forward to take
a closer look. I, on the other hand, stayed as far away
as I could, moving to stand by the pillar farthest from
my front door. Nobody seemed to notice. In fact, from
this point forward, amazingly enough, I actually got
to hang back and let Matthias do all the talking. This
is something I'd forgotten about having a man around.
Other men talk to him. Other men especially talk to
the man on the premises after something bad has
happened.

Watching Matthias discuss my door decoration with
Reed and Constello, I couldn't help recalling the time,
back when Ed and I were still married, when lightning
had struck our chimney. It had been Ed who'd ended
up talking to the insurance man and the repairman
and the lightning rod installation man. Ed, of course,
had not wanted to talk to all these men, but all these
men had definitely not wanted to talk to *me*. In fact,
they'd more or less sailed right past me and had
started discussing things with Ed before Ed even knew
what was happening.

Back then I remember being annoyed. In fact, as I
recall, after the insurance man and the repairman *and*
the lightning rod installation man had all gone, I myself had gone on and on to Ed about the entire situation. How I didn't appreciate being the Invisible
Woman. How it was *my* house, too. And how I was
woman, hear me roar, or words to that effect. In fact,
if I remember correctly, I believe I roared about the
whole thing for quite some time.

Today, after years of being single and having experienced many times the thrill of talking with insurance men, and repairmen, and every other kind of men, I must say I see things in an entirely different light. I stood there on my porch, quietly watching while Matthias took care of everything, and if I hadn't thought that the salt and pepper shakers would've looked at me even more strangely than they were doing already, I would've grinned.

As that old song goes: Isn't it nice to have a man around the house?

Evidently, the salt and pepper shakers had now stared at my door decoration all they wanted to. The significance of the thing being in the shape of a heart was not lost on them. They—you guessed it—exchanged yet another pointed look.

"Well," Constello drawled, "I reckon y'all had better wait out here while we have us a little look-see inside."

Reed must've decided that what Constello said needed further clarification. "Stay right here until we come get you," he said, looking first at me and then back at Matthias. Reed's voice was a familiar, flat, staccato monotone. Oh, my, yes, it was Joe Friday of *Dragnet* fame once again.

I was more than happy to obey the shakers' instructions. Matthias looked as if he might've wanted to accompany them inside, but in the end, he did as he was told. Thank goodness, I might add. I know it sounds unkind of me, but if anybody ran into a murderer in the next few minutes, I really preferred it to be Reed and Constello.

As it turned out, however, the salt and pepper shakers didn't run into anybody. "Looks like nobody's home," Constello drawled when he and Reed returned minutes later.

Reed elaborated. "There was nothing we could see

that would indicate a B and E, ma'am." As he finished saying this, his eyes darted to mine. I think he might've been expecting me to ask what a B and E was, but I didn't have to. Having read mystery novels from an early age, I'd known since I was twelve that a B and E meant breaking and entering.

I probably wouldn't have asked for a translation even if I hadn't known. I was too busy feeling a quick surge of relief. *Nobody had been inside.* I hadn't realized how unnerving the idea of someone breaking into my house had been until the shakers said it hadn't happened after all.

With my house pronounced murderer-free, we all moved inside to the living room. Matthias and I gave the salt and pepper shakers our statements, and the shakers took notes. I can't say the atmosphere was relaxed, but having eliminated meeting a murderer as a possible way to spend the evening, I did feel significantly less tense.

In fact, the only truly bad moment during the entire interview was when Constello mentioned that they intended to talk to my neighbors in the next few days to see if any of them had seen anybody on my porch earlier.

I all but gulped. "You're going to tell *all* my neighbors about what happened to my door?" Oh, *this* was going to be great. My problems with the phantom carver would, no doubt, be the talk of Harvard Drive. As if I hadn't already given them enough to talk about in the last year or so, what with Reed and Constello dropping by last summer during their investigation into the death of Matthias's father to search my house and car for murder weapons. And what with my coming across a body on the floor of one of my listings a few months ago. And now *this*? The way things were going, I'd be lucky if I wasn't featured on the front page of the *National Enquirer* before the year was up. I took a deep breath. "Is it really necessary to drag my neighbors into this?"

I immediately wished I hadn't said anything, because right away Constello started looking at me funny. As if maybe I might have an ulterior motive for not wanting my neighbors questioned. As if maybe I might not want my neighbors reporting what they'd seen.

I returned his look, feeling unbelievably tired. Did the man actually think I would take a knife to my own front door? "I just hate to get my neighbors all upset," I said weakly. "They're all elderly, you know, and—"

Reed interrupted me. "Ma'am, we're going to have to tell your neighbors." Joe Friday sounded as if the subject were closed. "They might be able to give us a description of the person who did this, ma'am."

Constello nodded his dark head. "You know, Miz Ridgway," he added, "you don't need to be a-worrying about your neighbors." Constello's eastern Kentucky accent sounded soft, but his eyes were still boring through me. "You need to be a-worrying about whoever did this to your door."

I shifted position on my couch, feeling uneasy. I couldn't decide if Constello was telling me that he thought I really *had* done this to my own door. In which case, I needed to worry about myself. Or if he thought it was somebody else. In which case, I needed to worry about whoever that might be.

Reed, a few minutes later, had it all over his partner as far as clarity goes. By then, he and Constello had moved back out to my front porch to take a final look at the heart carving. "Ma'am," Reed said, "we'll be sending somebody out to dust for fingerprints, but I don't think we're going to find any. It looks like whoever did this wiped the door clean after he was finished." He shuffled his feet a little and then looked at a point just over my left shoulder. "But you needn't worry, ma'am. We're going to catch whoever did this."

Reed sounded awfully confident. I might even have started to feel a little better if he had not added, "But, ma'am, *until* we catch him? Make sure you keep your doors and windows locked."

I stared at him. My, my. What great advice. I certainly wished *I'd* thought of it. "I'll do that, Detective," I said.

It did not exactly help my confidence level for the shakers to tell me three times before they finally left that if I saw any strangers hanging around I should give them a call *immediately*. The same went for any strange phone calls, any strange people following me around, or any strangers, period.

"Sure thing," I said. In other words, I should quit my job. And maybe enter a convent.

I couldn't help glancing over at Matthias the moment that last thought entered my head. Okay, quitting my job might actually be a possibility—one day, maybe. But the convent thing? It was a definite no.

I was even more convinced as the evening went on. In fact, shortly after the salt and pepper shakers had gotten into their Mustang, I made an amazing discovery.

Fear is a powerful aphrodisiac.

I'm serious. This could very well be the answer for every couple in America who's ever had sex problems. Forget about all those self-help books, or psychotherapy, or even Masters and Johnson. Nope, the next time your partner doesn't feel interested, you just hire somebody to call her up and tell her he's going to blow her away. Have your "hit man" tell her that he's not sure exactly when he's going to do the deed, but it'll be soon.

If the idea that you only have a limited time left to get in all the sex you can—combined with the idea that tonight might very well be the last night you'll ever get to make love to the one person in the world you're pretty crazy about—well, if that doesn't turn you into a Flying Wallenda in bed, there really *is* something wrong with you.

I blush to admit there was nothing wrong with me.

There was nothing wrong with Matthias, either.

Matthias had been standing at my elbow the entire time the shakers were warning me about strangers and cautioning me to keep my locks locked. Matthias didn't say anything, so right up until the shakers left, I'd been under the impression that he was just taking it all in. No big deal. I did notice, of course, that Matthias's green eyes seemed to be getting bigger and bigger the longer the shakers talked. And the more warnings they gave me.

The shakers' Mustang had only just started to back out of my driveway when Matthias reached for me. He kissed me long and hard, and then he said, sounding flatteringly upset, "Sky, I don't know what I'd do if you weren't in my life."

After that, he led me over to my living room sofa and showed me that he did know, however, exactly what to do when I *was* in his life.

Like I said before, it is nice to have a man around the house.

After Matthias and I made love on my sofa, we started to head for my bathroom with a shower in mind, but somehow we ended up making love again on the plushly carpeted floor of my hallway. After that, it seemed to me that I really had all the documentation I needed for my fear-is-an-aphrodisiac theory. Not to mention, I was having a little difficulty catching my breath, my heart was sounding like a freight train, and I really did prefer not to have to call 911 to be resuscitated. For one thing, there wasn't a doubt in my mind that if Matthias and I ever had to make such a call, we'd definitely be on an upcoming episode of *Rescue 911*. And maybe *Geraldo*.

So, after lying wrapped up in each other on my hallway floor for what seemed like a very long and wonderful time, we did what we always do after making love. Actually, I think what Matthias and I do is pretty much what every other couple in America always does, only this particular after-sex ritual never quite gets mentioned in romance novels or shown in R-rated movies. Matthias and I immediately headed for the bathroom to wash up, and then we returned to the living room to hunt for our clothes.

I finally had to give up on my panty hose. Lord knows where they went. I was pretty sure they'd turn up sooner or later, anyway. So I followed Matthias out to the kitchen, dressed pretty much the way I'd been before, only bare-legged. In the kitchen, while Matthias broiled two perfect sirloins and made a delicious sauce out of ingredients I didn't even know I had, I made the specialty of my house. That's right— two large Cokes, heavy on the ice.

We carried our plates out to the dining room, ate by candlelight, and then, when the meal was finished, Matthias did the most romantic thing. He cleared the table, loaded the dishwasher, and actually *started* it.

What a guy.

Then he started cleaning up my kitchen. Watching him move around the room in his snug jeans, actually scrubbing the drip pans of my stove until they shined, I found myself once again thinking what I always think when he does this. How the hell did this man ever end up divorced? Matthias cooks, cleans, and kisses—and, what's more, he does all three without being asked. So how on earth did any woman ever let him go?

I have yet to meet Matthias's ex-wife, Barbara, but to tell you the truth, the more I find out about Matthias, the more I think Barbara has to be totally deranged. I would never tell Matthias, but these days whenever he mentions her, I always get a mental picture of that poor woman they locked in the attic in *Jane Eyre*.

With my dishwasher rumbling romantically in the background, setting the mood, Matthias and I both seemed to realize at the same time that my theory about fear being an aphrodisiac needed additional documentation, after all. We began making love on my kitchen floor, but take my word for it, linoleum was not made with this purpose in mind. We ended up in my bed upstairs.

Afterward, I lay with my head on Matthias's chest, listening to the rapid beating of his heart, and feeling as if—for this one isolated moment—everything in my world was absolutely perfect.

I could've lain like that for, oh, say, the next five years or so, but Matthias broke the spell. He didn't mean to, but when his heart had finally slowed a little, he looked down at me and grinned. "Good *God*," he said. "Are you trying to *kill* me?"

It was a poor choice of words, and I guess I immediately tensed. Matthias's arms tightened around me. He took a deep breath and then said, "Don't worry, sweetheart. I'm not going to let anything happen to you."

I snuggled even closer to him, not saying a word. But I couldn't help thinking, How exactly are you going to accomplish this? The FBI, for God's sake, had over the years lost quite a few people they'd had under armed guard. So exactly—

Matthias interrupted my thoughts. "And Sky? I want you to think about what I said earlier tonight, okay? I want us to be together, I want to come home to you every night . . ."

I nodded, but with my head resting on his chest, I guess Matthias didn't realize that I was agreeing to do as he asked.

"I want to take care of you," he said.

I tried nodding again, but once more he didn't get it.

"You really shouldn't be alone, Schuyler. Not now, not with—"

Oh, dear. It looked as if Matthias wanted to discuss the entire thing all over again.

So, okay, I admit it, I'm awful. I immediately started breathing louder than normal, very slowly and rhythmically. Matthias tried for a couple more minutes, but after getting no response other than more slow, rhythmic breathing, he gave up. His voice sort of trailed off.

And, wouldn't you know it, *he* immediately fell asleep.

While I just lay there, in the circle of his arms, listening to *him* breathe.

I suppose it served me right.

You'd think that with Matthias lying right beside me I'd have felt protected and cared for and safe. And yet every time I closed my eyes, I kept seeing Trudi all over again. With that awful heart on her forehead. That awful heart that happened to be virtually identical to the heart now on my own front door.

Needless to say, it took me forever to finally drift off to sleep.

The next morning when I woke up, I realized that I was now actually a little afraid to go into the office. I wasn't about to let Matthias know it, though. If the man even had an inkling how I really felt, I had no doubt that he'd begin to move his things into my house in the next fifteen minutes.

Matthias bustled around my kitchen, making French toast, and I ended up eating more than I really wanted just to show him that I was fine. Hey, a little thing like a murderer leaving a memento on my door didn't bother me one bit. No sir. Not in the least.

After doing the dishes—really, the man actually unloaded the dishwasher from last night and loaded it with our breakfast dishes—Matthias drove us to my office, where the Roar Hog was waiting for him. When he pulled away, I actually waved cheerily.

I had every intention of getting so involved in work that I couldn't think about anything else. By ten it actually seemed as if my plan was working. The only other realtor who'd come into the office by then was Charlotte, and other than giving me one of those ultra-warm, ultrasympathetic smiles you give somebody terminally ill, she'd left me alone. I'd been able to concentrate on the mountain of paperwork on my desk, and I'd almost convinced myself that everything was pretty much business as usual. Another normal day.

And then the phone rang.

It was the kind of call that only two days ago I'd have been delighted to get. A woman's voice said, "Hi, there, I'm Gloria Glover, and I think I've just fallen in *love* with one of your listings." She hurried on to say she'd seen a listing of mine in *Homes,* a magazine published every two weeks by the Louisville Board of Realtors, featuring photographs and descriptions of properties for sale in Louisville and surrounding counties. "It's the Dutch Colonial on Carleton Terrace, and it looks like *just* what I've been looking for," she said. "I'd like to see it as soon as possible."

A shiver of fear actually traveled down my spine. "You *would*?" I said.

"I can meet you there in an hour," Gloria said.

"An hour?" I said. "Oh. My. Well, I don't know." Lord. Talk about low-pressure salesmanship.

Gloria was beginning to sound bewildered. "You don't *know*?"

I realized then that I sounded a little strange, so I hurried to explain. "What I mean is, I'll have to check my calendar. . . ."

There was silence on the other end. I could almost hear the woman thinking: *You have to check your calendar to see if you have an appointment in the next hour? If you had such an appointment, shouldn't you already know about it by now?*

I felt like an idiot. "Well, what do you know," I said, a shade too brightly, "as it turns out, I *am* free at eleven."

"Wonderful! I'll meet you there," Gloria said and hung up.

I sat there, staring at the phone. Either old Gloria wanted very badly to see the house on Carleton Terrace . . . or she wanted very badly to strangle me.

Chapter
12

I must've sat there at my desk, staring at my phone, for a good ten minutes after I hung up the receiver. While I sat there, all sorts of genuinely cheery thoughts chased each other through my mind.

Like, for example: Gloria Glover hadn't even given me the chance to suggest that she come by my office so I could drive us both over. Granted, I wasn't the best driver in the world. It was true that I'd once backed into a Kentucky Fried Chicken restaurant. I hasten to add, however, that this is an easy thing to do. If you're parked very close, the building completely fills your rearview mirror. It's easy to mistake the back of a white building for a very pale sky.

Then, too, I'd also at one time broadsided a parking meter, and to be painfully honest, I'd also once demolished a mailbox. These unfortunate incidents, however, have been extremely few and very far between. *And* I believe it's important to note that I have never in my life hit anything that was in motion. The way I see it, as long as all the cars and people in my immediate vicinity keep moving, they're safe.

Even admitting that my driving skills could stand improvement, I was still pretty sure that they weren't so bad that Gloria had heard about them and made up her mind never to get in a car with me. Not to mention, almost all my other clients seemed to prefer that I drive—mainly, I suppose, so that the extra mileage would go on *my* car, not theirs. And if anybody's gasoline got consumed, it would be mine, not theirs.

So, bearing all this in mind, the question was: Had Gloria wanted to drive herself because she just didn't like riding with somebody she didn't know? Or was it because she wanted to be able to leave immediately if she wanted to, so that she wouldn't be at the mercy of some high-pressure realtor—like, for instance, myself?

Or could it actually be that Gloria had insisted on driving herself because once she'd murdered me, she'd need a getaway car?

Once all these cheery thoughts went through my mind, something else occurred to me. It didn't present quite as pressing a problem as that last thought, but I did wonder: What kind of name was Gloria Glover, anyway? I mean, if that didn't sound like a name somebody had made up, nothing did.

I finally pulled my eyes away from that stupid phone and took a deep breath. Good Lord. Had it come down to this? Was I now afraid of a woman? What was left? Children and pets? And yet, when you came right down to it, there was no reason to assume that Trudi's killer could not have been a woman. Men certainly didn't have a monopoly on murder. In fact, from what I'd seen on the evening news nearly every day of my adult life, I'd say murder was becoming an equal-opportunity occupation.

As I considered this last, I reached up to brush a strand of hair away from my face and realized that my hand was actually shaking. I was so shocked to see it doing this that I actually found myself staring at my own hand for a long moment.

The moment ended, of course, when I realized that across the room Charlotte Ackersen was now doing a little staring of her own—straight at me, her eyes like large blue saucers. Since my hand was in the air already, I gave her a little wave with it, waggling my fingers and smiling my most winning smile.

Charlotte immediately returned my wave *and* my smile, but her eyes didn't get any less saucerlike.

I turned away from her, put my hands in my lap, and tried to calm down. I took cleansing breaths, I tried to picture myself lying next to a babbling brook, I repeated the word "peace" over and over again— all the stuff the self-help books say is supposed to work. What I found out was that all those self-help books are not written for people who think somebody might be trying to kill them.

Those people *should* be nervous.

Like, say, for example, me. My hands continued to shake. And I didn't even *need* a self-help book to tell me what my problem was. Scared shitless, I believe, would be the charming term both my sons would no doubt use to describe my current condition. I took another cleansing breath. Once again, it looked as if I were going to have to face facts. In my present S. S. condition, I wasn't going to be able to go to any appointment with Gloria Glover alone.

So, that brought up something else to think about. Who was going to be my escort this time? On Tuesdays and Thursdays, Matthias taught a studio class in printmaking at the Kentucky School of Art from ten till noon, so it sure wasn't going to be him.

In a way, I was almost glad that Matthias wouldn't be available. After all the speeches he'd made last night about it being the right time for us to move in together, I had no doubt that asking Matthias to accompany me one more time would just unleash another campaign.

Oh, my, yes, I would've hated to phone Matthias. On the other hand, I also hated phoning my sons. It didn't look as if I had much choice, though, because after my sons, the only other escort I could think of was *Jarvis*. My right hand was a blur as I reached for the receiver and started dialing my sons' telephone number.

Lately, phoning Nathan and Daniel has been like playing telephone roulette. Sometimes you win and their phone actually rings. Other times you're not so lucky. You get an odd-sounding ring, and then a terse automated message begins to play that goes something like, "The number you have dialed has been temporarily disconnected." This particular message, I've come to realize, should actually say, "The party you have called has not paid its telephone bill for two months, because it blew all its money on new CDs and Nintendo games."

I held my breath until the phone actually started ringing. When it did, I was listening carefully, trying to decide if this was a regular ring or a you're-outta-luck ring, when Daniel came on the line.

"Yo?"

This is how Daniel always answers the phone. All those *Rocky* movies I took him to when he was younger must've hit him hard.

"Hi, Daniel," I said. I sounded a little too cheery even to my own ears. "Is Nathan there?"

"Yo." Daniel apparently is convinced that this one monosyllable has multiple meanings. "I'll get him," he said. I heard him putting down the receiver, and then I heard, "Yo, Nathan! *Yo!*"

Nathan's and Daniel's voices are very much alike, both deep and rumbling. You'd never mistake one for the other, though. "Nathan Ridgway speaking." This is what Nathan said when he came on the line. This is how my younger son always answers the phone, except for those times when he also repeats his phone number right after his name. Oh, no, there's no way anybody would ever think this was Daniel.

"Hi, Nathan," I said. Now that I had him on the phone, I wasn't sure exactly how to go about explaining why I'd called, so I stalled a little while I tried to decide. "So. Hon," I said, "how are you doing? How's Anne?"

"I'm okay, Mom, but Anne is *really* upset," Nathan said. "Last night she told me that she couldn't get through all this without me. That's what she said. She said she really *needs* me."

I believe I'd heard this before. Once again, I wasn't sure how to answer him. He sounded so proud. "That's nice" seemed too cheerful. "Wow" seemed a bit strong.

Fortunately, Nathan didn't give me the chance to say anything. "Today is the, uh, visiting, you know, at the funeral home?" he went on.

I believe he meant visitation.

"It's from eleven to five, and Anne wants me with her every minute, you know, to, like, hold her hand?" Nathan continued. "It's going to be a rough day, I guess, but I want to be there for her."

By this time, of course, I was only half listening. Eleven to five? Uh-oh. "Then," I said, "you're going to be at the funeral home all day with Anne?"

"Yep, all day. I've gotta do it." Nathan was trying his best to sound long-suffering, but he couldn't keep the excitement out of his voice. "I have to be there,

Mom, I really do. To—you know—help Anne cope with her loss."

I swallowed. Scratch Nathan as an escort. He had been, hands down, my first choice. The boy might speak a little too loudly every once in a while, but on those occasions when I managed to convince him that shorts would not be the most appropriate wardrobe choice, I'd been able to count on him to look presentable.

This was, of course, because Nathan, Lord love him, would never, *ever* be seen in anything that didn't have a designer label. That included his shorts, his socks, and his underwear. I've always been secretly glad that they didn't have designer tattoos, or Nathan would no doubt be a carbon copy of Rod Steiger in that old movie, *The Illustrated Man*.

"Well, have a good time, dear." Obviously, I was a bit distracted. This last sort of fell out of my mouth before I could haul it back in. By the time I realized that it probably wasn't the best response to somebody telling you he intended to spend the day at a funeral home, it was already too late.

Nathan, would you believe, didn't even seem to notice. "Yeah, well," he said. What he meant by that I had no idea, and to tell you the truth, I didn't really care to ask him. "You're coming, aren't you, Mom?" he said.

I blinked. For a second, I wasn't sure what he was talking about. "Coming?"

"To the visiting. You're coming to the visiting, aren't you?"

I swallowed again. Actually, I'd seen poor Trudi with a heart on her forehead one too many times as it was. I supposed they'd do something to cover that up, but I didn't particularly want to find out what.

"I'll try to make it, hon," I said, "but I do have an appointment this afternoon."

And after that, I was pretty sure I had to shampoo my hair.

"You've *got* to come, Mom," Nathan said. "It's important that everybody who's closest to Anne and Trudi come and show their support."

He was making it sound like a pep rally. Not to mention, was Nathan under the impression that *my* name would be included under the general heading of Everybody Who's Closest to Anne and Trudi?

To begin with, Anne and I were hardly close. In fact, I barely knew the woman, having met her only a couple of times during the entire time Nathan and she had been dating. And, while I realized that she was "the one," I couldn't help recalling the long line of "the ones" before her, and the undeniable fact that Nathan had been dating her for only a short, short eight weeks. I could be wrong, but there did seem to be every chance that there was no good reason for the two of us to become closer.

And, as far as Trudi was concerned, *close* wasn't exactly the word for our relationship.

"Since Trudi was a coworker," Nathan was going on, "well, it just seems to me that—" These were Nathan's exact words. *It just seems to me that*—Apparently, this was an essay question I was supposed to complete in my own head.

Uh-huh.

I cleared my throat. "Hon," I said, "I'll do my best." And then, before Nathan could come up with any more Top Ten Reasons Why I Should Visit a Funeral Home Today, I said, "Can you put Daniel on? I need to speak to him."

Unlike with Nathan, I didn't have any problem at all deciding how to explain to Daniel why I needed him to escort me. That's because I knew without even thinking about it that I would have to lie. There was no way I could tell Daniel the real reason I wanted him along. If I did, it would be the first thing he'd say to Gloria Glover. "Yo, glad to meet you, my mom thinks you're a murderer, and that's why I'm here."

I realize that this sounds like something that could never happen, but believe me, a mother knows these things. If I needed proof that Daniel's tact and diplomacy could be a bit lacking, I got it as soon as Daniel got on the phone. He was chuckling. "Yo. Did ya hear what Nat said? He's going to be holding Anne's hand." He chuckled louder. "*Sure* he is. He's going to be holding Anne's hand—and anything *else* she'll let him hold."

Of course, Daniel had the tact and diplomacy to say this right in front of Nathan, so for the next several minutes, all I could hear over the line was:

"SHUT UP, DANNY BOY!"

"Yeah? Make me!"

"SHUT THE FUCK UP!"

"Lighten up, man, I was just kid—"

"YOU GO TO HELL! YOU GOT NO RIGHT—"

"*Fuck you!*"

"FUCK YOU *TWICE*!"

"*Fuck You Three Times!*"

What can I say? It was yet another proud maternal moment. I mean, can those kids count or what?

After the counting exhibition—and, yes, after I'd yelled "DANIEL!" only about ten times. Daniel finally got back on the phone. "Yo?" he said.

In the background, Nathan punctuated his departure with a door slam.

"Yo?" Daniel said again.

If I'd been a good mother, more like Marmee in *Little Women,* for example, I would've no doubt, launched into a heartrending appeal for Daniel to somehow reach down deep inside himself and make an effort to get along better with his youngest brother. Instead, I cleared my throat, and as I mentioned earlier, I went right ahead with my lie. "Daniel, I need you to come with me to show a house in an hour, okay? It's got a real sticky garage door, and I need you to help me open it."

What can I say? Marmee didn't have any sons.

"I dunno, Mom," Daniel whined. "Can't you get whoever you're showing the house to to open it for you?"

"It's another woman," I said. I was now, of course, hoping that Gloria wouldn't turn out to be a bodybuilder.

"Aw, Mom . . ."

Daniel whines better than anybody I know. He just does this so I'll say what I said next. "Five dollars."

"Twenty." Daniel's voice, I noticed, instantly sounded significantly more interested.

"Six dollars," I said.

"Ten."

I smiled. What an adorable little tyke. Trying to gouge his sainted, soon-to-be-gray-haired mother out of her last hard-earned dollar. How cute.

"Seven," I said.

"Deal," Daniel said. "When and where do I meet you?"

I told Daniel to meet me at the Carleton Terrace house ten minutes early, and he must've been in dire need of seven dollars, because he actually did it. His car was already in front of the house on Carleton Terrace when I pulled into the driveway.

Daniel drives a silver '84 Ford Thunderbird. His car—and I use the term "car" loosely—has a leather interior, power windows, power doors, power steering, power brakes, and an alarm. The only thing this car is not equipped with is a reliable motor, because most of the time this car is a couch with wheels. Today, however, it had apparently decided to see what the world looked like outside of a garage. Either that, or Daniel had gotten somebody to push him all the way here.

Daniel got out and started walking my way while I was still getting out of my car. I was still half-inside, pulling out copies of the listing sheet describing the Carleton Terrace property, and that's why I really didn't get a good look at him until he was standing right by my car.

"Yo," he said.

I glanced up when he spoke and stifled a scream. Oh, my God. Daniel had always been—how do I say this?—*distinctive* in the way he dressed. I knew this. Ever since he was a freshman in high school, I'd never seen my older son wear anything but jeans with jagged holes, T-shirts with jagged holes, and tennis shoes with jagged holes. He also pretty much took the Henry Ford view when it came to color selection. Daniel didn't care what color he wore as long as it was black. He also generally wore a tarnished cross dangling from whichever earlobe doesn't mean you're gay.

I had been prepared for Daniel to be wearing black, and for him to be sporting holes, and, yes, for him to have the nongay earring. I had, however, also expected him to have hair.

He didn't.

Unless, of course, you counted the peach fuzz now clinging to his pinkish gray scalp.

Daniel must've immediately picked up on my surprise. Of course, there was little chance that he'd miss it, considering I was standing there right in front of him, my eyes bulging, sucking in air for a full minute.

"Like the new 'do?" Daniel said.

I continued to suck air.

"I got it cut this way so I'd look mean," Daniel said. To emphasize his point, he flexed his muscles and scowled.

I continued to gape at him. Actually, now that he mentioned it, his hair did bring an M word to mind. It wasn't "mean," though. It was "mange."

Daniel was still flexing and scowling, when, oh, my dear God in heaven, I realized who he now looked like. It was Woody. Or rather, the guy who used to play Woody in all those old *Cheers* reruns, but who had turned his talents to playing a homicidal maniac in an Oliver Stone movie.

My son looked just like a Natural Born Killer.

"Cool, huh?" Daniel said.

Fortunately, he was spared my reply by a late-model beige Cadillac driving up in front of the house. We both turned to look as a plump woman in her sixties got out and began to walk toward us. She was dressed in a Burberry coat, carried a Coach briefcase, and she was moving quite briskly on heels I recognized as Cole Haan's.

I swallowed. I'd definitely brought the wrong son.

"Gloria Glover?" I said cheerily.

Gloria's expertly coiffed, frosted-blond head sort of bobbled up and down when I said her name. Her eyes, I couldn't help noticing, though, immediately ricocheted off me and bounced right over to Daniel.

My stomach was beginning to hurt. Idly, I supposed it was too late to ask Daniel if he had a hat.

Even when Gloria extended her hand toward me and introduced herself to me, her tiny, round black eyes never left Daniel.

"I'm so glad to meet you," I said, only a little more enthusiastically than somebody running for political office. "I'm Schuyler Ridgeway, and this—*this* is my son Daniel."

"Your *son*," Gloria repeated, her eyes still on Daniel.

"Yo," Daniel said. "I'm here to lift the garage door."

"The garage door," Gloria repeated again, now clutching her Coach briefcase tightly against her ample chest. She sounded a little dazed as she continued to stare at Daniel.

With Gloria's attention elsewhere, I couldn't help noticing the Gucci watch on the wrist of her left hand, and the diamond tennis bracelet on her right. Unless I missed my guess, those large clusters of pearls on each ear were genuine, as were the several diamond rings on each hand. Either murder was an extremely lucrative pastime, or I'd been a tiny bit off base here.

It could also possibly be that bringing Daniel along had been somewhat of a bad idea.

I suppose it's safe to say that I became more and more aware of just how bad an idea it had been as the minutes ticked by. Gloria, I am pretty sure, in the entire time she was at the Carleton Terrace house— which, take my word for it, wasn't long—never once took a good look at the place. That's mainly because she was too busy taking a good look at Daniel.

I do believe she expected him to make a grab for the tennis bracelet, or at the very least, the Coach briefcase, at any moment.

I, of course, tried to distract the woman, telling her about the self-cleaning range, the ultraefficient furnace, blah, blah, blah, but it was no use. After a while, I found myself staring at Daniel myself, trying to see in him what Gloria apparently did.

I guess, to anybody other than his mother, Daniel did look pretty scary. The boy had evidently been working out in a gym somewhere, because his shoulders and arms looked a lot bigger than I remembered them. Once we all went inside, he took off his black leather jacket, and I have to admit that the black T-shirt he was wearing was not exactly a confidence-builder. Actually, the T-shirt wasn't exactly black. It just looked black until you got close, and then you realized that all those black things were the empty sockets of very dark gray skulls. I believe Gloria realized this when we all went upstairs to take a look at the master bedroom. Because, from that point forward, it did seem that she kept me between her and Daniel. She also started staying, "Uh-huh. Uh-huh. Uh-huh," to just about anything I said. Until, of course, when we were all back downstairs, she finally said, as if it were all one word, "Thanks-so-much-for-showing-me-the-house-but-this-isn't-what-I'm-looking-for." Then, with a last wide-eyed glance at Daniel, she ran for her Cadillac.

She actually burned rubber as she roared off down the road.

"Well, that went well," Daniel said, as we both stood out on the front porch watching Gloria's car disappear around a curve. "Can I have my seven dollars now?"

I just looked at him.

And then, after a moment, I reached for my purse. It wasn't his fault that his mother was an idiot.

"I appreciate your helping me out, Daniel," I said. "I love you, hon." I even meant that last part.

Once Daniel had given me his usual kiss and taken off in the couch-with-wheels, I locked the Carleton Terrace front door, and then, feeling totally exhausted, I just sat out in my car for a moment or so.

Something had to be done. I'd lost two perfectly

good clients in as many days. If this kept up, I'd be out of business in a month.

Not to mention, I was getting to be afraid of my own shadow. Even now, just sitting out in this stupid driveway by myself, my heart was speeding up a little.

I certainly couldn't keep asking people to be my escort every five minutes. Matthias couldn't do it, because he had classes to teach. Nathan certainly couldn't, because he had hand-holding to do. And Daniel couldn't, because, well, to put it as kindly as only a mother can, he didn't quite have the professional image I wanted to project.

Even if I could hire somebody to be a bodyguard, was that any way to spend my life? Looking over my shoulder, being afraid without even knowing whether or not I should be?

I also couldn't wait for the police to come up with the answer. Clearly, if I waited for them, the only thing I would end up selling was pencils on a street corner.

No. What needed to happen was clear. I needed to find out who killed Trudi. And I needed to find it out quickly. Or Trudi's death might very well turn out to be the death of my own career.

When I'd first gotten into my little Tercel, I'd intended to go straight home. To maybe pull the covers over my head and cower for a few hours. I now decided that cowering is an unseemly thing for a grown woman to do.

I squared my shoulders, lifted my chin, and backed out of the driveway, heading toward Bardstown Road and the ramp to I-64. Maybe, on the phone earlier today, Nathan had been right. Maybe I *should* go by the funeral home during visitation. Anne would be there, and Derek, and—what was it Nathan had said?—*everybody* closest to Trudi and her sister.

Maybe I could find out which close friend could've wanted Trudi dead.

I glanced around, noting that all the cars in the lane next to me and even the pedestrians on the sidewalk were moving.

What the hey. I speeded up.

Chapter
13

Arch's Funeral Home is one of the better funeral homes in Louisville. Located just off Brownsboro Road, with stately columns out front, a sloping lawn, and a wide, tree-lined driveway, Arch's looks a lot like what you would've gotten if Scarlett had turned Tara into a funeral home.

If Arch's were not a funeral home, it would most definitely have been the sort of property that we real estate agents describe as "prestigious." In fact, as far as addresses around Louisville go, just the privilege of putting Brownsboro Road on your personal stationery is enough to add about thirty thousand dollars to the asking price. Add lawns a little larger than a postage stamp, and you've got homes lining Brownsboro Road on either side of Arch's that were in the two-hundred-thousand-dollar-and-up range. And, believe me, *up* was an extremely steep climb.

I was sure, as I walked through Arch's double front doors, that Trudi would've no doubt gotten quite a bit of satisfaction out of knowing that, as funeral locations went, she had hit the big time.

The first person I saw when I walked into the lobby was Barbi Lundergan. I couldn't help but stare at her. The outfit Barbi had selected as appropriate funeral wear was attention-getting, to say the least. Wearing five-inch stiletto heels, black fishnet hose, and a low-cut black knit dress that ended several inches above her knees, she looked as if she should be singing backup for Ray Charles.

It wasn't solely her outfit, however, that made me stare. It was her face—or, rather, something *on* her face. It was, in fact, something I never expected to see. Not on Barbi's face, anyway, and definitely not under the present circumstances. Would you believe, something that looked exactly like *tears* was glistening on Barbi's cheeks? Her eyes were red, her nose pink, and she was clutching a badly wrinkled lace handkerchief in one hand.

My goodness. If you didn't know better, you might actually get the idea that Barbi had been weeping. Either that, or she'd recently peeled an onion.

Recalling some of the things Barbi had said about Trudi, I personally leaned toward the onion scenario.

Barbi evidently didn't see me. Of course, her reddened eyes were focused on a sign prominently displayed in the lobby. It looked a lot like one of those black signs with movable white letters that they have in theater lobbies, the kind that has little arrows indicating the direction you need to go to get to the movie you want to see.

The only difference was, in this particular lobby, instead of movies being listed, it was the recently deceased. According to the sign, currently showing at Arch's was a Benjamin R. Strathmore to the left, an Edward K. Moorman III directly ahead, and finally, Trudi Vittitoe to the right.

Trudi apparently was part of a triple feature.

Barbi dabbed at her eyes once after reading the sign, took a deep breath, and then, squaring her shoulders, headed to the right. I followed her, moving soundlessly across the cream-colored plush carpet.

Barbi came to an abrupt halt just outside of an open door at the end of the hall. Putting a hand on one hip, she stood there in the doorway for a moment, surveying the room. It didn't take long for something to catch her eye, though, because almost immediately Barbi seemed to snap to attention. She smoothed any wrinkles in her dress, gave her platinum curls a little toss, and then headed purposefully through the door.

I went through the same door just moments after Barbi. Even though it was a large room, and it seemed to be filled with quite a few people, it didn't take any time at all to spot Barbi again. She was directly ahead of me, making a beeline toward a tall man in a black designer suit, standing in the middle of the room, talking in hushed tones to three women.

I stared at the man. It was Derek, Trudi's husband. As soon as the thought crossed my mind, though, I felt a quick pang. Derek wasn't Trudi's husband any longer. Derek wasn't anybody's husband any longer.

Evidently, this little fact had already occurred to Barbi. Arriving at Derek's side, she pressed her lace handkerchief to her lips and extended her free hand toward Derek. It was a pose I believe I'd seen Gloria Swanson do in that old black-and-white classic, *Sunset Blvd.*

"Derek. You poor thing." That's all Barbi said as she reached for Derek's hand. Apparently, however, it was not what she said, but how she said it. Derek broke off in midsentence and turned from the three women surrounding him to take Barbi's hand. As he did so, he gave the newcomer an appraising glance.

I, on the other hand, was giving Derek an appraising

glance of my own. I'd moved so that I was standing only about five feet away, on the other side of an enormous ficus plant. The plant didn't exactly shield me completely—its leaves were a little too far-spaced for that—but it was better than standing out in the middle of the room, obviously gawking at Derek and friends.

Oh, my, yes, in my humble opinion. Derek was movie star material, no doubt about it. Tall, tanned, and muscular, Derek Vittitoe even had one of those clefts in his chin, just like Kirk Douglas and Cary Grant. I stared at that cleft. I'd never noticed it before. Of course, the last time I'd seen Derek had been at the house on Saratoga, right after I'd gotten a good look at Trudi. I guess I'd not exactly been in a cleft-noticing mood. Then, too, as I recalled, Derek's chin had been trembling quite a bit at the time. That cleft had probably been a blur.

Derek's graying temples indicated that he had to be at least in his forties, but he had the physique of a man ten years younger. What's more, he either had very broad shoulders, or else the shoulder pads in his suit were a couple of sizes too big.

Barbi put Derek's shoulders to good use practically the instant Derek let go of her hand. "It was so kind of you to come by," he said as he released her. "I know Trudi would be . . ."

Barbi's face fell a little when Derek let go of her hand so quickly. Apparently, she'd been hoping he might hold onto it for the next several minutes. Undaunted, however, she immediately closed the gap between them and began hanging onto Derek's very broad, extremely handy shoulders. "Oh, *God,*" Barbi wailed. "How are we ever going to get along without Trudi?"

I just looked at her. Barbi's own answer to that

question would be, no doubt, "Much better," but—thank goodness—everybody present seemed to feel that this was a rhetorical question and didn't require an answer.

The other three women—who, before Barbi's arrival, had all apparently been vying for Derek's attention—were now looking at Barbi as if she were an insect. The thin one in the gray silk coatdress, standing on Derek's left, said, "I take it you and Trudi were close?" Disbelief was in her every word.

Barbi didn't even hesitate. "We worked together," she said without moving away from Derek. "I'm Barbi Lundergan," she added, tilting back her head to look for a moment into Derek's face. Then, turning back to the others, she continued. "Trudi worked right across the room from me." Barbi's voice was now actually trembling. In fact, if I hadn't known better, I'd have thought she was very near tears. "Oh, I'm going to miss her so-o-o much."

Barbi punctuated his last statement by leaning a little away from Derek, while, of course, still retaining her grip on his shoulders. This particular pose gave Derek an unrestricted view down the front of Barbi's low-cut black knit dress. An area to which Derek's eyes immediately traveled, oddly enough.

I blinked. Old Derek may have been in a funeral home, but he clearly wasn't dead.

"It's such a waste, *such* a waste." Barbi was now saying. Her asthma was acting up. She relinquished her grip on one of Derek's shoulders in order to dab at her eyes with her handkerchief. Her eyes appeared to be on the dry side for such extensive dabbing to be taking place, but since Derek wasn't looking at Barbi's eyes, anyway, it probably didn't matter. Barbi now leaned once again into Derek's chest and looked up into his eyes through fluttering lashes. "I know

Trudi wouldn't want you to be alone, though," Barbi said. "You must *try* to go on. . . ."

By now, of course, I was watching Barbi's maneuverings with something like awe. I mean, you had to hand it to her. She certainly wasn't letting any grass grow under her feet. Or even *over* Trudi, for that matter. Oh, my, no. And while there were those who might actually consider it tacky to hit on the new widower at the *wake,* clearly Barbi was not letting a little thing like public opinion stand in her way.

Barbi seemed, in fact, to care only about one person's opinion—Derek's. And, what do you know, he didn't seem the least bit appalled by Barbi's attention. In fact, the man actually seemed to enjoy holding Barbi close as she cried, "Oh, how I'm going to miss poor Trudi!"

Like a canker sore, I finished for her before I could stop myself. I, of course, immediately felt mean for even thinking such a thing. After all, it was entirely possible that Trudi's death might've made Barbi finally realize how much she'd genuinely liked Trudi.

I gave Barbi another long look. Her head was now resting against Derek's broad chest.

Uh-huh. *Right.* On second thought, it was also entirely possible that Barbi was just saying anything in order to be able to continue hanging onto one of the best-looking men she'd ever laid eyes on in her life.

My goodness, Barbi did seem to have old Derek in—if you'll pardon the expression—a death grip. I actually started to smile, watching them, when a truly horrible thought occurred to me. Barbi *had* been out of the office when I'd returned to find Trudi's memo on my desk.

So Barbi had been gone at the same time as Trudi.

Was it possible that Barbi and Derek had been carrying on for some time? Had the two of them decided

to do away with Trudi and were now setting it up to
look as if they'd become attracted to each other only
after Trudi was dead? I peered at them. Good Lord.
Could Barbi and Derek really have lured Trudi to
that house on Saratoga and done those terrible things
to her?

I immediately blinked that awful image away. What
was wrong with me? Barbi, for God's sake, was somebody I worked with. Somebody I'd known for years.
Next I'd be suspecting Jarvis's wife, Arlene.

To give myself something else to do besides stare
at Barbi and Derek, I turned to look around the room.
Unfortunately, the first thing my eyes happened to
land on was the casket.

And, of course, Trudi.

My mouth went dry as I stared.

Oh, God.

Poor Trudi didn't even look real. In fact, she looked
like a plastic figure.

I took a few faltering steps toward her, hoping that
maybe she'd start looking better as I got closer.

She didn't.

The heart on Trudi's forehead apparently had pre-
sented more of a problem than I'd originally expected.
Evidently it had not been possible to camouflage the
scar well enough so that the casket could be open, so
someone had come up with a creative solution. They'd
combed Trudi's hair forward over her forehead and
cut it into bangs.

Trudi now no longer looked like Farrah Fawcett.
She looked like a plastic Prince Valiant.

I couldn't stand it. I immediately shut my eyes,
turned, and had every intention of putting as much
distance between me and that casket as I could. I was
hurrying across the room when I spotted Anne and
Nathan. They were just walking into the room, coming

in through a side door. Apparently, they'd been taking a breather out in the hall. It must not have been a long enough break for Nathan, though. He looked grim, until he saw me heading toward him. Then his whole face lit up.

"Mom!" he said, waving me over. "Hey, Mom! Over here!" Almost immediately, though, Nathan seemed to remember where he was. And that, while waving your hand in the air and yelling might be fine at a football game, it probably wasn't the most appropriate behavior under the present circumstances. Not to mention, if Nathan hadn't realized it before he came in, I believe he got the hint when several people standing nearby turned to frown openly at him.

One of the frowners was Anne.

In fact, the look Anne gave Nathan looked suspiciously like one of the ones I myself had given Nathan when he was little and had acted up in church. I must say, Anne's look got much faster results. Nathan's mouth immediately snapped shut, and he started trying to rearrange his face into its former expression of solemnity. He apparently couldn't quite manage it, because he ended up with his mouth twitching in a sort of Bruce Willis smirk.

I had made my way around several people, and had just gotten to Nathan's side by the time he began doing Bruce Willis. "Mom," Nathan said.

I reached over and squeezed his arm. The poor boy actually sounded a little relieved to see me.

Once he'd said my name, though, you could tell he wasn't quite sure what came next in the funeral home etiquette books. Nathan's eyes went sort of blank for a second, and then he said, "Glad you could make it."

I just looked at him. One of these days I really needed to have a talk with that boy. I turned at that moment, though, to Anne. "I'm so sorry," I said.

Anne immediately nodded. "Trudi was special," she said.

Special was not one of the words I myself would've chosen, but I nodded anyway. "She was certainly one of a kind," I said. I comforted myself with the thought that at least I wasn't lying.

This was something I wasn't at all sure Anne herself could say. I'd hoped that maybe Anne would start talking, and that—as she talked—she would shed some light on who might've recently had arguments with her sister and therefore had a terrific motive for murder. I'd also hoped that Anne might have a few theories of her own about who might've done this awful thing.

All I heard out of Anne, however, was how terrific Trudi had been. In fact, to hear Anne tell it, Trudi had been a saint. "The best sister you could ever want," seemed to be a recurring theme. According to Anne, Trudi had no enemies, everybody loved her, and whoever did this to her must've thought that she was somebody else.

I just looked at her. *No enemies? Everybody loved her?* Obviously, we were talking about two different Trudi's.

Anne's theories regarding the murder didn't exactly blow me away, either. "It had to be either a case of mistaken identity," Anne said, "or it had to be a serial killer, picking out people at random. You know, like Ted Bundy, or somebody like that."

I kept right on nodding my head, no matter what Anne said, but to tell you the truth, the idea that a Ted Bundy clone was running around loose, knocking off real estate agents, seemed a bit far-fetched.

Particularly when so far there had been only one victim. I could be wrong, but in order to qualify as a *serial* killer, didn't you have to kill at least two people?

Up until then, all you were was just your plain, ordinary killer. Not to mention, was it really likely that a serial killer would lurk in an empty house on the off chance that some real estate agent would eventually turn up to show it to somebody?

Equally far-fetched, I thought, was Anne's portrayal of Trudi as God's gift to sisterhood. I mean, had Anne forgotten? I *knew* Trudi. Personally. A saint she wasn't. I mean, I certainly hoped she was up there with all the rest of the saints and all, but let's face it, if she was, she'd done the best sales job of her life.

After several minutes of listening to Anne going on and on about Trudi's generosity and her kindness, I decided I was going to have to be blunt. "Anne," I said when she finally paused for breath, "you don't happen to know if Trudi had recently received any threatening phone calls, or anything like that, do you?"

Anne's eyes sort of jerked in my direction, but she immediately shook her head. "No, no, nothing like—" At this point her voice stopped as suddenly as if it were a water faucet abruptly shut off. I peered at Anne. Her eyes seemed to be focused on something across the room. "—nothing like that," she finished. Her tone was now distracted.

I followed Anne's glance. The only people standing in Anne's direct line of sight were Derek and Barbi. Apparently, during the time I'd been talking with Anne and Nathan, Derek and Barbi had ditched the three women. They had also moved from the center of the room over to the side—I guess so that they wouldn't be blocking traffic—and now they were standing side by side, talking, his dark head bent over her platinum blond one.

I turned back to Anne. She *was* looking at Derek and Barbi. I wasn't sure exactly why at first, but the

way Anne continued to look at Derek and Barbi
struck me as odd. Like I said, I wasn't sure why right
off. I'd been watching Derek and Barbi myself, much
as Anne was doing now. And then it hit me. There
seemed to be an *intensity* in Anne's gaze that I was
pretty sure was totally lacking in mine.

Anne must've felt my eyes, because suddenly she
gave me a quick sideways glance. Her eyes met mine,
and as they did so, they seemed to do this odd flick-
ering thing. At least I think they did. The whole thing
was over so quickly, it was hard to say for sure I'd
seen it at all.

What I did see for sure was Anne abruptly moving
closer to Nathan. Linking her arm through his, she
stared up at him with a quick smile.

Nathan, of course, reacted the way he always seems
to act when a pretty woman grabs his arm. He looked
down at Anne with a big, goofy grin.

Once again, however, he seemed to remember
where he was. And that perhaps goofy grins might not
be altogether appropriate when there was a dead person in the room. Almost immediately, Nathan started
doing another Bruce Willis smirk.

What can I say? The boy obviously had talent.

Anne was still holding onto Nathan's arm. She indicated Barbi with a nod of her head. "Can you believe
that woman?" she said. "My poor sister isn't even in
her grave, and that—that *awful* woman is already
moving in on her husband!"

Nathan immediately said what sounded to me like
the first thing that occurred to him. He looked over
at Derek and Barbi, and said, "Derek sure doesn't
look as if he minds."

Anne's head went up, and she immediately removed
her arm from Nathan's, reaching into the pocket of
her suit for a tattered Kleenex. "Well," she said, dab-

bing at her eyes with the Kleenex. Her eyes looked dry to me. Much like Barbi's had earlier, oddly enough. "I think it's disrespectful. At the very least." Anne dabbed at her eyes again as she glanced once more at Barbi and Derek.

Barbi was at that moment looking up into Derek's face and batting her lashes. I could almost feel the wind all the way across the room. Derek must've been feeling something himself, because he moved so that he was standing even closer to Barbi. He leaned over and said something so close to her ear that his face was partially obscured by platinum waves.

Beside me, Anne caught her breath. "No, it's not just disrespectful. It's *cruel,* that's what it is. I mean, my poor, sweet sister is—is—"

Apparently, getting the Kleenex out was a good idea, after all. Tears were now trickling down Anne's cheeks. "Ex—excuse me," she sort of gasped. "I've—I'll—I—ladies' room."

That was pretty much an exact quote. Having made this extremely lucid statement, Anne turned, and balling up the Kleenex in her hand, fled from the room.

Nathan immediately started to go after her, then hesitated just long enough to tell me over his shoulder, "She's kind of upset."

"I'd say so," I said.

The question was, though, was she upset about Trudi? Or about something else?

"Be right back," Nathan said, and then he was gone.

Left standing all by myself, I turned to look over at Derek and Barbi again. They had been joined by a middle-aged couple who were now obviously extending condolences to Derek. Even from where I was standing, you could tell that Barbi would definitely prefer that the newcomers make it snappy. She even tapped her foot for a second or two, but the couple

did not take the hint. When the woman leaned forward and gave Derek a hug, Barbi looked away. And
happened to meet my eyes.

Lifting her hand, she moved away from Derek and
the couple and started walking straight toward me.
Swaying her hips, of course, in a blur of motion. In
that tight dress, it was quite a show. One, I noticed,
that swiveled the head of almost every man Barbi
passed on her way.

When Barbi got to my side, she actually giggled.
"Goodness, look at all these old coots. Isn't it a shame
that they've all got their wives with them?"

Now, what was I supposed to say to that? "A pity."

Barbi nodded, tapping her front teeth with a fingertip lacquered the exact same shade as her crimson
mouth. "I mean, " she said, surveying the room with
a speculative air, "some of these guys have got to be
in their seventies. They look like they're not long for
this world. And—"

"And?" I said. I was trying not to smile. I have
always thought that part of Barbi's unique charm was
that she said the most outrageous things right out
loud.

Now she pulled at a platinum curl absently. *"And,"*
she said, "their dried-up old wives are going to inherit
their loot, and what in hell are *they* going to do with
it?"

"Buy moisturizer?" I suggested.

I forgot, of course, that I was talking to Barbi. She
stopped in the middle of what she was saying, let go
of the platinum curl, and blinked heavily mascaraed
lashes at me. "Huh?" she said.

I didn't particularly want to explain. Especially since
two of the dried-up old wives to whom Barbi had so
kindly referred were now looking our way. My luck,
they could read lips. Or they had really powerful hear-

ing aids that could pick up sounds in the next county. I'd really prefer *not* to be attacked by a gang of elderly women in a funeral home. "Never mind," I said, waving my hand as if to erase what I'd just said.

Barbi apparently was accustomed to people abruptly dropping the subject with her. She just shrugged. "Well," she said, pulling on her hair again, "like I was saying, it's a damn waste. Because if one of those old coots left his money to me, *I'd* know how to spend it."

I nodded. Fact was, I didn't doubt her for a minute. I'd seen her in action. In Victoria's Secret alone, Barbi could blow a month's salary in an hour, tops. The woman was an inspiration to us all.

Now she looked back over at Derek and frowned a little. He was still talking to the middle-aged couple. "Schuyler," Barbi said, "what do you think of Derek?"

I followed her eyes. "He seems nice."

Barbi blinked and stared at me. "*Nice?* Girl, he's better than nice," she said. She leaned closer to me and said, hardly lowering her voice at all, "I mean, old Shitty-toe was right about one thing. Her husband is a *doll.*"

I just stared at her. Somehow, with Trudi lying right there in the same room with us, quite irrevocably dead, it seemed particularly unkind to continue to refer to her as Shitty-toe. "You know, Barbi," I began, "I—"

I didn't get to finish, though, because at the same time as I began to speak, another woman's voice sounded behind me. "What? *What?*" Barbi and I turned in unison to see Anne standing not five feet away, in back of us. Apparently, Anne had just gotten back from the ladies' room. "*I said,* what did you just say?" Anne was looking straight at Barbi, and her eyes looked as if a tiny fire burned behind each one.

Barbi didn't even miss a beat. "I said *Trudi* was a doll," she said, waving a hand in the air. "We're all going to miss her." Glancing over at me, she said, "Isn't that what I said, Schuyler?"

For a moment I didn't say a word. I was thinking, of course, *Gosh, thanks, Barbi, for putting me in the middle. What are friends for?*

"That's what she said, all right," I said through my teeth.

Anne obviously didn't buy any of it. As Anne's eyes turned into little bonfires, Barbi must've decided this would be a good time to leave. "Be seeing you," she said, looking straight at me. Turning on a heel, she headed back to Derek, tapped him on the shoulder and said something to him. Then she walked out of the funeral home without a backward glance.

Barbi's departure, of course, left me standing there alone with Anne—a woman clearly not in her best mood. I immediately started looking around for Nathan. Where *was* that boy when you needed him?

I'd just spotted him, coming through the side door again, when we all heard it. Outside, a woman screamed.

Chapter
14

For a moment there, right after I heard the scream, it was like being an extra on one of the episodes of that old TV show, *Rawhide*—right after a gunshot had spooked the herd.

I don't recall consciously making a decision to run out to the parking lot as fast as my feet could carry me, but I found myself doing it, anyway. Mostly because everybody else in the room seemed to be headed that way. It wasn't so much curiosity as an urgent need not to be trampled that caused me to accompany them.

On the way, Nathan pretty much summed up the entire situation in a single sound. *"Aarrgh!"* he yelled. What's more, with a frenzied expression on his face not unlike that of stampeding cattle, Nathan kept making this admittedly odd sound as he took off with the rest of us toward the funeral home front door. He'd started out behind me, but by the time we'd almost reached the front door, he'd passed me. "That was a scream!" he told me as he was going by.

I had slowed down to a fast walk. Most of the herd

was ahead of me by then, and those that were left straggling behind me were in worse physical shape than I was, and certainly not in trampling condition.

"It was a scream, Mom!" Nathan yelled again.

I just looked at him. There are times when I'm convinced that my sons don't think I'm very bright. In this instance, he apparently felt I would not have come to this conclusion on my own, but needed *his* assessment. "A scream? Really?" I said.

Sarcasm is pretty much wasted on Nathan. He nodded his head. "Yeah, Mom," he said, "it was a scream! I'm sure of it."

I didn't even blink. The kid was serious. He was giving me news.

"Who screamed?" Nathan shouted at me.

He didn't wait for my answer, though. He picked up speed and sprinted by me. It was just as well. My answer, of course, would have been that, at that particular moment, it was Nathan himself, bellowing at the top of his lungs.

The scream we'd all heard shortly before Nathan's, however, clearly had been Barbi's doing.

As soon as I went through the front door, I saw her across the parking lot, standing next to her car. Actually, she was doing less standing and more *leaning* than anything else. She was kind of draped across the driver's side of her car, looking pale and shaken.

Derek, oddly enough, got to Barbi's side first.

I glanced over at Anne, and what a surprise, she did not look at all impressed by Derek's speed and endurance. In fact, punctuation marks had formed between Anne's brows. Deep punctuation marks.

"Barbi," Derek said, his handsome face filled with concern, "are you okay?" As he spoke, he ran a big, tanned hand through his dark, wavy hair.

It was a gesture not lost on Barbi.

She responded by batting her eyelashes. "Oh, Derek, I am so sorry." A trifle belatedly, Barbi seemed to realize that there were indeed actual other human beings standing around who probably should be acknowledged.

Barbi gave the rest of us a cursory glance. "Sorry, everybody," she said. "I'm so stupid."

I couldn't help but notice that nobody jumped to disagree.

"I didn't mean to alarm anybody," Barbi hurried on, "but there was a—a—um—wasp in my car."

Everybody's reaction to that one was pretty much what you'd expect. Everybody first looked at Barbi, and then they looked at each other. A few people in the crowd rolled their eyes.

I felt a bit inclined toward eye-rolling myself. Barbi had let loose that bloodcurdling scream over an *insect*? While I realized that wasps did happen to be insects equipped with stingers, still, unless they were also toting around .357 Magnums, Barbi's reaction seemed a bit overdone.

Even Barbi herself seemed to realize that her reaction needed defending. "Why, that wasp scared me to death," Barbi was now saying. "I guess I'm just silly when it comes to wasps!"

Glancing around at several faces in the crowd, I'd say Barbi was not going to get any argument on that score, either.

Quite a few people in the crowd began to make their way back inside, mumbling a little among themselves.

Oddly enough, though, Derek was one of the ones who remained. Anne and Nathan also stayed behind. Anne was holding Nathan's hand, but her eyes were on her brother-in-law. They seemed to narrow quite a bit when Derek immediately moved to Barbi's side.

"Nonsense," Derek told her. "You're not silly. You're just careful, that's all. Here, why don't you let me get that wasp out of your car for you?" As Derek said this last, he gave Barbi a little wink. "We wouldn't want you to get stung, now, would we?"

I looked over at Barbi. I'd seen Barbi practically curl up in a man's lap with far less encouragement than an outright wink. Barbi, however, didn't budge. She remained where she was, sort of leaning against her car door, staring at Derek with eyes that seemed to be growing larger by the minute.

What was the matter with her? I might've thought that Barbi felt that it was inappropriate to flirt with a new widower whose wife was not even buried yet. And yet that had clearly not bothered her only moments earlier, when the wife in question had been lying in her casket in full view in the very same room. If Barbi was actually bothered by improprieties, she should've been far more bothered inside Arch's than out here in the parking lot.

And yet, obviously something was bothering her out here. When Derek made a move as if to reach for the handle of Barbi's car, Barbi didn't budge.

"Here," Derek said smoothly, "let me—"

"No!" Barbi said the word so quickly, it sounded like a shout.

Derek drew his hand back so fast, you might've thought Barbi had hit him. "What?" he said.

Barbi's eyes grew even larger for a second, then she quickly said, "I—I don't want you to see the inside of my car," she said. "I mean, it's, uh, it's a mess. You'll think I'm a terrible housekeeper."

Nobody seemed to want to point out to Barbi that she was talking about her car, so the term "housekeeper" probably didn't apply. For his part, Derek was now looking at Barbi the way I've seen quite a few men look at her over the years I've known her. Derek was wearing the expression on his face that a lot of men seem to get the moment they realize that inside Barbi's pretty little head, there could possibly be a stiff breeze blowing.

Barbi gave a careless little shrug. "Besides, that wasp is all gone now. It—uh—it just flew out the door. That's what it did, all right. It just flew right out the door." Barbi followed all this up with a little smile, but I thought her smile looked a little shaky.

"Oh," Derek said. "Well, then."

I wasn't sure what he meant by this, but once he said it, he shrugged his broad shoulders, looked at Barbi, looked at her car, and then slowly turned to walk back toward the funeral home.

Barbi looked as if she might've liked to reach out and stop him, but still she didn't move. "Uh, Derek?" she said to his retreating back.

He turned and looked at her.

"Thanks anyway," She lifted her hand and waggled her fingers at him. In what I knew she thought was a sultry wave.

It didn't look sultry to me, but since I wasn't the one being waved at, maybe I wasn't a good judge.

Derek didn't exactly look blown away by it either. He nodded at Barbi, his eyes still puzzled, and then continued to move back inside. When Derek left, Anne and Nathan followed him. "You coming, Mom?" Nathan said. I wish I could say my son said this right away, concern for his beloved mother never being far from his mind. Clearly, however, it was an afterthought. Nathan had immediately started off with Anne, and then several steps away, he'd stopped and looked back at me.

What can I say? The way a son dotes on his mother can bring a tear to your eye.

I waved at him. "Be there in a minute. You go on."

When Nathan had stopped, so had Anne. Now I noticed she gave me and Barbi a speculative look before she and Nathan continued to follow Derek inside. I wasn't exactly sure what Anne was speculating about, but to tell you the truth, I didn't think about it long. My mind was on other things.

When I was sure everybody else had moved out of earshot, heading back inside, and that just Barbi and I remained, I turned to Barbi. "Okay," I said. "Let's have it. What really happened?"

Barbi tried to bluff. "Why, Schuyler, I don't know *what* in the world you're talking about."

I choked back a laugh. She was trying the Southern innocent bit on *me*? I started to tell her, *Barbi, get real. I* invented *the Southern innocent bit.* I was afraid, however, that I might actually have to explain to Barbi what the Southern innocent bit was—since it seemed to me that Barbi could possibly be operating purely on instinct here. Then, too, there was the chance that she might want to argue with me as to exactly who the inventor of the Southern innocent bit really was. Instead of getting into all this extraneous stuff, I cut to the chase. "Barbi, move away from the car."

I believe I've heard this exact phrase on that television show, *Cops*. I don't want to brag or anything, but I believe I said it with every bit as much authority as the policemen on that show.

I wouldn't have believed it possible, but Barbi's eyes got even bigger. "What do you mean?"

I was getting tired of this. "I mean, if you don't move away from your car, I'm going to call my son Nathan back over here." I gestured over my shoulder, toward Nathan and Anne. They were almost to the front door of the funeral home, but they were walking pretty slow. "I'll have Nathan pick you up and deposit you somewhere else. Like maybe over there." I indicated the expanse of lawn on our far left.

Barbi thought it over. She took her sweet time about it, too. I believe, however, in Barbi-time her mind might've been racing. She stared at me for a moment, and then she looked over at Nathan and Anne. Having done all this, Barbi then went through the entire routine all over again.

Then she actually moved.

I stood there, surprised my little threat had worked. I mean, I wasn't even sure myself that I could get Nathan to leave Anne's side long enough to come back over here and wrestle with Barbi. On the positive side, there was the distinct possibility that, for the opportunity to wrestle with a woman wearing the low-cut dress Barbi had on, Nathan would walk barefoot over ground glass. On the negative side, Nathan might prefer not to be caught Barbi-wrestling in the immediate vicinity of a woman he now considered to be "the one." The way I saw it, it could go either way.

Barbi must've been convinced, though. She moved so that she now stood right by my side, facing the car. I followed her gaze, and that—of course—was when I saw exactly why Barbi had been leaning up against the door of her car. She'd been hiding something.

Someone had scratched a heart into the door of the driver's side of Barbi's Mustang.

I stared at that awful thing, and it was all I could do to keep from screaming, just like Barbi had so recently done. Instead, I drew in a long, gasping breath and grabbed Barbi by the arm. "Come on," I said, "we shouldn't be out here by ourselves. We ought to go inside with the others." As I said this, I did a quick scan of the parking lot.

Unfortunately, the lot was filled with cars, which didn't exactly make for easy viewing. As best as I could tell, the entire cast of *Natural Born Killers* could be hiding out here, squatting down between the cars, and I might not spot them. My heart began to pound. "Barbi? Did you hear me? It isn't safe out here." In fact, the asshole who'd decorated Barbi's car could be watching us right this minute. The thought made the hairs on the back of my neck stand up. He could be close to us even now, hiding behind a shrub, or a car, or just about anything, just so he could see our reaction to his artwork.

I gave Barbi's arm a yank. "Come on," I said.

Barbi wrenched her arm away. "Cut it out," she said. She actually sounded irritated.

I stopped and stared at her. "Barbi, we need to get *inside*."

Barbi shook her platinum blond head stubbornly. "Baloney," she said.

I stared at her all over again. This was her entire reaction? To mention a lunch meat? Was she *kidding*?

I also had a few unkind thoughts with regard to her intelligence. Was it possible she really didn't grasp the significance of the heart on her door? Well, I hated to break it to her, but I was going to give it one last try, and then she was on her own. "Barbi, listen," I said. My tone was not patient. "Whoever did this probably is the same guy who murdered Trudi. Understand? So, we need to get inside, and we need to call the police."

Barbi cocked her platinum head to one side. "What for?"

I was scanning the parking lot again. Nothing caught my eye, but then again, I wasn't sure what I was looking for. "Come on, Barbi," I said, summoning up every last bit of patience I had. "You know damn well you've got to call the police."

"Oh, no, I don't," Barbi said, folding her arms

across her chest. "There's no use getting them involved."

What? No *use*? If the police weren't any use in catching the sort of person who took a knife to cars and people, then what use were they? Selling raffle tickets?

"Look, Barbi, I don't want to leave you—"

Barbi, unbelievably, smiled at me. "Oh, that's okay," she said cheerfully. "You go on."

"Barbi—"

Barbi was still smiling. "Look, Schuyler," she said, "somebody's just trying to scare me. That's all."

"Barbi," I said, "you could be in real danger. The guy who murdered Trudi could also be after you."

This sounded perfectly logical to me, but from the look on Barbi's face, you wouldn't have thought so. "Nonsense," she said stubbornly. Reaching over, she actually patted my arm. "I'm going back to the office now. I think I've paid enough respects to Shitty-toe for one day, don't you?"

I blinked at that one, but I refused to be derailed. "Barbi, if you don't call the police, then I'm going—"

Barbi may not have been a brain trust, but she figured out what I was about to say this time pretty quick. "Oh, no, you aren't," she said. "I don't want to talk to the police, and I'm not going to. Hell, if you call them, we'll be here all night. I've got things to do."

"But, Barbi—"

Barbi gave her hair a stubborn little shake. "This is just somebody playing a stupid practical joke."

Her tone implied I was making a mountain out of a molehill.

"I'm *going* back to the office," Barbi said.

And that's what she did. I headed inside, and then I stood there, staring after her, from just inside the front door of Arch's. I watched Barbi back out of her parking space, then turn around and drive away.

Barbi didn't look the least bit scared.

The way I saw it, there were only two explanations for this. One, Barbi was not bright enough to realize that she should be scared. This was a distinct possibility.

Or, two, she knew beyond a shadow of a doubt that there was no reason to be frightened.

My stomach wrenched. I didn't want to be thinking what I was thinking, but there was no getting around it. The day Trudi had disappeared, Barbi had returned to the office after Trudi had been gone for quite a while. In fact, Barbi had come into the office after I myself had returned.

Moreover, the memo I'd thought was Trudi's had been partly printed and partly written out in longhand.

A lot of times I myself didn't bother putting the person's name at the top to whom the note was sent. I'd just left the note on the desk of whomever it was for, and a formal address didn't seem particularly necessary.

Hell, everybody in the office had to do this some of the time, because I got notes with no name at the top all the time. What this meant was, if Trudi's memo had been originally intended for, oh, say, *Barbi,* for instance, but Trudi had left off Barbi's name, it would've been an easy thing to print TO S. R. at the top and give it to me. In fact, now that I thought about it, the top of that note had been torn. So, it could even be that the original name really had been torn off.

I crossed my arms and actually shivered. I couldn't believe I was seriously considering the possibility that *Barbi,* of all people, could've strangled Trudi. Barbi was somebody whom, before she'd begun the Great

Manhunt, I'd considered a good friend. Nonetheless, there was no denying it; Barbi could've done it. She outweighed petite Trudi by quite a bit; she would've had no trouble overpowering her.

And yet, just because a person *could* do a certain thing, it didn't necessarily follow that they really would do it.

I mean, for God's sake, I *could* lose twenty pounds. Enough said.

Besides, before I started accusing an old friend, there *were* other possibilities.

Squaring my shoulders, I turned and headed inside. Almost the instant I walked into the large room to the right of the lobby, I spotted Derek. It wasn't hard, of course. Once again, he was surrounded by quite a few people offering condolences, almost all of whom were women, oddly enough. I spotted Anne and Nathan right away, too. They were standing almost directly across the room from Derek. I started in their direction, and then I realized that neither Anne nor Nathan seemed to have seen me yet. So I retraced my steps, ending up leaning against the wall, on the other side of a large Schefflera plant this time, out of Anne's and Nathan's direct view.

Where, yes, I admit this shamelessly, I could watch Anne without her realizing I was watching.

And, what do you know, I hadn't been wrong earlier. Almost immediately I noticed that Anne's eyes did seem to stray in Derek's direction about every other minute. How strange.

Shortly after I noticed this, I noticed something even more strange.

Derek never once looked at Anne.

I mean, you'd think that old Derek would at least give his sister-in-law a quick *glance* every once in a while. If nothing else, just to see how she was bearing up.

I stood there, watching the two of them, and I began to get a sickening feeling. I did hope I was wrong, but it looked to me as if maybe my baby son, Nathan, was being used as camouflage. This could definitely explain why an older woman with more education would suddenly be so attracted to him.

Other than, of course, his quite nice looking legs.

Anne must've realized that she might possibly be the object of scrutiny in this public a setting, because all of a sudden she moved closer to Nathan's side, looping her arm through his. Her eyes scanned the room.

I moved back to lean against the wall again, thinking. Anne knew that I'd stayed behind to talk to Barbi out in the parking lot after everyone else had moved back inside. She had given me and Barbi that speculative look as she turned to go.

I took a deep breath, stepped out toward the middle of the room so that Anne could easily see me if she looked my way, and started walking resolutely toward her and Nathan, shouldering my way through the crowd. Anne and Nathan spotted me right away, and if I didn't know better, I'd say Anne actually started looking a little wary. Nathan, of course, started doing Bruce Willis again.

When I reached their side, before either of them had a chance to speak, I gave Anne's arm a maternal pat. "You poor thing, this has got to be such an ordeal."

Anne gave her dark head a quick nod, biting her lip.

Over Anne's head, Nathan winked encouragement at me. Evidently, according to Nathan I was doing the right thing. "And, as if you didn't have *enough* to upset you, there's this thing with your brother-in-law and Barbi Lundergan." I clicked my tongue sympathetically.

Nathan, of course, was staring at me now. Tongue-clicking is not exactly something I do on a regular basis. In fact, the only reason I even know how to do it is because I've learned at my mother's knee, so to speak. My mother is a tongue-clicking champion.

Anne's eyes had sort of jerked open. "What do you mean?" she said, her eyes traveling once again in Derek's direction.

I looked straight at her. "I just talked to Barbi out in the parking lot, and I found out that what Nathan said earlier was absolutely right." I shook my head, trying to look disgusted this time. "Your brother-in-law really didn't mind Barbi flirting with him a bit."

It was odd, watching Anne's face right after I spoke. Her face suddenly seemed to tighten up all over. As if an unseen hand were pulling on every muscle. "What are you talking about?" Anne asked. Her voice sounded oddly shrill.

I looked away, at the rest of the room, and then said, in the tone of someone sharing a scandalous secret, "*Well,* Barbi just told me that she and Derek have a dinner date." I glanced back at Anne. "That man certainly isn't wasting any time, is he?"

For a moment there, I was certain I saw a flash of fury in Anne's eyes, but it was gone as suddenly as it had come. Had I been imagining it because I'd *wanted* to see some reaction?

Anne's voice did seem to be shaking a little. I wasn't imagining that. "I can't believe Derek cared so little about—about Trudi," she said, "that he'd start dating when she isn't even buried yet!"

"That's a man for you," I said. I did some more sympathetic tongue-clicking.

I was still watching Anne closely. Was her anger

excessive, or was she just feeling outraged on her sister's behalf?

Other mourners arrived then to offer condolences to Anne, and I moved away. Returning, of course, to the other side of the Schefflera plant again.

It was almost a half hour later that I saw what I'd been watching for. Anne moved quickly to Derek's side, leaned toward him, and whispered something. Whatever it was must've been important, because Derek immediately shot Anne a look.

Anne didn't wait. She turned on her heel and headed straight out of the room, without looking back.

Derek, on the other hand, stood around for a moment. He nodded hello at a few new arrivals, went over and stood in front of Trudi's casket with his head bowed for a minute or so, and then—with a quick look around the room—went out the same door Anne had gone through.

I, on the other hand, didn't even bother to take a quick look around the room. I just followed Derek as fast as I could.

The door Derek had gone out opened into a hallway with a single door on the left. I headed for the door, leaned forward to listen for voices, and when I heard none, I opened it very slowly, making as little noise as I possibly could.

As it turned out, I could've made more noise, because it was clear right from the start that Anne and Derek were not listening to anything but each other.

"Idiot!" Derek was saying.

"You're the idiot if you think you can run around on me. Right under my own nose!"

It was all I could do to keep my mouth from dropping open. Anne was accusing Derek of running around on *her*?

Chapter
15

Derek's voice was a low growl. "Keep your voice down, you little fool," he told Anne. "Somebody might come in and hear you."

What could I say? The man definitely had his finger on a real problem. I'd opened the door enough by then to see that the only thing between me and the happy couple was a long portable coatrack standing against the wall on my right. Fortunately, the rack wasn't empty. With Kentucky weather in March being the roller-coaster ride I'd mentioned earlier, the coatrack was holding quite a few coats. Holding my breath, I edged my way through the door, tiptoed soundlessly across the plush beige carpet, and huddled next to a navy blue London Fog.

"Oh, spare me the melodramatics, Derek," Anne was now saying. "Nobody's coming in here."

Anne obviously did not have quite the grasp of the situation that Derek did.

"I'm not being melodramatic," Derek said. "I'm being careful." As he said this, Derek evidently decided he ought to demonstrate just what being careful

entailed. He turned away from Anne and began taking
a long, long look around.

I saw Derek's head turning in my direction, and I
froze. I don't think I even breathed until Derek's eyes
had moved past me. He continued to scan the immediate vicinity, and then finally turned back to Anne.
Who was, by this time, tapping her foot.

"So, tell me, Anne, what in God's name were you
thinking of?" Derek sounded angry. "I thought we'd
discussed all this. I thought we'd decided exactly what
we had to do. Are you trying to ruin *everything*?"

Anne cleared her throat before she answered, but
even still, she sounded close to tears. "But, Derek, I
had to know—"

Derek interrupted her. "—had to know? Had to
know *what*?" He lowered his voice to barely above a
whisper. I, of course, moved closer to the London Fog,
leaning as far forward as I could without falling into
the rack. A tricky proposition, believe me. "What
could you possibly need to know so badly that it was
worth taking this big a risk?"

Anne did not sound the least bit apologetic. "I need
to know what's going on between you and that
Barbi person!"

Derek's voice now sounded puzzled. "Me and
Barbi?" He spoke the name with considerable disdain.
A thing like this could really hurt poor Barbi's feelings. "Are you *joking*? There's nothing going on between me and Barbi, of all people. Whatever gave you
that idea?"

You could tell Anne really wanted to believe Derek.
What's more, hearing Barbi's name mentioned with
such contempt had clearly been music to her ears. Her
voice suddenly sounded a lot less angry that it had
before. "It wasn't a *what*ever. It was a *who*ever,"

Anne said. "Schuyler told me. She said that Barbi told her that you and she were going out to—"

Derek forgot to be quiet this once. "Wha–a–at?" he said. You might've thought he was choking on the word.

Anne was now nodding her blond head emphatically. "That's what Schuyler said, all right. She said that you and Barbi had already made a dinner date, and that—"

Anne appeared not at all reluctant to repeat word for word what I'd told her earlier, but I decided to spare her the effort. I stepped out from behind the coatrack. As I did so, both Anne and Derek's heads swiveled in my direction. Neither of them said a word, but each had the same expression—that of a deer caught in the headlights of an oncoming car.

"Okay, so I admit it," I said with a shrug. "I lied. You two don't seem to have been all that honest, either. In fact, I think the police are going to be fascinated to hear all about you two lovebirds."

Anne's mouth dropped open. Turning to Derek, she said, "Derek?" As if she fully expected him to do something about this sudden turn of events.

What Derek came up with must've been a real disappointment. First, he wheeled on her, glaring. If looks could kill, Anne would've joined her sister out front that very moment. Then Derek turned back to me. The glare had been replaced by a look of bewildered innocence. "Why, Schuyler," he said. "I really don't know what you're talking about."

I didn't even blink. "Are you trying to tell me that there's nothing whatsoever going on between you and Anne here?" I asked.

Derek smirked. "Well, of course not," he said. His tone implied that the idea was preposterous. "Do you really think I'd have anything to do with *her*?"

Derek said this last word with just about the same amount of disdain with which he'd said the name, Barbi, earlier. Apparently, old Derek felt that if something worked, you should stick with it.

I was pretty sure, however, that Anne would've preferred that Derek simply deny that there was anything going on and let it go at that. His backing up his argument by implying that Anne might not be attractive enough to sustain his interest was probably ill-advised.

"What the hell do you mean by that?" Anne took a step away from Derek and glared at *him*. "Who the hell do you think you are, acting as if I weren't good enough for you? *You're* the one who was married, buster! I'm single! I haven't made any promises I didn't keep!"

Anne's point did seem to be well-taken. However, I was pretty sure that, had Trudi been consulted on the matter, she probably would've felt that while no overt promises had indeed been made, it was pretty much a *given* that your own sister refrain from running around with your husband.

With Anne continuing to stare at him as if he were something disgusting that she'd just discovered on the bottom of her shoe, Derek took no time at all to realize that he'd misspoken. He was now doing major salvage work. "Anne, dear," he said, spreading his hands out in a conciliatory gesture, "what I was trying to tell Schuyler is that you and I are practically brother and sister. That we would never—"

I had to hand it to old Derek. He was pretty fast on his feet. No doubt, he'd be sending Anne flowers before the day was out.

As soon as the thought crossed my mind, I turned to stare at Derek with new eyes. Hold the phone. Wait a minute. *The flowers Derek always sent to Trudi on*

Tuesday were never delivered. That meant that hours before her body was found, Derek had already started behaving as if he knew that his wife was never going to return to the office.

So how exactly had he known that?

"—I mean, for God's sake, Anne, you and I are family," Derek was now saying. "That's what I meant when—"

I broke in. "Derek, what happened to your flowers?"

Derek looked irritated that I'd interrupted his salvage operation. "Flowers?" he said, frowning.

I nodded. "You know, the bouquet you sent Trudi every Tuesday afternoon? This week it didn't come," I said. I wagged an index finger at him. "You know, a thing like this could make a person think that you knew *in advance* Trudi wouldn't be around to receive them."

Derek just looked at me. He shook his dark head, as if he couldn't believe I was actually saying such a thing. His tan, though, suddenly looked a couple of shakes lighter.

Anne must've noticed how pale Derek had gone, too. His distress apparently brought out all her protective instincts, because she immediately jumped right in. "Oh, for God's sake, Schuyler," she snapped. "That doesn't mean a thing. So what if he didn't order the damn flowers; maybe he just forgot. I mean, Trudi *had* been missing since lunch. A thing like that *can* be upsetting, you know." Anne's tone was scornful. "It certainly doesn't prove Derek killed her, or anything like that."

I didn't answer Anne right away. I just looked at her, while a lot of puzzle pieces seemed to fit together in my mind. No wonder Trudi had suddenly become a matchmaker for Nathan and Anne. Trudi must've suspected that Anne and Derek might be attracted to each other, and that was why she fixed up Anne with Nathan in the first place. Trudi had been trying to pair Anne up, just in case Anne really did have her eye on Derek.

Lord. How pathetic.

I folded my arms across my chest. "The way I see it," I said, "you two have one terrific motive for murder."

Anne's chin went up. "So what? We didn't do it." She, too, folded her arms across her chest and met my gaze head-on.

I swallowed uneasily. If Anne was lying, I had to give credit where credit was due. She was very good at it.

Still, I wasn't totally convinced of their innocence. I looked straight at Anne, and then over at Derek. "Why don't we just let the police decide whether you two did it or not?"

Anne and Derek instantly looked stricken. "No!" Anne said. "There's no reason to bring the police into this. I am telling you the truth."

"Sure you are," I said.

Anne's chin went even higher. "Look, I'll *prove* that I'm telling you the truth," Anne said. "I'll even admit that we *planned* to kill her!"

Now that little admission was something of a shock.

It apparently was a shock to Derek, too. He was now staring at Anne as if he were seriously considering killing *her.*

I, of course, was staring at Anne, too. If Anne and Derek had been planning to murder Trudi, that certainly explained Anne's instant *amore* with Nathan. It also explained why Anne had willingly let Trudi pair her off, and why for the last eight weeks she'd been dating Nathan. She'd been trying to throw suspicion off herself and Derek.

I could feel my eyes narrowing as I looked at Anne. Then she had been *using* my son.

My son who, at this very moment, was actually entertaining the notion that she was "the one."

I uncrossed my arms and took a little step away from Anne. I needed to put some distance between us. Because I suddenly wanted very badly to slap her smug little face.

Anne, unbelievably, was now looking triumphant. "You heard me right, Schuyler. Derek and I have been planning to kill Trudi for months!"

I blinked. Lord. Anne actually sounded proud to have had such a project on her calendar.

"For God's sake, Anne, will you shut up?" To his credit, Derek did not sound proud. To his discredit, however, Derek did sound as if, at that particular moment, he could easily strangle *Anne*. He was actually clenching and unclenching his hands as he hurried on. *"Shut your stupid mouth!"*

Anne ignored Derek's rude suggestion. As a matter of fact, she didn't even glance in his direction. Shrugging her shoulders, she went on, "Divorce was out of the question, of course."

"Of course," I said, nodding.

I must've answered too quickly. Anne's eyes darted toward mine, her mouth pinched with distaste. "Divorce *was* out of the question. It would've been impossible."

This time I didn't nod. And I didn't say a word.

Anne tossed her hair. "I think you know as well as I do that our beloved Trudi was not the sort of woman who would ever leave Derek and me alone." Anne shook her dark head from side to side to punctuate that last statement. "Oh, no. If Trudi knew for sure that Derek and I were together, why, she would have taken extreme satisfaction in making the rest of our lives a living hell. You know she would have.''

What could I say? That *did* sound like the Trudi I'd known.

Anne must've interpreted my silence as agreement, because she hurried right on. "Really, it wasn't like we *wanted* to kill her. But what else could we do? Trudi herself left us no choice.''

I nodded again. Now wasn't that just like a murder victim? Always backing you into a corner. Always leaving you no options. Always being so damned *inconsiderate.*

Anne was shrugging again. "So, of course, I had to lure Trudi to a vacant house so that we could do what we had to do without being seen.''

Once again, I didn't blink. Let me see now, I bet I could guess the exact address of the vacant house Anne had chosen.

Can you believe Anne actually had the gall to smile at this point? I don't think she meant to, but she began to sound eager—eager and, yes, a little *excited* to have the chance to tell the whole thing to somebody. "It was *so* easy to get her there, it really was! And Trudi always thought she was smart; well, we found out just how smart she really was, didn't we? Hell, all I had to do was tell Trudi that Nathan and I were planning on buying a house together. After that, all she could see was that fat commission. I could've gotten her to meet me just about anywhere!''

I continued to stare at Anne, frozen-faced. Anne seemed to be leaving out a significant part here. The part where she'd led Trudi to believe that the reason she and Nathan were buying a house together was that she and Nathan were getting married.

This could possibly explain why Nathan had not

known that he was engaged. The bride-to-be had ne-
glected to mention it to him.

"Of course, I didn't want Trudi to tell anybody that
she was meeting me, so I told her that the engagement
was a big secret. That Nathan and I wanted to make
the announcement ourselves after all the contracts
were signed."

Anne now glanced over at Derek, almost as if she
were expecting praise from him for a job well done.
He was staring woodenly straight ahead. Anne turned
back to me. "I told Trudi that I was going to meet
her at that house on Saratoga, but I knew all along
that it was Derek and me who were really going to
meet her."

Derek sort of winced when his name came up this
time. He held up a big hand, like a traffic cop signaling
Anne to stop. Turning toward me, he quickly put in,
"But, Schuyler, you've got to believe us, we didn't
meet Trudi there after all," he said. "I mean, *Anne*
called her, all right, and *Anne* told Trudi to meet us
at that empty house, all right—"

I glanced over at Anne. Did she notice that old
Derek here seemed to be putting a little extra emphasis on her name every time he said it? A person could
get the idea that he didn't feel equally to blame.

Anne, however, didn't even seem to notice. She just
stood there, listening to him, even nodding a couple
of times to back up what Derek was saying.

I almost rolled my eyes. If I'd liked Anne better—
like, for example, *at all*—I would've told her, *Anne,
wake up! The coffee is emitting an odor, already. Take
a whiff!*

"—but we didn't do anything to Trudi. Absolutely
nothing!" Derek finished.

"Uh-huh," I said. My tone was skeptical.

Anne, unbelievably, looked *offended* that I didn't

take Derek's word at face value. Once again, she leaped to his defense. "I'll have you know," she said, uncrossing her arms so that she could point an index finger at me, "Derek is telling you the truth!"

Right. He'd run around on his wife with her own *sister,* he'd plot to murder said wife, and he'd even admit it right to your face. But, oh, no, the man wouldn't lie. Not Derek. He was too decent for that.

"We didn't get the chance to do anything," Anne said. She did not sound pleased. "Because, wouldn't you know it, Trudi was already dead when we got there."

My own chin went up at that one. "She was already—" I repeated, trying to take this last in.

Anne was nodding. "You heard me. Somebody got to Trudi before we did."

I couldn't help it. My mouth dropped open.

Anne was shaking her head now. Those two deep punctuation marks that I'd noticed earlier once again appeared between her brows. "Derek and I drove my car, and we parked a couple of blocks away. You know, so that nobody would see the car and be able to recognize it later. Then we walked the rest of the way, and when we got there, we found the back door unlocked." Anne shook her head again. "Then we went in and found her. Down in the basement." Anne did not look the least bit distressed to be recalling such a memory. In fact, her eyes seemed to be dancing with excitement more than anything else.

Derek's eyes were not dancing. He was back to staring woodenly straight ahead. "It was terrible," he muttered. "Anne went down the steps first, and then I followed her. Oh, God, it was awful! I couldn't even look—"

Anne interrupted. "Can you believe, he barely

glanced at her, and even then, he had to run back upstairs to throw up?"

I looked over at Derek. Then he had been taking his second look at Trudi yesterday, after I'd phoned him. He probably hadn't noticed the heart the first time when he'd taken such a quick glance. No wonder he'd looked so genuinely stunned when he'd returned from the basement.

Anne was rolling her eyes. "Derek barely made it to the bathroom in time. Men can be such babies."

I just stared at her. Good Lord. When Anne had rolled her eyes, she'd looked exactly like Trudi.

Derek was now turning to glare at Anne. "For God's sake, Anne, it *was* terrible." His tone was defensive.

Anne stared right back at him, unyielding. "It was terrible, all right. It was terrible that Trudi was already dead." She ran a careless hand through her dark waves. "I mean, we'd made all those plans, and I'd been waiting all that time to finally show that little bitch exactly what I thought of her, and then we were too late. Somebody else got to her first. *Damn.*"

That touching little sentiment actually made me go cold all over. So much for sisterly devotion.

Derek also seemed a bit startled by what Anne had just said. His eyes widened considerably as he turned to look at her all over again.

"I mean, can you believe it, somebody beat us out!" Anne added.

That had to be a real disappointment.

I hated to admit it—because after leading Nathan on the way she had, Anne certainly deserved to have a few bad things happen to her—but I was pretty sure Anne was actually telling the truth. For one thing, her anger at not being able to carry through her plot against Trudi certainly had an air of authenticity about it. Surely Anne wouldn't act that nasty if she didn't really feel that way.

It had not exactly been her finest moment.

I stood there, trying to put it all together. If Anne and Derek really didn't kill Trudi, but had—as they said—lured her to the empty house on Saratoga, then there never had been any nameless client. I cleared my throat, looking from Derek to Anne and back again. "You mean to tell me, what Trudi wrote in that note was just—"

Anne finished my sentence, already nodding. "—just Trudi's little joke. She knew how everybody at the office felt about her stealing other people's leads, so she must've left that note behind, just to put in a little dig." Anne smiled bitterly. "That was Trudi all right. That little bitch had *such* a terrific sense of humor."

I certainly hoped Anne would not be called upon to say a few words at the funeral.

I rubbed my forehead, still thinking. If there never was a client, then Trudi's killer had to have been someone who'd known where Trudi was headed that day.

If it had not been Anne and Derek, it had to have been someone who'd read the note that Trudi had left. The note with the ragged top. The note that had looked as if it had been torn from a memo pad.

Or had the name of the person to whom the memo had really been sent—had that name alone just been torn off? As I recalled, my initials had been printed in all caps—as if the writer were afraid to write anything more, for fear the handwriting might be recognized.

I suddenly felt even colder.

On the morning I got the memo, there had been only one other person in the office, besides me and Trudi.

"So, Schuyler," Anne was now saying, "there's no reason for you to tell the police anything. You've got no proof that Derek and I have been seeing each other. We'll deny everything. And it won't bring Trudi's killer to justice. It'll just muddy the waters so that—"

I didn't wait to hear the rest. I just spun on my heel and headed straight for my car. Minutes later, I was driving as fast as I could toward my office.

Chapter
16

The office was full of people when I walked in. Jarvis was seated at the desk to the right of the door, going over a mortgage application with a young couple. These two were evidently buying their first house, because both the young woman and the young man were wearing the stunned expressions a real estate agent gets used to seeing on the faces of people signing away their next thirty years for the very first time.

Charlotte was over at her desk, showing the multiple listings book to another couple. This last couple was in their forties, and the house-buying thing must've been old hat to them. They looked a little bored.

I gave all these people just a cursory glance, however. The only person I really focused on, in fact, was Barbi. She was still wearing the tight, low-cut black knit dress she'd been wearing earlier at the funeral home, only she'd added a black linen blazer on top of it. More suitable as business attire, I suppose, although the suitability of any particular outfit for the office had certainly never seemed to bother her before.

Like Jarvis and Charlotte, Barbi was also not alone at her desk. There was a plump woman in a navy blue sweat suit sitting there, going through a folder of papers. From where I stood, it looked to me to be Xeroxes of several pages out of the multiple listings book.

I tried to act casual, as if nothing unusual were going on. I meant to just glance Barbi's way very innocently, so that she hardly even noticed, but I must not have a very good poker face. The second I looked her way, Barbi's head sort of jerked in my direction.

When Barbi looked over at me, it was all I could do to keep from turning on my heel and running right out of there. Instead, I gave her a quick nod and tried to follow this up with an easygoing, gosh-isn't-it-a-nice-day sort of smile, trying to act normal. The only trouble was, what exactly was normal in a situation like this? I mean, how do you smile normally at somebody you actually think might be guilty of cold-blooded murder?

I went straight to my desk, relieved not to be looking in Barbi's direction anymore. I stowed my purse under my desk as usual, and then I hurried into the back room to do what I always do under stress. That's right. I intended to find the biggest glass I could and fill it full of Coke, extra heavy on the ice.

I also intended to wait until Barbi was free and then talk to her. Unfortunately, that little plan never quite got off the ground. While I was pouring my Coke, I felt something hard being pushed into my back.

"You've figured it out, haven't you?" It was Barbi, her voice so low I could barely hear it.

Barbi must've tiptoed in, because I hadn't heard so much as a footstep before she spoke. Of course, the ice cubes rattling into my glass had made quite a bit of noise. Almost as much noise, in fact, as my heart started making right after Barbi spoke.

"Damn it, Schuyler, why the hell did you figure it out?" Behind me, Barbi actually stamped her foot like a frustrated child.

I started to turn around, but Barbi jabbed me in the back again. "Don't turn around," she hissed. "You'll be sorry if you do."

Hell, I was sorry I'd even come in here. I was particularly sorry I hadn't turned and run out of the office moments ago when I'd had the chance. "Look, Barbi," I said, "I don't know what you think, but I haven't figured anything out. I mean, I'm not exactly the figuring-out type." I was clearly babbling at this point. "I mean, I'm still trying to figure out how to program my VCR, for God's sake, so—"

"Shut *up!*" Barbi's voice was almost a sob. "I know you've figured it out, and now I'm going to have to do something I never wanted to do."

I swallowed uneasily. I didn't particularly want her to go into detail as to what precisely she was talking about. So I just shook my head. "Look, I don't have any idea *what* you're talking about," I said. "Really, you're going to have to explain it to me, because I don't have a clue." Barbi had still not let me turn around, so it was a little disconcerting to be saying all this to a large glass of Coke.

Still, I was doing my best to sound convincing. After all, I was a sales professional, wasn't I? While standing behind me was, let us not forget, a woman who'd once asked me how many quarters there were in a football game. It would seem, then, that I ought to be able to sell Barbi on anything. "Really, Barbi, I mean it, you've got the wrong idea, you—"

"*Shut up!*" Barbi managed to sound as if she were screaming, and yet she was still whispering. Quite a feat. "I *know* you know. I know it!" Apparently, Barbi wasn't quite as dumb as I'd hoped. She backed up her last little comment with another painful poke in my back. I winced. I also idly wondered exactly what the chances were that what was currently pressing into my back was just one of Barbi's very long, heavily lacquered fingernails. I started to turn around again.

"I *said,* don't turn around," Barbi snapped. "This *is* a gun, you know, in case you're wondering."

I immediately abandoned all thoughts of turning around. I did, however, give my head a little shake, as if to indicate that, no, now that Barbi mentioned it, I did *not* happen to be wondering. Not at all. In fact, I didn't see how I could possibly be *less* curious.

This certainly explained why Barbi had decided to wear the blazer. It would've been impossible to conceal a gun in that tight, skimpy dress. Not to mention, I wasn't sure that little frock even had pockets.

Can you believe, all this actually flashed through my mind? You might've thought that I had all the time in the world to think things over. When, in actuality, it certainly looked as if I were rapidly running *out* of time.

It particularly looked that way when Barbi went on. "Come on, Schuyler, let's go."

My mouth felt as if I'd just eaten a sandwich, heavy on the sand. I had to swallow once before I could speak. "Barbi, before we go, would you mind if I took a tiny sip of Coke?"

Behind me, Barbi gave out with an impatient little sigh. "Oh, for God's sake, Schuyler," she said, "you are sometimes really cuckoo about your frigging Coke."

She actually said that. Standing there, right in back of me, holding an actual gun pointed at my actual back, Barbi was telling me that *I* was cuckoo. I mean, apparently this woman standing behind me had been able to bring herself to *strangle* another human being. And yet she couldn't bring herself to say the F word out loud. Instead, she said "frigging." So, let's go over this again, *I* was the cuckoo one?

No frigging way.

I didn't want to make any sudden moves for obvious reasons, so I decided it would probably be best if I asked again before I reached for my Coke. "Then I *can* take a drink?"

I shouldn't have asked. Barbi may have been a tad slow, but apparently it didn't take all that long for it to occur to her just exactly what I could do with a glass in my hand. Things like, oh, for example, spin and throw it in her face. Break the glass and cut her with it. Maybe drop it on her foot.

I'm not sure I would've had the courage to do any of these things, since Barbi's gun did seem to be pressing against my back. The possibilities of Barbi missing me at that distance looked pretty much nil. As it happened, though, I never had the chance to find out just how courageous—or, for that matter, just how foolhardy—I was. "No, you can*not* have a drink!" Barbi hissed. "What do you think this is, Burger King?"

Under any other circumstance, I think I would've laughed. Right out loud. Having a gun pressed against your back, however, makes seeing the humor in a situation a lot more difficult.

"I *said*, let's go," Barbi said, and gave me a nudge with the gun.

I didn't move. Instead, I tried to speak calmly. "Barbi, this isn't a good idea."

Barbi's sense of humor such as it was, was still apparently intact. She actually chuckled a little. "Yeah, well, it's a little too late to talk about whether something's a good idea or not. I mean, Schuyler, you *know*—you know what I did."

There seemed to be little use in denying it. "I guess," I said, "out in the parking lot at the funeral home earlier, this was why you weren't afraid the killer was after you. Because the killer was *you*. It was you all along." I was surprised, listening to myself. From my tone, you might've thought I was telling her the ending to a movie.

Barbi didn't even try to deny it. "Yeah, well, I didn't do the heart," she said. "I don't want you thinking that I could do something like that. I mean, that heart thing was pretty sick." Barbi actually said this as if she truly believed that just *killing* Trudi was not as bad as disfiguring her.

I immediately decided that this was a topic probably not worth discussing. I mean, it seemed obvious Barbi and I had differing viewpoints on the subject.

By now my hands were so damp, I wanted to wipe them on my skirt, but I was still afraid to move.

"I couldn't do an awful thing like that heart," Barbi was going on. "I mean, *that* was really disgusting."

I nodded. "I believe you," I said. I wasn't lying. I was pretty sure she *was* telling the truth. For one thing, Barbi had looked too appalled when I'd first told her about it. As a matter of fact, now that I thought about it, I even had a pretty good guess as to who really *had* done the heart on poor Trudi.

Actually, once Trudi's killer was eliminated as a possibility, the identity of the phantom carver was pretty obvious. Disappointed at not being able to actually kill Trudi, but wanting to do something to express how angry she was with her, this particular person had done the only thing she could think of.

How creative, *Anne*.

And today, after seeing Barbi openly flirting with

Derek, Anne had pretended to go to the ladies' room, but instead, she'd headed out to the parking lot to be creative once again. How Anne had known which car belonged to Barbi, I wasn't sure, but Barbi's TRU LUV license plate was something that, once noticed, you remembered. Anne might've noticed Barbi's tag just about anytime Anne had come by the office to see her sister. Hell, Anne could even have noticed the thing just passing Barbi's car in traffic.

"Trudi deserved what I did to her, Schuyler, you know she did." Barbi punctuated this little statement by giving my back another poke. If I lived to see tomorrow, I was going to have a black-and-blue mark there for sure.

Of course, let's face it, at the moment bruises were the least of my worries.

"Trudi ruined my entire life, Schuyler," Barbi said. "She robbed me of *everything* when she blabbed to Sam and Mason."

I blinked, still looking at my Coke. Barbi had indeed lost two men, yes, but did that mean her entire life was ruined?

Barbi evidently was convinced of it. "Before Trudi opened her big mouth, I'd had it made. *Made!*" Barbi's voice was shaking now. I rather hoped her trigger finger was not doing the same thing. "Those guys were talking marriage, Schuyler. *Marriage!* I was going to have *everything* I ever wanted. Cars, clothes, travel—" Lord. Barbi made marriage sound as if it were roughly equivalent to winning the lottery. Obviously, Barbi had a slightly different view of the entire marriage concept than I did. "—and," Barbi hurried on, "it wasn't as if I were really doing anything all that awful, either, dating both of those guys at the same time. I was just trying to make up my mind which one would be the easiest to live with. . . ."

I blinked again. She hadn't been trying to decide which one she really loved. She'd been trying to choose which man would require the least of her. Lord. Had this self-centered, shallow, vindictive human being been the person Barbi had been all along? Had I been fooled that badly?

"And then Trudi had to ruin everything." Barbi's voice now shook with rage. "She did it on purpose, too, Schuyler; she just couldn't stand anybody else having anything."

I couldn't exactly disagree with Barbi. Trudi might very well have done the whole thing on purpose. Of course, Barbi was omitting the part where she'd called Trudi "Shitty-toe" in front of the entire office.

I cleared my throat. How did that saying go? Paybacks are hell. In this case, they certainly had been. For both women.

"And," Barbi went on, "as if she hadn't done enough, Trudi had the nerve to leave me that smart-alecky memo."

I didn't even blink. The memo had not been sent to me, after all—just as I'd suspected. It had been left with malice aforethought on *Barbi's* desk.

"Trudi was such a shit! She left me that note just to make me mad!"

I took a deep breath. Well, Trudi, I'd say your little memo had done the trick, all right. After what Trudi had done with the S & M, her memo had been all it took to make Barbi so mad she could kill.

Obviously, it had been Barbi who'd added the salutation to the note, TO S.R. After Barbi had printed that on the top of the paper Trudi had left her, Barbi had left the note on my desk. So it would look as if she herself had never seen it. Then she'd followed Trudi to the vacant house on Saratoga. Where she'd killed Trudi moments before Derek and Anne had arrived.

Barbi must've heard Derek and Anne going around to the back door, and had been able to escape out a side door just in time. My guess was she'd probably slipped out through the door in the utility room off the garage. In fact, it would've been easy. Barbi had shown the house herself before, so she would've known exactly where all the doors were located—and exactly where those doors led.

"Trudi was such an *asshole*," Barbi said.

I tend to agree with anybody currently holding a gun on me. Call me fickle. I immediately nodded. "Trudi was a stinker, all right," I said.

"You know, I'm really sorry, Schuyler," Barbi said.

I swallowed, surprised. Barbi actually sounded genuinely sad. For a moment there I thought she was talking about Trudi—that, after all was said and done, Barbi had thought it over, and she really did regret what she'd done.

I knew better than to turn around, but I started to say, "Oh, Barbi—"

That's when she jabbed me again. "But this isn't my fault," she said. "It's *yours*. I wouldn't have to do what I have to do if you hadn't stuck your big nose in where it doesn't belong."

If I hadn't been afraid to move, I would've slapped myself on the forehead. I should've known. Barbi wasn't sad about having to kill Trudi. Barbi was sad about having to kill *me*.

There really didn't seem anything for me to say. Lord knows, I wasn't exactly elated at the prospect myself.

"And I tried to warn you," Barbi said. "I carved that dumb heart on your door and everything, just so you'd back off. But, no, you wouldn't listen."

So it had been *Barbi* who'd decorated my front door. Of course. She'd probably headed for my house minutes after Matthias and I left to meet Irving Rickle. Now she was doing her best to make it sound as if she'd carved up my front door in order to keep me from finding out too much. I couldn't help recalling, though, how terribly angry Barbi had looked when I'd left with Matthias—yet another man she'd tried for and lost. Barbi may not want to admit it, even to herself, but I knew she'd left that little memento on my door partly to punish me. She'd known it would scare me as badly as it did.

Behind me Barbi abruptly cleared her throat. "So see? *You're* making me do this." At this point she actually shook her head regretfully. "Oh, well, come on, let's get it over with."

Personally, I didn't see any reason to hurry. "Now, Barbi," I said, opening my arms in a gesture of appeal.

"Put your hands in your pockets and turn around."

I believe I mentioned earlier how much I hate being bossed around. However, in this instance I didn't hesitate. I put my hands in my pockets, and I turned around. As soon as I could make eye contact with Barbi, though, I said, "Barbi, for God's sake, what are you doing?"

I'd expected Barbi to, at the very least, look away. I guess because if I'd done the things she'd done, I would've had trouble meeting anybody's eyes. Barbi, however, stared right back at me, without even blinking.

It was all I could do to keep from shivering. My God. Who *was* this woman? I'd had dinner with her, I'd told her all about Ed—hell, I'd even met her family. Had I never really known her at all?

"Let's go," she said, waggling the gun a little.

"Barbi," I said. I really hated to hear it, but a pleading tone had crept into my voice. "For heaven's sake,

think of your kids. Jennifer and Shawn, Jr. are going
to—"

That was about as far as I got with that little train
of thought. Barbi reached out and dug her fingernails
into my left wrist. Jabbing the gun in my side, she
snapped, *"Shut UP!"*

She didn't have to ask twice. I shut up. I also
wrenched my wrist out of her grasp. Three crimson
half-moons were now etched into the skin just above
my left hand. Two of them looked as if they had broken the skin. I stared at them almost as if I were in
a daze, actually thinking, *Oh, yeah, I'm going to need
a tetanus shot.*

I really hate getting shots. Of course, on the up side,
it didn't look likely I'd live to get this one.

"That was a shitty thing to do—bringing up my
kids." Barbi's voice was almost a growl. "That was a
damn shitty thing to do. Hell, I could shoot you right
here just for mentioning their names!"

I stopped staring at my wrist and started staring at
Barbi again.

God. This woman really was a total stranger. A total
stranger who was waggling her gun as if it were the
most natural thing in the world for her to do, and
whispering, "Now *move.* We're heading out the front
door, and we're getting into my car."

I just looked at her, feeling for the first time a quick
surge of anger. I guess by now I've made it abundantly
clear just how much I dislike taking orders. In this
particular situation, however, what else could I do?

I took a deep breath and, like a good little girl,
started moving toward the door.

Chapter 17

Funniest thing, when somebody is holding a gun on you, the strangest things go through your mind. Especially when you've got an entire office to walk through, and it gives you some time to think.

The first thing that occurred to me as I was moving out of the small kitchen in the back and heading toward the door leading to the outer office was that everything suddenly looked a little odd. It took me a moment to realize what was different, and then it came to me. Everything—the kitchen, the hall, even the pictures decorating the walls—now seemed much more in focus. It was as if somewhere in my mind, an invisible hand had fine-tuned everything to startling clarity. I don't know, maybe this is something your body does, a defense mechanism it goes into. When it thinks you could be taking your final look around, it makes sure you get a very clear view.

Since I had a pretty good idea as to what was going to happen once Barbi and I were out of the office, I was trying, of course, to move as slowly as I could. Once I must've slowed down a little too much, because Barbi nudged me with the gun. "Move," she whispered.

She didn't have to tell me twice.

When we got to the doorway, I could see Jarvis again over at the desk by the door. God. Every feature of his face seemed to stand out in bold relief. Incidentally, not a pretty picture. Our fearless leader was even smiling a little as the stunned young couple in front of him signed yet another form.

Across the room I could see Charlotte at her desk, still looking through the multiple listings book with the bored middle-aged couple. Turning my head, I saw again the plump woman in the sweat suit that Barbi had been talking to. Barbi had apparently been gone too long, because the woman was beginning to frown as she crossed and uncrossed her legs, her Reeboks slapping softly against the floor.

I started to go through the door, still marveling at how unbelievably crystal-clear everybody and everything suddenly looked, and then—without really meaning to—I hesitated.

Barbi reacted instantly. "I said *move,*" she whispered. "Move!"

That's when something else occurred to me. People always seem to expect women to do as they're told. Even other *women* expect women to meekly obey.

Barbi was poking my back with that damn gun again. "Hurry up!" she hissed.

I blinked. Wait a second now. Let me understand this. Barbi was telling me to *hurry* to my own death? What was wrong with this picture?

"Schuyler," Barbi said, her voice now barely audible, "get going."

Almost automatically, I took a couple of steps forward, and then once again, I came to an abrupt halt. We were now standing in full view of everyone in the outer office. Oddly enough, though, not a single person turned our way. I suppose it wouldn't have mattered if they had. Barbi was standing close enough to me so that you couldn't see that she had a gun. It was odd, though—as if suddenly she and I had become invisible.

"Move!" Barbi's whisper now sounded angry.

I started once again to do what Barbi said, and then just like before, I stopped. I swallowed once so that my voice wouldn't crack when I spoke, and then before I lost courage, I said, "Barbi, I don't think I'm going anywhere." I was actually a little surprised to hear myself say such a thing.

Barbi was quite a bit more than a *little* surprised. I could hear her gasp. "Oh, yes, you are! Now get going!"

I shook my head, and then turned to look at her.

Good Lord. Barbi's eyes seemed to have explosions going off inside them. "Come on, Schuyler!" she said. "Get going. Right now!" She sounded angry, and for the first time since she'd come up behind me, a little scared. "And you'd better not cause a fuss."

A *fuss*? This time several things occurred to me all at once. One thing was: Did Barbi actually expect me to *cooperate* in my own death? *Was she kidding?*

Another thing was: Did Barbi really think that I ought to make this whole thing easy for *her*? Because, when you came right down to it, what Barbi was asking me to do was to walk quietly out the front door, attracting as little attention as possible, so that nobody would particularly notice. And, also, so that she could take me someplace very nice and very remote and put a few bullets into me.

Well, all I can say is, it could be that I really do have a big problem with taking orders. The words *I don't think so* sprang to mind.

"Get a move on," Barbi was now hissing at me.

You can guess what I said. "I don't think so."

Barbi took in another long breath. "Schuyler, I mean it, I'm going to shoot you! And after I shoot you, I'm going to shoot everybody else."

I said it again. "I don't think so." I glanced around the office. The woman in the sweat suit had spotted Barbi, and she was now lifting a plump index finger, trying to get Barbi's attention. "Look around you, Barbi. There are too many people here. You can't shoot them all before somebody jumps you." I listened to myself saying this, and I actually sounded reasonable. As if these were the kinds of choices I myself contemplated every day of my life. My goodness, what to do, what to do? Should I shoot everybody in the room, or should I just leave without hurting anybody? Let me think. "Barbi," I said, "in all honesty, your only chance is to get the hell out of here as fast as you can."

Barbi actually whined. "You've *got* to come with me," she said. She tried to brandish her gun, waving it back and forth, but even that thing didn't look as scary anymore.

I barely gave her gun a glance. "Barbi," I said, "if you don't get out of here right this minute, I'm going to step away from you and yell at the top of my lungs that you've got a gun. I'm betting that young guy over there talking to Jarvis tackles you before you can get off a shot."

I was bluffing big-time now. The young guy with Jarvis was probably still so shell-shocked from seeing how much interest he and his wife were about to fork over for the next thirty years, if he found out Barbi had a gun, he'd probably beg her to shoot *him* first.

Barbi, however, bought every word I said. She took

one horrified look around the large room, her eyes as wild as those of an animal caught in a trap, and then she bolted for the front door.

I had to stop the plump woman in the sweat suit from running after her.

Chapter
18

The second Barbi was out of sight, I called the police.

They caught up with her on the other side of Nashville. Would you believe she was driving her own car, the one with the TRU LUV license plates? This certainly sounded more like the woman who'd asked me about the number of quarters in a football game.

If Barbi had been driving any other car, it might've taken them a little while longer to catch her. As it was, she was in custody in time to make the eleven o'clock news.

When I heard the newscaster talking about it, I knew I should've been feeling glad or relieved or something. All I felt, though, was sad. I listened to the guy on Channel 3 going on about how the suspect had been spotted on I-65, and apprehended without incident. He started talking about extradition and arraignment and things like that, and before I knew it, I was sitting there on my couch with tears rolling down my cheeks.

Barbi had been a friend of mine. She and I had gone to the movies together, we'd cooked dinner for each other, and we'd spent lazy evenings together, drinking Bloody Marys and talking about our ex-husbands and our kids.

She hadn't seemed all that different from me.

And yet, she'd *murdered* somebody.

She'd wrapped a scarf around another woman's neck, and she'd brutally taken away all the remaining moments of that woman's life.

How could something like this have happened? How does a person get to the point where all her options dwindle down to, *Oh, I know what'll solve everything. I'll just kill her.*

My God, Barbi, what the hell had happened?

That was the question that kept nagging at me. I suppose one reason I couldn't get it out of my mind was that, up until she did this terrible thing, Barbi and I had seemed to have so much in common. Our kids were close in age, and even though Barbi's children were a girl and a boy, her problems with them were much the same as my own with Nathan and Daniel. Barbi had been a real estate agent, just like me, and she'd worried when her sales fell off, just like I did. With only two years' difference between us, we were for all intents and purposes the same age. Barbi was a lot like me. Or, what was even worse to contemplate, I was a lot like *her*.

So were we all, then, so close to committing murder? If pushed, were we all capable of such horror?

To say I was depressed for a long time after Barbi's capture would be an understatement. I couldn't help wondering if there had been something I could've done to prevent what had happened. Had there been some clue that I should've picked up on? Or did my own intense dislike of Trudi keep me from seeing how very much Barbi herself had grown to hate the woman?

What really got me down was that I finally had to admit a terrible truth to myself. That even today, even after everything that had happened, I still liked Barbi a lot more than I'd liked Trudi.

Oh, my, yes, by the end of the week following Barbi's arrest, I was not exactly what you'd call the life of the party. By Friday even Charlotte had begun to leave the room when I walked in. I guess everybody was tired of hearing me rehash the entire incident. Hell, I'd even had Jarvis himself take me aside and say, "Look, Schuyler, it's over. Barbi's in jail where she belongs. Let it go. None of it was your fault, understand?"

I would've liked to have taken Jarvis's word for it, but let's face it, he wasn't exactly a man known for his concern over moral issues. As he talked, I couldn't help recalling that this was the man who'd once told clients that a certain property he'd just listed had very quiet neighbors—when, in reality, every other real estate agent in the office knew that these so-called "neighbors" happened to be a cemetery.

When I'd called him on it, Jarvis had actually argued with me. "I wasn't lying," he said. "You don't get any quieter neighbors than that!"

Like I said, Jarvis wasn't much help.

The only person, in fact, who helped me start feeling a little better about everything was Matthias.

"Schuyler," he said that following Saturday night when we were over at his place, "you're being too hard on yourself. I mean, how could you possibly have known what Barbi was planning?" He'd put his arms around me and pulled me close. "Give yourself a break, okay, sweetheart? Murder is not exactly the first thing civilized people think of as a problem-solving technique. You shouldn't be blaming yourself for not seeing it coming."

I wish I could say his words suddenly hit home, and a huge weight seemed to fall from my shoulders. In reality, I was still pretty depressed. It was comforting, though, to have him hold me close and rub his big hand through my hair. And, yes, to have him kiss me.

I have mentioned, haven't I, how well this man can kiss?

When Matthias finally pulled away, he drew a long, ragged breath. I knew, of course, what he was going to say.

"Schuyler, have you done any more thinking about our moving in together?"

I may have known what he was going to say, but I hadn't realized until that very moment that I'd finally made up my mind.

I moved closer to him so that I could look into his eyes.

Those damn green eyes.

Who could resist this man?

I reached over and took one of his big, strong hands in mine, feeling the familiar surge of pleasure I always felt just touching him. Without a shadow of a doubt, I loved Matthias more than I'd ever loved any man in my life.

Love, I knew, was a fragile thing. The slightest little thing could kill it. Like, oh, say, for example, doing a little creative carving on a person's forehead. Oddly enough a tiny thing like that could actually sour a romance.

I found that out right after Barbi was arrested. I'd thought Derek probably needed to hear exactly what Barbi had told me with regard to the artwork on Trudi's forehead. So when he phoned me asking for details regarding what had happened at the Arndoerfer Realty office the day Barbi tried to get me to leave with her, well, I simply told him. Not only how

I'd figured out the Barbi was guilty, but also how I'd figured out exactly who the phantom carver had to have been.

I think Derek had already figured it out for himself. Even though up till then Anne had been trying her best to convince him that the heart had been the handiwork of the killer, Derek didn't sound at all surprised.

Shortly after Derek and I had our little chat, Anne phoned me at the office, wanting to know what in hell I'd told Derek. Oddly enough, Derek was refusing to have anything more to do with her.

Can you believe when I told her the truth she hung up on me?

I also told Nathan the truth. All about Anne's little creative project. It certainly snapped him out of pining away for the woman.

Oh, yes, I'd say love is fragile, all right.

All of this was going through my mind as I took Matthias's hand. "I love you, Matthias," I said. "I want you to know that." I swallowed once, and then I said as quickly as I could, "I also want you to know that I don't want to move in with *anybody* right now."

Matthias's handsome face immediately fell. And, yes, my stomach immediately wrenched. I wouldn't have hurt him for the world. That's why I spent so much time right then and there trying to explain all of it to him. How I wasn't ready to give up my independence just yet. How I'd decided that I needed to make very sure that, when and if I ever moved in with him, I was doing it for the right reason.

Not because I was afraid that if I didn't agree to it right this minute I might lose him.

Not because I just didn't want to remain alone in a society mostly made up of pairs.

Not because I was thoroughly weary of having to

support myself, and I wanted to take the rest of my life off.

And certainly not because I was afraid that, without a man at my side, I was not quite a whole person.

Barbi had shown me just how desperate a woman can get if she ever becomes convinced that life without a man is not worth living.

I told Matthias all this, taking my time, telling him just exactly how I felt. When I was finished, Matthias nodded his big, shaggy head and pulled me close. "I understand," he said. And yet, I wasn't sure he really did. His green eyes looked infinitely sad.

So I took another deep breath and began again. Hey, I had all night. And I did want him to believe me. I needed him to understand that my not moving in with him didn't mean that I wasn't in love with him.

It didn't even mean that the idea was permanently out of the question.

All it meant was that I wanted to wait a while. So that if and when I decided that I wanted to move in with Matthias, it would simply be because I wanted to share the rest of my life with him.

Nothing more.

And certainly nothing less.

Don't miss the next Schuyler Ridgway mystery,
TWO-STORY FRAME,
coming from Signet in 1997.

I was already angry, even before the phone call that sent me hurrying out into the rain. In fact, on that damp Tuesday in early October I'd pretty much spent the entire morning sitting at my desk at Arndoerfer Realty, working very little—and, more than anying else, watching the wall clock across the room slowly tick away the minutes. I was alone in the office, and that was okay with me. In the mood I was in, I didn't want to see anybody.

I was angry at my boyfriend, Matthias Cross. I was angry at my ex-husband, Ed Ridgway. And I was angry at both my sons, Nathan and Daniel. I was angry at all of them for talking me into doing things that they all knew very well I didn't want to do.

Most of all, though, I was angry at myself. In fact, I think I might've been angrier at myself than I was at all of the others put together. The thing I kept asking myself over and over again was: Why was I such a wimp? Why couldn't I do like all the drug posters said and just say no, for God's sake?

Heading the list of people I should've said no to

was Matthias. I mean, okay, so Matthias happened to have the greenest eyes I'd ever seen. And so he also happened to have a wonderfully thick beard, peppered here and there with gray, that I loved running my fingers through. And so he also happened to have a slow, lazy smile that could turn my knees to jelly. So what? I was not some love-struck teenager. I'd passed the Big Four-Oh two entire years ago, and I do believe that at this age, when warning bells start going off in my head, I should listen.

Those bells had sounded like a four-alarm fire the night before, right after Matthias had asked me to do him "a little favor." Oh, yes, that's what he called it, a *little* favor. If Matthias considered this a little favor, I'd hate to see what he thought qualified as a big one. It would probably involve organ donation.

Actually, now that I thought about it, I believe I'd much rather donate a kidney than what Matthias had asked. "I'd really appreciate it," he said, "if you'd go with me to meet Barbara at Standiford Field." Standiford Field is the main airport in Louisville, Kentucky. Before Matthias said this, he and I had been sitting quietly on a wicker bench out on my screen porch, enjoying a cool evening breeze already hinting of rain on the way. After Matthias spoke, I stiffened, and for a long moment, I just looked at him. Barbara? He wanted me to meet *Barbara*?

Even though Matthias and I had been dating over a year, I had yet to meet either Barbara, Matthias's ex-wife, or their daughter, Emily. I didn't think there was anything particularly ominous about my not having met them, however. After all, Barbara and Emily did live in Boston these days, and the last time I checked, Boston was quite a distance from Louisville.

Mother and daughter had moved back to Barbara's hometown right after she and Matthias split up. According to Matthias, Barbara had told him at the time that she was moving to be near her aging parents. However, since Barbara up and married a guy by the name of Phil Coleman a mere two days after hers and Matthias's divorce was final—and this Phil person happened to own a house in Boston—it seemed to me that Barbara might've overstated her parents' influence a bit.

Shortly after establishing residence in Boston, Barbara opened a boutique, and from what I gathered from Matthias, this boutique didn't run very well without her. Emily, on the other hand, was attending Boston College not only during the regular semesters, but during summer school, too—and holding down a part-time job. So, it didn't take a genius to figure out that, in the last year or so, neither Barbara nor Emily had really had any time to come down for a visit.

Until, of course, *now*.

I cleared my throat, and immediately asked the first incredibly stupid question that came to mind. "You mean, Barbara is coming to town?"

If I were Matthias, I'd have been tempted to reply, *No, I just thought we'd go hang around Standiford Field on the off chance that she might show up.*

Instead, Matthias just stared at me for a moment, and then he nodded. "Her plane arrives at two tomorrow afternoon." He ran his hand over his beard, and went on. "I can't imagine why Barbara has suddenly decided to come down for a visit."

I didn't say a word, but what Matthias had told me a few days ago did immediately spring to mind. He'd mentioned that his ex-wife had just filed for divorce from the Phil person. Now, maybe Matthias couldn't imagine why Barbara would be dropping by all of a sudden, but *I* sure could.

"I'd really appreciate your coming with me," Matthias hurried on. "I really don't want to meet Barbara all by myself."

I forced myself to smile at him. When Matthias and I first started dating, I'd been pretty curious about Barbara. Mainly because I couldn't imagine what kind of deranged female would let a man as wonderful as Matthias get away. Now, though, suddenly faced with the prospect of meeting Barbara face-to-face, I didn't feel anywhere near as enthusiastic. This was the woman, mind you, who'd spent far more years with Matthias than I had. The woman with whom he'd had a child. The woman who today might very well be regretting her decision to leave.

Lord. If I never met Barbara, it would be too soon.

My smile was beginning to feel like something I'd pasted on my face. "You won't be all by yourself," I told Matthias. "Emily will be there, too, won't she?"

I thought I sounded positively casual as I asked the question. I must not have sounded quite as casual as I thought, though, because Matthias's eyes darted in my direction. "It's almost time for midterms," he said, looking straight at me, "so it looks as if Emily won't be able to get away."

I blinked, and looked away. Barbara was coming down all by herself? Correct me if I'm wrong, but wasn't it a little odd that only Barbara would come for a visit? Leaving Emily behind?

Those weren't the only questions that occurred to me either as I sat there on the screen porch, pretty much avoiding Matthias's eyes. Another was this: Where exactly was Barbara going to stay while she was in town? I was not, of course, about to broach this particular subject with Matthias, but it definitely weighed on my mind.

What also weighed on my mind was how I'd recently turned down Matthias's invitation to move in with him. It occurred to me right that minute that if I hadn't turned Matthias down, I'd at least have some say in where Barbara would be staying.

"How about it, Sky?"

Sky is Matthias's nickname for me. Short for Schuyler, I suppose. Every time he says it, I'm reminded of the only other person I've ever heard of whose name was Sky—Sky King. Sky King was this cowboy/singer/airplane pilot on television in the fifties. As I recall, Sky was always whipping his guitar out of the cockpit and bursting into song. Whenever Matthias calls me Sky, he always says it so fondly. I've never had the heart to tell him that I've always thought Sky was a boy's name. And a geek boy's name, at that.

I looked back over at Matthias, and gave him another smile. "I'd be glad to go with you to the airport," I lied. "In fact, I'm really looking forward to finally meeting Barbara."

I was surprised to hear my own voice. I actually sounded sincere.

That, of course, is how I ended up on this rainy Tuesday, sitting at my desk, gloomily watching the wall clock march toward two o'clock. Apparently, I'd sounded so sincere, Matthias hadn't even questioned it.

I don't know why I should've been surprised. Hadn't I sounded every bit as sincere two weeks ago when I'd agreed to do what my ex-husband Ed had wanted me to do?

As a matter of fact, Ed was the next name on my list of people, right after Matthias, to whom I should've just said no.

Actually, I guess my sons, Nathan and Daniel, should be listed on the same line with Ed, because it was my sons who'd done the actual asking. Ed had evidently known that what he wanted me to do was pretty outrageous, so—basic coward that he is—he'd gotten Nathan and Daniel to discuss the entire thing with me.

I'll have to hand it to my sons. They didn't beat around the bush. "Yo, Mom," Daniel began. *Yo* accounts for a major portion of Daniel's vocabulary. I've decided that I should never have taken him to see all those Rocky movies when he was little. Those movies obviously hit him hard. "We got something we need to ask you."

Nathan jumped in. "How about helping Dad and the Kimster house-hunt, okay?"

The Kimster is the boys' name for Kimberly Metcalf, Ed's fiancée. I would say, *current* fiancée—Ed has gone through quite a few fiancées in the years we've been divorced—except that this one, I think, might turn out to be the real thing. The two of them have actually set a wedding date—in a scant four weeks—and sent out invitations. Something none of Ed's other fiancées ever got around to doing.

Unlike Barbara and Emily, I *had* met the Kimster. Several times. In fact, I suspected Ed had gone out of his way to make sure I'd met her. Kimberly, Lord love her, was just twenty-seven, only five years older than Daniel, Ed's and my oldest. Kimberly was also very petite, and very curvy with shoulder-length blond hair and blue eyes so large, she looked perpetually surprised. To be cruelly honest, Kimberly was not quite as pretty as some of Ed's previous fiancées, but from what I gathered from Ed, she had something that none of the others had.

Connections.

Ed had told me more than once that Kimberly was one of *the* Metcalfs of Lexington, Kentucky. I don't really keep up with Who's Who in Kentucky, but even I had heard that particular name. Around the Bluegrass state, the Metcalf family name meant money so old, nobody really knew how they'd first come by it. What everybody did know was that the Metcalfs had spread a good deal of their money liberally around Kentucky, making endowments to the ballet, the arts, the University of Kentucky scholarship fund, and various other charities.

Ed had also told me several times that he met Kimberly at the opening of a regional art exhibit at the J.B. Speed Museum. Ed seemed to feel that Kimberly's appearance at such a function was further proof of Kimberly's superior bloodline. It was, no doubt, not a bit kind of me to think such a thing, but Kimberly's pedigree certainly seemed to explain why good old social-climbing Ed had decided to really get married this time.

Kimberly, for her part, seemed to believe that marrying somebody twenty years older automatically put you in their age group. Kimberly has actually told me more than once not to worry—that she has no intention of trying to replace me as a mother-figure in the *boys'* lives. Really. She actually said this. I, of course, immediately assured her that I wasn't worried. I mean, the Kimster might be a sister-figure to Nathan and Daniel. But a mother-figure? I didn't think so.

I had known, of course, the second that Nathan and Daniel popped the question, so to speak, that I would regret giving in to them, but I couldn't seem to think of a good excuse not to help Ed and Kimberly with their house hunt. Not without sounding as if I had a problem with Ed getting married again, anyway. In fact, it was while I was talking to Nathan and Daniel that I—in an effort to convince them both that I had no problem whatsoever with their father's upcoming nuptials—actually agreed to kick back part of my commission as a wedding present.

Kick, of course, was the operative word here. I'd

been kicking myself ever since. Too late, I'd realized that this was what Ed had wanted me to do in the first place—reduce my commission. This kind of maneuver was just like cheapskate Ed. He was, after all, the very same man who'd insisted back when we were still married that I wash out plastic bags and reuse them.

Lord. What a sweetheart that man was.

And yet, I couldn't exactly renege after telling Nathan and Daniel I would do it. So I'd spent the last two interminable weeks escorting Ed and his child-bride-to-be all over Louisville and surrounding counties. During those two god-awful weeks I'd listened to Ed lecture Kimberly on everything from the quality of carpet to how many bathrooms they'd need. It had been a painful reminder of all the times I myself had listened to Ed's lectures back when he and I were married. By the time I'd spent fourteen days herding the happy couple through countless houses, I firmly believed what up to then I'd only suspected: The *Ed Encyclopedia* would rival the *Britannica* easy.

Kimberly didn't seem to mind Ed's lectures anywhere near as much as I did. In fact, the young woman seemed to hang on Ed's every word. Kimberly had even told me during one of our first house hunting expeditions that she considered Ed to be absolutely perfect. I believe the Kimster's exact quote was, "Ed is so wise, so mature." I'd just stared into those huge blue eyes. Only somebody in her twenties would think that Ed, of all people, was mature.

Kimberly apparently believed that Ed was so perfect, she couldn't understand how he ever came to be divorced. She'd actually taken me aside one afternoon, and bluntly asked why Ed and I got divorced. "Was it really because you two had just grown apart? Like Ed said?" Kimberly asked.

I'd had to bite my tongue to keep from telling Kimberly about Ed's joining the Girlfriend of the Month club during the last years of our marriage. Or, at least, that was what I thought he must've done, since a new girlfriend seemed to show up about every four weeks or so.

I didn't feel, however, that it was my place to drag out all Ed's dirty laundry. If Ed wanted Kimberly to know what a jerk he was, it seemed to me that he should be the one to tell her. Besides, what did I know? Maybe Ed had finally finished sowing his wild oats, and was ready at last to settle down.

"I guess Ed and I just grew to be two very different people," was what I finally told Kimberly that afternoon. Hey, I was telling her the truth. I had grown to be someone who was faithful. And Ed had grown to be someone who wasn't.

Ed had also grown to be someone who based his judgments of people pretty much entirely on what they drove, where they lived, and whom they could claim as ancestors. Or maybe Ed hadn't grown to be like this. Maybe he'd always been this shallow, and I just hadn't noticed until I'd been married to him for a while.

When Ed and Kimberly at last made up their minds about a house, it was all I could do to keep from weeping in sheer relief. Naturally, the house Ed and Kimberly decided was perfect for them turned out to be one of the houses that I'd shown them on Day One of their house hunt—a two-story frame on Willow Avenue.

The two-story was one that I'd been trying to sell for some time. It was a charming Victorian, and the main reason it had been on the market for so long was that it was being sold as a result of a pending divorce. From what I understood, the separation agreement stipulated that the wife, Adrienne Henderson, could stay in the house until it was sold. Adrienne's estranged husband, Frank, had already moved into his own condo, but Adrienne apparently had not wanted to move. *Ever.*

Whenever I'd tried to sell the house, Adrienne had followed along in back of me, telling the prospects anything and everything to discourage them from buying. Unfortunately, it had taken me a while to catch on to what Adrienne was doing.

In fact, it was only after Adrienne had told Ed that she was "sure that Schuyler had mentioned the roach problem," but for him not to worry, she was "pretty sure it had already been taken care of," that I finally got wind of what was being said behind my back.

Having been through a divorce myself, I admit, I was sympathetic with Adrienne. It was all too clear that the divorce was all Frank's idea, and that Adrienne was doing everything she could to keep from having the thing finalized. It was equally clear, however, that Adrienne was just putting off the inevitable. Judging from the hostile looks I'd caught Frank Henderson giving his wife, I'd say the man was more than a little anxious to untie the knot.

Not to mention, I had to do my job. When I told Frank how Adrienne had been sabotaging sales, he swore under his breath and then said, "Mrs. Ridgway, I can assure you that it wouldn't happen again." Whatever he said to Adrienne, I didn't know, but after that, Adrienne kept to herself when the house was being shown.

After Adrienne's input, it seemed practically a miracle that Kimberly and Ed had finally decided that the house on Willow was the one for them. Kimberly and Ed had already written a contract on another house before this one, only to back out at the last minute because Kimberly decided she didn't like the people next door. Rednecks, Kimberly called them.

Kimberly's little discovery that their prospective neighbors were of the redneck variety had cost Ed his five-hundred dollar deposit. And yet, Ed—can you believe it—hadn't even acted as if he minded. This was a surprise. The man who'd yelled at me for leaving a light on whenever I'd left a room—the man who'd wanted plastic bags washed and reused—this was the same guy who'd simply shrugged when the Kimster blew five hundred smackers? What's more, the house on Willow cost fifteen thousand dollars more than the first house. And still, Ed had not seemed to mind.

It could very well be that the man was in love.

Ed and Kimberly's offer on the Willow Avenue house had been accepted the day it was made, and the closing was set for the end of the month. I should've been elated, and yet, as I sat there at my desk, listening to the rain pattering on the roof overhead, and more or less glaring at the wall clock across the way, I was still angry at myself for giving up any of my commission. Hell, I'd earned every penny. Twice over.

What was wrong with me, anyway? Why did I let all the men in my life walk all over me? If this kept up, I might as well just lie down and stencil "WEL-COME" on my chest.

When the phone rang a little before noon, I remembered as I reached for it that this was the day that Adrienne was supposed to let Kimberly come in and measure for drapes and such. I was sure this had to be one of them, complaining about something.

"Schuyler?"

The second I heard the tremor in the voice, sure enough, I knew something was wrong. "Kimberly?"

"Look, you've got to get over here right away."

My first impulse was to tell Kimberly that I was busy. "I'm pretty tied up—" I began.

Kimberly interrupted me. "Look, there's a problem here, understand?"

"A problem?" It crossed my mind that Adrienne Henderson might've been up to her old tricks again. Had Adrienne told Kimberly that something else was wrong with the house? "Let me speak to Mrs. Henderson," I said.

Kimberly's answer was quick. "Mrs. Henderson's not here. She left."

"She left? What do you mean, she left?"

Kimberly went right on, as if I hadn't said anything. "Look, Ed's going to be mad, and I don't think I should have to deal with this all by myself—"

"Deal with what?"

Kimberly was now sounding angry. "Just get over here *now,* OK? I'm afraid—"

The phone suddenly went dead. It was so unexpected that I just sat there, staring stupidly at the receiver for a long moment. Had Kimberly hung up on me? Or had she been cut off? I looked up the phone number for the Henderson place in my current listings file, dialed it, and got a busy signal.

I dialed two more times, only to hear the busy signal again and again.

The last time I couldn't help sighing. My boss, Jarvis Arndoerfer, didn't like his office left unmanned, but he made an exception when a client called with a problem.

There seemed to be only one thing to do.

I put on my coat, grabbed my purse and umbrella, and cursing under my breath, I hurried out into the rain.